The
HOME FRONT
GIRLS

The
HOME FRONT
GIRLS

SUSANNA BAVIN

bookouture

Published by Bookouture in 2024

An imprint of Storyfire Ltd.
Carmelite House
50 Victoria Embankment
London EC4Y 0DZ

www.bookouture.com

ISBN: 978-1-83790-786-1
eBook ISBN: 978-1-83790-785-4

In memory of Jeremy Snape
Looking at the clouds from the other side

And also to my friend Kath Breen
with thanks for all those afternoons spent talking about writing

CHAPTER ONE

END OF JULY 1940

This was the part of her job Sally hated. It didn't matter how many times she had to do it; she knew she would never get used to it. First-time nerves, she had called it six months ago when, dry-mouthed, she had stammered and fluffed her lines, her face ablaze with guilt. But here she was all this time later, and with nearly forty tests under her belt, and her butterflies were on the rampage yet again. She might not blush or stammer any more, but her insides still tied themselves in knots. She loathed tricking people. Not just tricking them – trapping them.

She blew out a sharp breath, hearing Mr Morland's plummy voice in her head. 'This is our patriotic duty, Miss White, unpleasant though we may find it.'

Liar, Sally thought. She was certain he didn't find it in the slightest bit unpleasant. She had seen him positively swell up with complacent pride when he had the chance to present evidence before a judge rather than a magistrate.

It was quite a long road and there was a shop on nearly every corner. Sally came to the one on her list, Tucker's Groceries, and hovered outside, steeling herself to go in. Now would be a good moment because there wasn't a queue. She always tried to enter the selected shops when there were no other customers, partly because her heart ached for the unsuspecting shopkeepers, but also because her skin prickled in embarrassment if she had an audience, even though she was the only person present who knew what was happening.

Seeing a couple of housewives with shopping baskets coming along the road, she hung back in case they were heading for Tucker's. One of them was wearing a tin hat on top of her headscarf. Had her husband made her promise to wear it every time she went out, now that a bomb had been dropped locally at long last?

One of the women caught her looking. 'Morning, love,' she said, and Sally forced a smile, feeling caught out. Never engage with the locals: that was one of her rules. To break it, as she had learned from wretched experience, left her feeling even more of a heel.

The little bell tinkled above their heads as the two women entered the shop. Through the window criss-crossed with anti-blast tape, Sally saw the shop assistant greet them. She was a young blond woman – and not just blond but golden-blond. Not like Sally. She was fair, but not properly fair, not pure fair. Others called her hair dirty blond. Even Mum called it that.

The presence of the two housewives let Sally off the hook for a few minutes. She walked further along the street, all red brick and lace curtains with glimpses of the thick blackout curtains pushed over to the sides.

Deborah's words came floating back. 'Are you going to have a look? You won't be far away, you know.'

Should she – or would it be too morbid for words? Sally had to admit to feeling curious. Who wasn't, after all these months of waiting? The phoney war, they called it. The outbreak of war had been preceded by months of preparations – air-raid shelters and gas-masks, the blackout, the never-ending stream of pamphlets on everything from evacuation to growing your own vegetables and how to protect windows to lists of items to keep in your air-raid shelter. Then war had been declared, but the dropping of high explosives and poisonous gas-bombs that everyone had dreaded simply hadn't happened. Hence the name 'phoney war'.

Well, it was real now. Several bombs had been dropped in this area of Salford the night before last. Not far from where Sally was now, a transport timekeeping office had been hit. Rumours were rife about the extent of the damage, which was why Deborah had encouraged her to go and take a look.

Stopping when she reached the corner, Sally looked back the way she had come. The woman in the tin helmet appeared on the pavement, glancing over her shoulder to carry on nattering to her friend as they left the shop.

No sightseeing today. Sally wasn't sorry to forgo the opportunity. The thought of seeking out the site of a bombing just to be nosy made her skin crawl, all the more so because she would have to ask for directions, these streets being unfamiliar to her. They never did their testing in places where their faces were known. Sally lived in Withington on the south side of Manchester.

She walked back down the pavement, past a couple of women in turbans and wraparound pinnies gossiping on their doorsteps. One housewife had evidently got off to a late start and was still busy donkey-stoning her front step. She had pulled the doormat onto the pavement to kneel on it while she washed the step and then rubbed the donkey-stone all over it to leave behind a cream-coloured coating, which she patterned into swirls. Along the road, all the doorsteps were freshly donkey-stoned, showing off each housewife's respectability and providing the morning with an air of normality in spite of the damage recently inflicted close by.

Children were playing out, enjoying the start of the summer holidays. Girls of various ages were skipping together, chanting, 'Loopy – miss a loop... loopy – miss a loop...' as the lines of skippers jumped expertly through the rope and out the other side without getting tangled up. Grubby-kneed boys played British Bulldog from pavement to pavement, giving it their all, dodging and grabbing. A breathless yell of 'British Bulldog, one, two, three!' was accompanied by an ominous ripping sound as the boy who had been caught dragged himself free and flung himself to safety in the nick of time.

Were these children among the thousands who had been evacuated last September, only to be brought back when the feared bombing raids had failed to materialise? Or were they children whose parents had refused point-blank to part with them?

Halting outside Tucker's, Sally peered through the window. There were no customers; she already knew that, but she checked all the same. Curling her fingers around the door handle, she used her thumb to press down the small brass plate that lifted the latch, walking past a display of Morning Glory polish and Vim as she entered the shop. The golden-haired girl wore a starched white apron and a white cap. Behind her, wooden shelves bearing Fry's Breakfast Cocoa, McDougalls flour, Spry vegetable fat, Heinz Salad Cream, small boxes of Oxo cubes and dark glass bottles of Bovril stretched up as high as the ceiling. There was a stepladder over to one side.

'Morning.' The fair-haired assistant smiled warmly and a dimple appeared in her cheek. 'You've come just at the right moment. There was a queue earlier. What would you like?'

Drat. She was a friendly one. It was always worse when they were friendly. Sally steeled herself.

'Good morning. I haven't been to your shop before. I wonder if you could let me have some butter?'

'You aren't registered here, miss.'

'I know, and I wouldn't ask, only I'm visiting family nearby and they've run out. It made me feel guilty – you know, the extra mouth to feed.'

'You ought to have given your ration book to the lady of the house.'

Sally didn't miss a beat. 'I'm only here for a day or two. I didn't think I'd need it. I'll know better next time.' She gave the girl a winning smile.

It was odd. Sometimes, in spite of feeling so uncomfortable, or maybe because of it, she threw herself into the part so thoroughly that she could almost believe the words coming out of her mouth. Afterwards, that made her feel grubby, but at the time it was strangely compelling.

'You do see what a scrape I'm in,' she added, inviting understanding.

The assistant pulled a face, but her blue eyes were sympathetic. 'You know I shouldn't serve you.'

Shouldn't. Not *can't.*

Sally groaned in a humorous way. 'Couldn't you stretch a point just this once?'

The girl sighed, then dipped her head and glanced to right and left, as if there might be an audience watching from the wings. 'Seeing as you're in a fix – but not a word to anyone or we'll both be for it.'

Sally felt a moment's pleasure, as if she really were in dire need of butter, but it was instantly followed by that heavy sinking feeling she experienced every time her prey fell for her act. The kind-hearted assistant cut a piece of butter, using the wooden paddles to pat it into shape. Sally shifted the string of her gas-mask box further onto her shoulder as she lifted her handbag to open the clasp fastener and remove her purse. She glanced at her wristwatch, noting the exact time of the illicit transaction.

'There you go, love,' said the assistant. 'And remember...' With one finger, she tapped the side of her nose, her blue eyes twinkling as she smiled.

Sally got out of there as quickly as she could.

CHAPTER TWO

Sally sat at her big wooden desk with an in-tray on one side and an out-tray on the other. In between the two a long groove in the desk's polished surface provided a place for pens and pencils to lie in. At the end of the groove was the inkwell. Beside Sally, on top of a small cupboard, stood her typewriter, which she had to heave across onto the desk each time she needed to use it.

Across from her sat Deborah, her best friend. She was dark-haired with an attractive smile. Their two desks butted up against one another, all the better for having a secret chat when they were alone. They loved working together. Before this, they had both worked in the typing pool. Then they had been plucked from there to sit tests in English and maths, after which they were both allocated posts here in the Food Office.

They had been friends all their lives, in and out of one another's houses in Withington. They had attended the same school, then both got shop jobs when they'd left aged fourteen. They had gone to night school together to learn typing and eventually joined the Corporation typing pool together – and now here they were in the Food Office together.

'Like sisters,' everyone had always said of them.

Deborah asked about that morning's test and Sally gave her head a little shake. Just thinking about it made her uncomfortable.

'You know how I hate doing tests,' she said.

'Don't let it get to you,' said Deborah, not for the first time. Her bright-blue eyes, so like her brother Rod's, were sympathetic. 'I don't let them upset me. If a shopkeeper isn't obeying the rules, they deserve everything they get.'

'It wasn't the grocer in the shop today,' said Sally. 'It was an assistant – but it's the grocer who'll get it in the neck.'

The door opened and both girls looked round as Miss Greening from Housing walked in. She was a short, full-figured girl with a bubbly personality. She glanced around to make sure Mr Morland wasn't present. Holding up her left hand, she waggled it to show off the ring that had been the talk of the canteen yesterday after she had come to work flaunting it to all and sundry.

'My boss is out at meetings all day, so I'm going round showing everyone my ring.' She held out her hand over the place where the two desks joined.

'It's beautiful,' said Sally, looking at the pretty pear-shaped sapphire.

'D'you want to have a go?' Miss Greening started to pull the ring off.

Deborah immediately held out her hand for it, sliding it onto her finger and holding it out to admire it. 'Here you are.' She half-rose so she could lean across and give it to Sally. 'Your turn.'

Sally put it on her right hand. That seemed politer somehow when trying on someone else's engagement ring.

'Left hand!' Deborah chided and waited for Sally to comply. 'That's better. What do you think?' she asked Miss Greening.

'Looks like a perfect fit to me, Miss Grant,' said Miss Greening. She took the ring back and replaced it on her wedding finger.

When the door closed behind her, Sally remarked, 'We've had

a stream of engaged girls passing through our office recently, all showing off their rings.'

Deborah giggled. 'And we've tried them all on. It's been fun.' Her blue eyes sparkled.

'So many girls getting married,' said Sally. 'My mum says it's because of the war.'

The door opened again and the two girls bent their heads over their work as Mr Morland walked in. He was a middle-aged man, tall and well built with an upright posture, who always looked crisp and smart in pinstripes and a silver watch-chain. He had a kindly demeanour but his eyes were unexpectedly sharp and nothing got past him.

'You're back, Miss White. How did the Salford test go?'

Sally felt like saying, 'There was a young assistant and she fell for it, poor girl,' but she said formally, 'I was able to purchase the butter, sir.'

'Good, good.' Mr Morland always said, 'Good' when they trapped a wrongdoer. He never said, 'Good' when the shopkeeper was honest and refused to be caught out. 'Have you written up your report?'

'I'm just about to,' said Sally.

She had a form to fill in, giving all the details, including her own statement of what had taken place and when. Afterwards, she and Deborah went down to the canteen for their dinner. The room was noisy and a layer of grey tobacco smoke hung in the air above the tables. The choice today was fish-and-leek pudding or baked vegetable roll. Sally always paid attention to what was on offer. She might hate testing shopkeepers for honesty, but she loved the rest of her job and took it seriously. In these days of rationing, she wanted to be able to advise housewives on how to make tasty and nutritious meals. She was proud of the way she had come up in the world from shopgirl to Food Office clerk.

She and Deborah sat opposite one another. Deborah picked up the water jug and poured drinks for them both. A couple of girls from Transport, Miss Hill and Miss Brelland, joined them. Tall Miss Hill moved with languid grace. Miss Brelland was something of a beauty, with masses of reddish-gold hair.

'That's a pretty brooch,' Deborah told Miss Brelland.

'It's my birthday.' Miss Brelland touched the old-fashioned cameo on the lapel of her linen jacket. 'My mother gave it to me. It isn't new. It used to belong to my great-aunt.'

'Happy birthday,' said Sally. 'Are you doing anything special?'

'I'm on fire-watching duty tonight.' Miss Brelland pulled a face, but she didn't sound grumpy, just matter of fact. 'But me and the girls are going to the flicks tomorrow night and then we're going dancing on Saturday.'

'What film are you going to see?' Deborah asked.

'The others let me choose,' said Miss Brelland, 'so it's going to be *It's a Wonderful World*. I love James Stewart. He's so handsome.'

'It's a good film,' added Miss Hill. 'I saw it when it first came out. It's got everything – comedy, mystery, romance.'

'Not to mention a handsome hero,' said Sally.

'I hope you enjoy it,' Deborah added.

'I will,' Miss Brelland said. 'I've been on fire-watching duty for six nights, so I'm looking forward to some time off.'

'We'll be at a party on Saturday evening, won't we, Miss White?' said Deborah. Office etiquette required them to be formal in the presence of their colleagues. To the others, she said, 'It's my brother's birthday. He's at home for a few days. My mum is thrilled to pieces. We haven't seen him since war was declared.'

'I remember you saying when he went away.' Miss Hill nodded, her brow furrowing slightly above her brown eyes as she recalled. 'He's an engineer – that's right, isn't it?'

'Yes,' said Deborah. 'He used to work on the docks at the Manchester Ship Canal. He's a caulker. That means he makes ships watertight. When he lived here, he did repair work, but once the war started he was sent off to the shipyards in Barrow-in-Furness to work on actual shipbuilding for the war effort.'

'It sounds like he's earned his birthday party,' said Miss Brelland.

'Mum and Dad have hired the church hall for the occasion,' said Deborah. 'It's not just for his birthday. It's to give him a good send-off as well because he'll be heading back up north next week.' She gave Sally a smile. 'It's going to be a wonderful night.'

'I hope so,' Sally agreed.

She smiled back at Deborah. She was looking forward to the party. Rod was important to her. When they were all children, Deborah had thought it great fun to tease her big brother and generally make a nuisance of herself, but Sally had always looked up to him. He was so good-looking. He had the same bright-blue eyes as his sister, and they both had hair of such a dark brown as to verge on black, but, while Deborah's face was heart-shaped, Rod's was narrow with higher cheekbones.

Last year, as preparations for war had got under way, Rod had helped Sally's dad dig the huge hole they needed in their back garden for the Anderson shelter. Sally and Rod had grown friendlier and Rod had taken Sally out a few times without Deborah, which had never happened before and felt very exciting. Sally had felt Mum and Mrs Grant looking at her in a new way, as if she was more grown up now. She enjoyed that because, as the daughter of older parents, she often felt she was wrapped in cotton wool.

Sally had explained this to Rod. 'I think Mum and Dad can see I'm not their precious little girl any more.'

'No – you're my girl now,' Rod had replied, and he had grasped her hand tightly, pressing it to his chest. 'I'll take care of you.'

Something had squirmed inside Sally. She didn't like the suggestion that she was someone else's possession – but that was just Rod's way of speaking, that's all. It didn't mean he felt he owned her. Even so, she'd worked hard to train as a typist and had done well for herself. It would have been nice if Rod had acknowledged that.

It would have been nice too if he didn't always hold her hand so tightly. On the couple of occasions when she had murmured a protest, he'd smiled and asked, 'Can you blame me?' as if holding her hand so firmly was a kind of compliment.

Sally had tried linking arms with him after that. She often linked arms with Dad, loving the cosy affection and companionship, enjoying the thought that the world could see they were special to one another. But Rod's idea of linking was more like being clamped to his side.

When Rod was packed off to Barrow-in-Furness, it had happened at short notice, causing a great flap in the Grant family. Rod's mum in particular was really upset and that upset Sally too because she loved Mrs Grant. When Rod had asked Sally if she'd write to him, she said yes, but the truth was she felt torn and uncertain. Did she truly want to be clamped to Rod's side? But it was impossible to hint at her thoughts when everyone else was shocked and agitated at Rod's imminent departure. He had received just forty-eight hours' notice of his move. Mrs Grant was struggling to get his packing done, all the while on the verge of tears.

That had been at the start of the war. Now Rod was back, but, even though he had only just come home, the time was already fast approaching when he would have to return to Barrow. Sally knew what a wrench it would be for his family. They were extremely fortunate to have him in a reserved occupation, especially after what had happened at Dunkirk just a matter of weeks ago.

Something caught in the back of Sally's throat. The thought of Dunkirk was still raw and she was sure the rest of the country felt the same. The shock and fear caused by the retreat of the British Expeditionary Force to the northern shores of Europe was not to be forgotten, even though it was mingled with the enormous pride and gratitude at the courage and resilience of the many ships, both large and small, that had crossed the Channel repeatedly to rescue as many men as they could, snatching a potent moral victory from the jaws of what would otherwise have been a crushing defeat.

After the way the ships and boats of all types had rallied to save the army at Dunkirk, Sally was even prouder to think of Rod working in shipbuilding. This party on Saturday for his birthday was going to be the best possible send-off he could have. She wanted him to have that. He deserved it.

And afterwards he would go away again.

CHAPTER THREE

Sally and Deborah walked down the aisle between the seats and stepped down onto the platform at the rear of the bus, ready to get off at their stop. There was a yell from behind them.

'Miss! You've left your gas-mask behind.'

'Cripes,' muttered Deborah, hurrying back to fetch it.

The bus pulled in to the side of the road and they jumped off, walking arm in arm along the pavement through the soft golden glow of early evening, discussing whether Clark Gable was more handsome than Robert Donat and whether they should go and see *Gone With the Wind* again.

'That would make three times,' said Deborah, 'and there are lots of other films we want to see.'

At Deborah's garden gate, they parted and Sally continued down the road to her family's house. Each house had a small front garden. The Whites' was paved over and Dad, fully aware of the need for everyone now to grow as much of their own food as they could, had installed some wooden troughs for growing salad. For weeks, while Sally and Mum exchanged amused and indulgent glances, he had been talking about the importance of successive sowing and how he intended to keep them supplied with lettuce, radishes, spinach and beetroot until the first frosts.

Sally let herself into the house, smiling at the familiar, comforting scents of lavender polish and tobacco. She hung up her gas-mask box on one of the pegs attached to the wall in the narrow hallway. Mum and Dad were in the parlour, as they always were when she arrived home from work. Dad was reading the paper and Mum was knitting, a cigarette sitting in the ashtray beside her, a thin plume of smoke curling as it rose.

'There you are, love.' Mum looked up with a smile as Sally bent to kiss her. 'I'll finish this row and then do the tea.'

All three of them ate their dinners in the middle of the day, Sally in the canteen or occasionally, as a treat, in a cafe, Mum and Dad at home. Really, they were old to have a child of Sally's age. Mum's hair, which had been salt-and-pepper while Sally was growing up, was now grey. Dad had hardly any hair left at all, just the thinnest of wispy layers around the sides and at the back. Sally remembered when he had been full-faced. Now his cheeks were sunken beneath his blue eyes.

When she was little, it had never really struck Sally that her parents were so much older than everyone else's. It wasn't until she was twelve and went into Miss Delaney's class that it hit home. Miss Delaney had taught for donkey's years and in fact had taught many of her pupils' parents. When she punished a child – and she was a demon with the leather strap for all that she looked like she could barely withstand a puff of wind – she would often turn away muttering darkly, 'Just like his father,' as if this was the worst thing that could possibly be said about anybody.

Nearly all the parents of the sixty children in Sally's class, including Deborah's mum and dad, had been taught by Miss Delaney – but Sally's mum had gone to school with her. It was as if the White family had a generation missing, because Sally's parents were of a similar age to everyone's grandparents. Deborah sometimes moaned about her own mother, but Sally loved Mrs

Grant because she seemed so young and approachable. When Sally's mum said, 'When I was your age,' it felt like a hundred years ago. When Deborah's mum said it, it seemed entirely real and believable. Back when Sally's mum had been Sally's age – twenty – Queen Victoria had only just died. Deborah's mother hadn't turned twenty until after the Great War – in fact, not until after the Spanish flu.

Mum had endured several 'unhappy events' before having Sally. As a child, Sally had had no idea what this meant, but now she knew this meant Mum had suffered miscarriages. Not that Mum had said any such thing. It was Deborah's mum who had taken Sally aside one day for a quiet word.

Dad was older than Mum and he was retired. He had been forty when war had broken out in 1914, which meant that when conscription was introduced he was too old to be called up. Dad never talked about it, but Mum had whispered to Sally that Dad had been presented with white feathers by women who considered him a coward for not fighting and he had been taunted for having White as his surname. In fact, it wasn't until the final desperate months of the war, when the conscription age was raised to fifty-one, that Dad had been called up, but instead of being sent across the Channel to fight in the trenches he had been given a job in the south of England in the stores, responsible for checking and sending out equipment.

He was extra-determined to do as much as he could this time round and had signed up for Air Raid Precautions the moment the lists had opened. Sally had been taken aback when she glimpsed tears in his eyes when he received his tin helmet and ARP armband. As much as she sometimes wished that her mum was younger, she had never wished the same about her dad. She thought the world of him just as he was. She loved everything about him, from the sweet scent of his pipe tobacco to the two deep vertical lines in between his bushy eyebrows. Dad always wore a tweed jacket with leather patches on the elbows when he was indoors. It had to be blazing hot, like it had been that last summer before the war, before he would divest himself of his jacket – and even then he only took it off indoors. He would never have been seen outside the house unless he was properly dressed.

It could be a bit of a bore having an older mother, but there was something special about having an older father. Sally felt deeply loved. It tugged at her heart sometimes when she thought how her darling dad was of a comparable age to her friends' grandads. She couldn't bear to think about how she wouldn't have him for as long as Deborah would have her father.

Mum went into the kitchen to make the tea and Sally went to help. Sometimes she stayed in the parlour with Dad, and Mum didn't mind; but at other times Mum would get huffy, though without saying why. Likewise, when Sally did go to help with the tea, Mum sometimes shooed her out of the kitchen, saying, 'You go out to the office and do your job. My job is to look after you when you come home.' But on other occasions she would accept Sally's assistance without a murmur. It was important to try to do the right thing with Mum, though you couldn't always tell what that might be.

Their kitchen was old-fashioned. It still had the huge black range from goodness knew how many years ago. The most modern thing was a kitchen cabinet with a drop-down surface and various shelves, cupboards and drawers, and even that must have been the best part of twenty years old.

'It's only stewed kidneys on toast,' said Mum, slicing the loaf, 'and the kidneys are ready. They just need warming through. I've already set the table. Go and sit with your dad. He's got himself worried because of women and children arriving here from Gibraltar. It's only a few days since people were trying to escape from the Channel Islands.'

'The more who escape the better,' said Sally.

'Your dad's taking it all to heart. Things seem to be going Hitler's way.'

'Only for now.' Sally straightened her spine. 'He'll soon see he can't push us around.'

She spoke staunchly, but the fear of invasion was in every heart and it hadn't helped that Jerry had snatched the Channel Islands. With that and what had happened at Dunkirk, where would it end?

Victory. It had to end in victory. The alternative was unthinkable.

Picking up the *Radio Times*, which this week featured a photograph of the actor Jack Buchanan on the cover, Dad flicked through until he reached today's programmes. Sitting opposite him in her comfy old armchair, Mum lit a Craven A and inhaled deeply, shutting her eyes as she blew out the first stream of smoke. She enjoyed a cigarette at various points during the day, though only inside her own house, of course. She wouldn't dream of smoking outside the home. Sally sat drinking her cup of tea. She was enjoying a cigarette too. The Whites always ended their teatime meal in the parlour with a cup of tea and a ciggie, or in Dad's case a pipe.

Dad chuckled. 'Did you say you're off to the pictures, Sally? Me and your mum will be listening to *General Release* later on. That's music from the films.'

Sally chuckled too. 'Maybe they'll play the music from whatever I'm watching. We haven't chosen the film yet.'

She finished her tea, then went upstairs to get changed, putting away the cream blouse and navy skirt she wore for the office and choosing her fawn dress dotted with tiny white spots. She'd had the dress for several years and had turned up the skirt to the fashionable knee length. Over it she wore a pretty, white cardy with short sleeves that Mum had crocheted for her.

She was ready to walk along the road to Deborah's house when there was a cheery rat-tat at the front door and she opened it to find that Deborah and Rod had come to fetch her. Deborah looked trim in a boat-necked mauve dress she and her mum had made together. The colour suited her blue eyes and dark hair. As for Rod – well, he would look good whatever he wore. This evening he was decked out in a suit comprising a single-breasted jacket with pocket-flaps and trousers with turn-ups, together with items Sally was familiar with: his blue-and-grey-striped tie, his grey trilby and black leather lace-ups.

'Well! Don't you look smart,' Sally said, feeling proud of him.

'Don't you start,' said Deborah. 'You should hear Mum going on about how handsome he is.'

Rod grinned. 'Sally thinks I'm handsome – don't you, Sally?'

'Don't encourage him,' Deborah said at once.

That saved Sally from answering. She hadn't expected to see Rod this evening and she felt a little uncomfortable. While he had been away, writing to him had been made easier by the fact that he wasn't much of a letter-writer and she had only written in reply, never sending extra letters. She'd kept her tone cheerful and friendly, not lovey-dovey. She hadn't wanted to commit herself – although hadn't the simple fact of writing been a kind of commitment?

So far during Rod's few days at home, she had avoided being on her own with him. With their two families being so close, she couldn't help feeling hemmed in. Hemmed in? Now she was being daft – dramatic – and that wasn't like her.

Rod was looking at her now, his bright-blue eyes gazing into her face as he waited for her to speak.

'Is it a new suit?' she asked.

'I'm earning more up in Barrow than I did on the Ship Canal,' said Rod, 'so I thought I'd treat myself.' He thrust out his chest, looking pleased with himself.

'Come in and say a quick hello to Mum and Dad,' said Sally, leading the way to the parlour.

'Are you going with them, Deborah?' asked Mum, and Sally groaned silently.

It was Rod who answered. 'It's not Debs who's the extra one here, Mrs White. It's me. I count myself honoured to be allowed to go out with these two. Everyone knows they're inseparable.'

That made everyone laugh. Sally put on her linen jacket, picked up her handbag, slung her gas-mask box over her shoulder, and they set off. They met up with a couple of chums and went to the pictures. As Abbott and Costello larked around on the screen, Sally sat beside Rod in the tobacco-scented darkness. He took her hand. Took it. He didn't reach out and touch it, seeking permission, but took it and held it. Pure instinct prompted Sally to try to pull away, but Rod didn't let go. Sally gave in. She didn't want to surrender, but what else was she supposed to do? She didn't want to cause a fuss.

At the end, when everyone respectfully stood up, she tugged free. Rod would have kept her hand, but she whispered, 'Not during the national anthem.'

Rod chuckled but he complied. Soon they joined the crowds leaving the cinema and heading outside into the blackout. There were those who claimed it was a good idea to stand still while their eyes adjusted, but Sally thought the truth was that your eyes simply never got used to it. This blackout darkness was deeper than any she had ever experienced and it still had the power to take her by surprise. There had been both hilarity and alarm on so-called 'black Friday', the day the blackout started on the first of September last year. To start with, even a faint torchlight had been forbidden, but that had soon proved unsustainable and by the middle of the month it had become legal to use a torch, as long as you dulled the beam using at least two thicknesses of tissue paper and pointed the light, such as it was, downwards.

But Sally had learned to look upwards as well at the beauty of the night skies, ink-black and speckled with brilliant pinpoints of starlight, though she had soon learned not to say so, because there was always someone who would say, 'Oh aye, perfect for Jerry. He'll see exactly where to drop his bombs.' That hadn't happened yet round here – well, apart from the bomb over in Salford a day or two ago. It gave Sally a shivery feeling to think that maybe there were more bombs to come. It wasn't just high explosives everyone was scared of. It was the thought of having gas-bombs dropped on them.

She, Deborah and Rod headed for home, Rod in the middle with a girl on each side. They took particular care as they stepped onto or off kerbs. Everyone knew someone who had twisted an ankle that way. They stopped off at the Grants' house. When Deborah said goodnight, Sally gave her a swift hug, which gave her a reason to free herself from Rod.

'Don't do anything I wouldn't do,' Deborah called to them as she turned the key.

'That gives us plenty of scope,' retorted her brother.

Deborah slipped inside, batting her way past the blackout curtain without letting so much as a sliver of light peep out. Rod took Sally's hand and they walked along the road to her house. Reaching the gate, he gave her hand a tug, turning her to face him and drawing her close. Sally placed her free hand lightly on his chest.

'I'd better go in.' She glanced towards the front door. 'Mum and Dad will be waiting up for me.' She laughed as she added, 'And if you don't get home pretty sharpish, we'll have your sister making meaningful remarks to us.'

'Pesky little brat,' said Rod.

'Hey, that's my best friend you're talking about.' Sally pretended to give him a slap. She stepped away. 'I'd better go in.'

Rod pulled her back to him, seeming unaware of her reluctance. 'A goodnight kiss first.'

CHAPTER FOUR

Sally walked into the church hall near the big crossroads in Fallowfield. Before the war it would have been used for parish committees, fundraising amateur concerts and the knitting circle. No doubt those things still took place, but the hall also had other purposes now. The war might yet have to start in earnest at home, but all the preparations were in place. You only had to look at the information on the noticeboard, all those lists and dates to do with the Women's Voluntary Service, first-aid training, ARP duty rosters and lectures on gas attacks. Sally knew all about gas attacks, because she'd had special training for her voluntary night-time war work. She was up there on the noticeboard too, on the list headed AUGUST. She came here twice a month to give advice on the first and third Thursday mornings. Today was not only the first Thursday, it was the first of the month, so she was right at the top of the list.

This morning, the Citizens Advice Bureau had a trestle table at one end of the room. People awaited their turn, sitting on a line of wooden chairs along the wall. Sally passed a small group of WVS ladies talking about providing care and support for a woman who had come out of hospital following an operation.

Mrs Jasper came towards Sally, dressed in the dark-green uniform of the WVS. Mrs Jasper was nicely spoken with a calm manner. She had lost her husband in the last war and both her grown-up sons were in the merchant navy.

'Good morning, Miss White.' Mrs Jasper lowered her voice to add, 'You've already got a customer. She was on the doorstep when I arrived to open up. I've parked her over there until you get set up.'

Sally glanced down the long room, trying not to be obvious about it. She saw a thin lady in a fox-fur and a small, angled hat with a brooch pinned to the front. She caught Sally looking.

'I'll be with you in a minute,' Sally called.

She quickly set up her table, opening the advice box and removing pamphlets and stationery. In this place, her 'desk' was a green-baize-topped card table. It stood next to a shelf, so she always arranged the pamphlets on that. It looked more professional than having a cluttered table. Popping her handbag and gas-mask box beneath her chair, she took a few steps down the room, the heels of her two-tone leather shoes tapping loudly on the bare floorboards. She smiled an invitation at the woman, who stood up.

'Please take a seat,' said Sally when the lady came to her table. 'I'm Miss White. What can I do for you?' She took care to keep her voice and her expression neutral until she knew the nature of the query.

'I'm Mrs Bradbury and I've come for the new ration books for my family.'

'What happened to your old ones?'

'The gentleman from the Food Oversight Office took them. He said they were part of a lot where the printing had been botched and that I should apply to you for a new set.'

The Food Oversight Office? That was a new one. Usually it was the Food Control Office when this happened. Sally smothered a sigh. How long had they had ration books now and how many times had folk been warned?

'I'm sorry to tell you that you've been the victim of a confidence trickster, Mrs Bradbury,' she said. 'There was nothing wrong with your ration books, but not to worry. I can deal with this for you, and I'll also need some details for the police.'

Poor Mrs Bradbury opened and closed her mouth like a goldfish, then burst into tears. Honestly, the advice box ought to contain a stock of spare hankies – large ones, not silly little lace-edged confections such as the one Mrs Bradbury was now using to dab at her cheeks.

'Have you finished?' Mrs Jasper asked, edging forward, when Sally finished writing and put the cap on her fountain pen. She gave Mrs Bradbury a sympathetic look. 'I couldn't help noticing...'

'This is Mrs Bradbury,' said Sally. 'She's had rather a shock.'

'I'm sorry to hear that, dear,' said Mrs Jasper, guiding the lady away. 'Let me make you a cup of tea and you can tell me all about it.'

Sally's next clients were already waiting, a middle-aged lady and a redhead of about eighteen, probably mother and daughter judging by the identical oval faces and straight noses. Sally waved them towards the chairs on the other side of her table.

'I'm Mrs Langtree,' said the woman, 'and this is my daughter Florence.'

'I'm Miss White. What can I do for you?' Sally asked in her neutral voice.

'Our Florence is getting wed,' said Mrs Langtree.

Sally smiled. She was going to enjoy this one. 'Congratulations. When's the big day?'

'End of September,' said Florence.

'We've come to see about extra coupons,' said her mother. 'We thought it best to come in plenty of time.'

'You did the right thing,' Sally assured her. 'Are you aware of the ban that's coming into force next week about icing on cakes?'

'That's why we're here today,' said Mrs Langtree. 'We want to get our order in before the ban starts.'

'I'm sorry,' said Sally, 'but wedding rations are based on the date of the wedding, not the date of applying. I'm afraid this week's brides will be the last to have iced wedding cakes.'

Florence's face fell a mile and Sally's heart reached out to her.

'Oh well,' said Mrs Langtree. 'What can we have?'

Sally knew it by heart. 'Quarter-ounce butter and eight ounces sugar per person; and one pint of milk per twenty guests.'

'It doesn't sound much,' Florence lamented.

'You're the one who insisted on getting wed in wartime,' said Mrs Langtree. 'Don't forget Auntie Mavis has those two tins of peaches.'

'You'll be allowed extra rations for a maximum of forty people,' said Sally.

Florence brightened. 'That means we don't have to invite Mary's brats.'

Sally stood up and took two pamphlets off the shelf. 'This is a reminder of the rations available and this one is a cake recipe.'

Before handing them over, she hole-punched each top left-hand corner and treasury-tagged them together. All the Town Hall girls were hole-punching like crazy at the moment and saving all the tiny circles of paper for confetti, because several girls were tying the knot in the next few weeks.

'Remember to get your cherries and candied peel before the end of the month,' Sally advised. 'You won't be able to get them come September. This is your application form for the extra rations. If you fill it in now, I can get matters under way for you.'

She helped them to fill in the form and saw them on their way. She had a little queue now. She approached the man who was first. He was about Dad's age, with big bags under his eyes.

'Would you like to come to my desk?' she said.

As he got up, the woman beside him rose as well and he ushered her forward. Sally waited for them to take their seats before she resumed her own.

'I'm Miss White. What can I do for you?'

The woman uttered a gurgle and pressed a screwed-up hanky to her mouth. The man patted her arm. Sally knew what was coming next.

'We're organising a funeral,' said the man.

'We want to give him a good send-off,' the woman added in a choked voice.

'I can help you with that,' Sally said gently.

Sally spent the afternoon in the office. Sunshine poured through the windows, the shadows of the anti-blast tape creating zigzag lines on the floor. Mr Morland had dictated a couple of letters to Deborah earlier. The dictation had been pretty slow, because the girls hadn't learned shorthand at night school, only typing. As Deborah typed the letters, her gaze rested on the piece of paper beside her and her fingers flew confidently across the keys. Sally smiled to herself, remembering how hard it had been to learn the layout of the keyboard. The teacher at night school used to place a board over each typewriter and the girls had to slip their hands underneath to do the typing, so nobody could cheat by looking at the letters. It had felt like hell on earth at the time, but now she and Deborah were glad of it.

Seated behind his desk, Mr Morland unfolded a sheet of paper and nodded complacently.

'The lists for the magistrates' courts for next week. You shall accompany me on Monday afternoon, if you please, Miss White.'

'Yes, Mr Morland,' said Sally.

Rising from her seat, she took the list and pinned it to the noticeboard on the wall above the radiator. As she glanced down the list, the words *Mr Tucker & female asst* caught her eye. What a pretty smile that girl had had. The dimple had showed it was a real smile too, not just a polite stretch of her lips. Sally felt bad for her. She didn't deserve to land in hot water – well, she deserved it, obviously, because she'd flouted the rules, but... oh, Sally hated performing the tests, hated setting out to trip people up, especially folk like the girl with the dimple. She had only wanted to be kind.

The time ticked its way towards six o'clock. Sally and Deborah kept on working. When it was just the two of them, they started packing up and getting ready to go so that they could leave on the dot of six, but that wasn't allowed when Mr Morland was here. He was a real stickler. When the clock struck, the girls tidied their desks and Mr Morland locked the filing cabinets before putting on his bowler hat.

The girls helped one another into their jackets and put on their hats. Deborah sported a beret, which she wore at a jaunty angle, while Sally wore a straw hat with a floral band round the crown.

'You can't go wrong with straw,' according to Mum. 'They never go out of fashion and you can use different bands to ring the changes.'

Mr Morland held open the office door for them and the girls bade him a polite goodbye as they left, gas-mask boxes swinging from their shoulders. They headed downstairs, running down the second flight. As they reached the bottom, Sally missed her footing and stumbled. She cried out in surprise and might well have measured her length on the chessboard-tiled floor except that a strong pair of hands caught hold of her, steadying her. She found herself standing very close to her rescuer, looking up into a pair of warm brown eyes beneath the brim of a cloth cap.

Sally's breath caught, which of course was natural because she'd almost suffered a fall; except that she knew that wasn't the real reason. A layer of the tiniest tingles shivered across her skin. For a moment her thoughts scattered in all directions, then rushed back together again.

'Found your feet?' The man's square jawline was softened by a boyish smile. He smelled of soap, fresh air, tobacco and something that Sally took a moment to recognise. Yes – wood shavings.

Sally nodded, laughing at her clumsiness. 'Thanks. I thought I was going to land head first. Not very elegant.' It wasn't her clumsiness that had made her laugh. It was the racing heartbeat drumming in her chest.

The man let go of her but made a play of staying close, hands at the ready. 'Just making sure you aren't going to topple over.' There was a playful twinkle in his brown eyes.

When he smiled at her, Sally smiled back. Heavens, was she blushing? She didn't feel uncomfortable, though. The young man might have made a joke out of her stumble, but he'd done it kindly and light-heartedly, creating a moment of closeness between them.

'Thank you,' she said.

He was tall and good-looking and his hands had been swift and strong. 'My pleasure.' He touched the brim of his cap to her.

Deborah was waiting. 'Idiot,' she said affectionately when Sally joined her, and they walked on. Others were leaving the building and the two girls slowed as they came to the doors. Sally looked back over her shoulder. The young man stood at the foot of the staircase, watching her. Their glances caught for one final time and Sally's heart thumped.

CHAPTER FIVE

The following afternoon, Deborah was out of the office doing tests on the unsuspecting shopkeepers of Ordsall. Sally had never understood how Deborah could remain unaffected by having to undertake this task, but Deborah didn't seem to mind it at all.

'It's just another duty,' was her attitude. 'It's nice to get out of the office.'

She had set off with her list tucked into her handbag and her gas-mask box hanging from her shoulder. She looked neat in her crisp blouse and dark skirt. There was no uniform as such for the office girls in the Town Hall, but they all wore either a dark dress or a dark skirt with a white or cream blouse. It was the done thing. Deborah had once suggested to Mr Morland that on days when they were to go out doing tests they should be allowed to wear ordinary clothes, something summery and pretty so they didn't look like office girls, but he wouldn't have it.

'The shopkeepers might suspect we're there to test them if we dress this way,' she had said.

'They don't seem to have suspected it thus far if the results are anything to go by,' was the firm reply.

Deborah hadn't gone out until after their tea break and was

due to go straight home after completing her final test. Sally got on with her work. She had a lot of filing to do. Deborah thought filing was boring, but Sally liked the precision it involved. There was one correct place for each paper or each folder and to put something in the wrong place might mean it couldn't be found quickly when it was required.

As she did her filing, she thought about tomorrow's birthday party for Rod. A smile touched her lips. Mr and Mrs Grant had organised what they called 'the best bash' they could. They had hired the bowls club hut – which made it sound small and poky, but actually it was a decent-sized room. Not as big as the church hall, but plenty large enough for a party for family and friends, and it had a little kitchen attached. Deborah and Sally had spent ages working on a party menu, to which everyone was contributing a plate of something, and Mr Grant was going to bring his gramophone, so there would be music and dancing.

Sally was looking forward to the party. She knew how much effort had gone into putting it together and wanted it to be a success. She also knew she had to do some serious thinking about Rod. Everyone else was delighted for them to be a couple, but Sally wasn't so sure. It had been easy to ignore her doubts while he was away in Barrow, but now she was forced to confront them again. Not that she could do anything about them during Rod's birthday weekend. That would be too unkind.

When she went downstairs to the ground floor at the end of the day, her heart leaped at the sight of her rescuer from yesterday standing beside the front doors. His stance was casual, with one shoulder leaning against the wall, and he stood up straight when he caught sight of her. His build was slim and athletic, his face narrow with a firm sweep of jawline. Tiny pulses jumped in Sally's wrists and in the base of her throat. Her senses seemed ultra-aware. She went straight to him. Any other action would have been impossible.

He raised his cap to her. His brown eyes were warm with a clear gaze.

'I wasn't expecting to see you again.' Even as she uttered the words, Sally questioned whether they were true.

'I've been standing here trying to think what to say to you if you appeared. "No ill-effects after your tumble?" was the best I could come up with. But that would be a daft thing to say, because you weren't hurt. It was just an excuse to speak to you. The truth is... I wanted to see you again. Are you free for a cup of tea? Please? Right now?'

'I have to get home. My mother will be expecting me.'

'Just a few minutes.'

She ought to say, 'No, thank you.' She ought to say, 'I have a boyfriend.'

'Just for a few minutes, then,' she said.

He smiled and something inside Sally melted.

'Andrew Henshaw.'

'Sally White.'

There was no handshake. It was safer that way – now where had that thought sprung from?

They went to the Worker Bee cafe on Deansgate. Sally had been there a few times before, though not for some time. It wasn't as smart as a Lyons Corner House, but it was clean and unpretentious and the food was tasty. Andrew opened the door and Sally entered, glancing up at a tall wooden frame immediately inside.

'The owner has rigged up an intricate blackout system,' Andrew explained. 'If you come here after dark, you find yourself in a small area surrounded by blackout fabric. When you've shut the door behind you, you can move the fabric aside and walk in properly.'

'Like a magician's magic cabinet,' said Sally.

There were two free tables, one in the window and the other

in the corner near the wooden counter. Sally went to that one, instinctively wanting to hide herself away. Did that mean she was doing wrong? It didn't feel wrong, but that didn't mean she wanted to be seen by anyone she knew.

Andrew wasn't handsome the way Rod was, but he was definitely good-looking. His brown eyes, as well as being warm and kind, were intelligent. But he wasn't in uniform – and why not, at his age? A knot of guilt immediately tightened in the back of Sally's throat as she thought of Dad being presented with white feathers in the last war. She would never do that to anybody, not even in her thoughts. It was wrong to make assumptions.

Sally poured tea for them both from the brown earthenware pot and drew her cup and saucer towards her. What was she doing sitting here with a stranger? What had got into her?

Andrew took out Capstans from his pocket and offered her the open packet. She shook her head. Mum would throw a fit if she smoked in public.

'Well, Sally White,' said Andrew after he had inhaled and blown out a stream of smoke, taking care not to blow it across the table. 'What job do you do in the Town Hall? Or aren't you allowed to say?'

Sally hesitated. Everyone was constantly being reminded not to hand out information willy-nilly, no matter how unimportant it might seem. It wasn't just a matter of what to say or not say to a stranger. There was also the question of who might be listening.

But there was no harm in saying, 'I work in the Food Office. You know, rationing, things like that.' She wouldn't mention the way they tested shopkeepers for honesty.

Andrew nodded. 'Important work. Are you tied to the office or do you get out and about?'

'We run advice sessions in church halls and places like that. I enjoy meeting people and the feeling that I'm helping them.'

Andrew smiled. 'So you don't have to face too many complaints about rationing?'

'Some folk have a bit of a grumble, but mostly the public understands that it's fair shares for all. I'm always on the lookout for nutritious recipes to share.'

'Is that part of your remit?'

'No,' said Sally, 'but I like to give housewives fresh ideas when I can – and I like them to give me ideas too.'

Andrew nodded, smiling. 'That shows you care about your work. You're going above and beyond what's required. Good for you.'

The praise was delivered in a matter-of-fact way that made it all the more sincere and Sally was warmed by an inner glow. 'I want to do my bit, that's all, same as everyone else. What job do you do?'

'I'm a teacher,' Andrew told her. 'My father was a cabinet-maker and I followed in his footsteps, though not in the way he'd intended – I became a carpenter and joiner, but what I really wanted was to teach. I was lucky. I spent a couple of years at night school and after that I was awarded a college place.'

'That doesn't sound like luck. It sounds like you must have worked jolly hard.'

'There's a lot to be said for following your heart,' said Andrew, and Sally's own heart took the next few beats at a rush. 'I'm a woodwork teacher now. I want to give my lads the best possible training, so that for the best ones an apprenticeship to a carpenter or even a cabinetmaker is a real option. The ones who aren't up to that standard will still be able to do all kinds of useful jobs around the home for the rest of their lives. Not just putting up shelves but building the shelves in the first place; or making a new leg to go on a rickety table or stool. I love carpentry, but what I love most is passing on my skills to others and seeing young lads blossom.'

'That's a funny word to use.'

'It's accurate, though. Most of the boys I teach have a tough time in the classroom because they're not academically inclined. I want them to see that there's more to education than subordinate clauses and knowing the kings and queens of England by heart. Once a boy finds something he's good at, it changes his attitude to everything else.'

Sally wanted to praise him, but felt shy. Anyway, after the compliment he had paid her about her own work, it might sound as if she was just commending him for form's sake. Instead she asked, 'Weren't you evacuated last September with the schools?'

'Not all the kids went away. A lot of parents simply refused to part with them, so some schools have been merged together. I was told to stay here.'

'What are you doing with your summer holiday?'

'Is that a polite way of asking if I'm whiling away my days smoking and doing crosswords?'

'Sort of,' Sally admitted. She badly wanted him to be engaged in something worthwhile.

'Fair enough,' said Andrew with a grin. 'The Corporation has got me doing repairs in their Corporation houses. I also run a youth club near where I live.'

'Where's that?' Heavens, what a forward question!

'Chorlton. Cum-Hardy, not on-Medlock.'

Sally felt tingly with pleasure. She smiled and then quickly reined it in. Honestly, why was she so delighted? 'I live in Withington.'

'So we're not far from one another.' Andrew was suddenly serious. There was a suggestion of vulnerability in the set of his lips. 'Which is as good a way as any of asking... can I see you again?'

CHAPTER SIX

Sally hurried home, half-dazed, half-alarmed. She had spent far too long with Andrew. She had only realised how long because the Worker Bee had become busier and the waitress had asked them if they were going to be much longer. A flush had crept across Sally's cheeks. They had drained the teapot some time ago.

Hastening into the house, she kissed Mum. 'Sorry I'm late. I had to finish a piece of work.'

The lie slipped out before she knew it and she turned cold inside, but what else could she have said? She couldn't say she'd gone to a cafe with a man she didn't know and they'd lost track of time because they were so busy revelling in one another's company. No respectable girl who already had a sort-of boyfriend could possibly say that. And what had she been thinking of to do such a thing? Anyhow, it didn't matter, because she had told Andrew she couldn't see him again.

Her life was complicated enough with Rod to cope with. Seeing another man was out of the question. She had dashed aside the temptation to ask Andrew if he would wait for her, because that would be a shabby thing to do to Rod, whatever her real feelings about him. He was entitled to better treatment than that from her. At the same time, she was aware that meeting Andrew had made her more willing to take a stand. She just had to get the timing right.

She and Deborah were due to go on duty in the wartime mortuary in Embden Street that night, starting at ten o'clock. Before that, Sally was to spend the evening with Deborah and, for the first time in her life, she didn't want to. That time spent with Andrew had left her feeling raw and defenceless, as if she needed to recover. Recover? Nonsense! It had been a ridiculous thing to do and she shouldn't have done it. If she felt guilty and unsettled now, it was her own fault. The last thing she wanted was to be disloyal to Deborah and Rod. They had been there all her life and they deserved her loyalty even if she was having second thoughts about Rod. And then there were the four parents. They would be shocked if they knew what she was thinking. They were her real life. Andrew Henshaw wasn't. If she hadn't missed her footing on the stairs yesterday, she would never even have met him.

But she had met him and the memory made her insides flutter.

For tea, Mum had made spinach soup with dumplings. It was a recipe that Sally had been given by a lady who came to one of her advice sessions to ask about extra rations for her daughter, who was expecting a happy event early next year.

'This is good, Mum,' said Sally. 'I'll be able to give it a personal recommendation when I hand out the recipe.'

'Tell your ladies to add a bit more seasoning,' said Mum. She was a great one for adding herbs. She kept her own little herb garden in terracotta pots on the roof of the coal-hole outside the back door.

After tea, Sally got changed out of her office clothes and went round to the Grants' house. Rod wasn't there and Sally didn't know whether to be relieved. Then she felt guilty for wondering. It was a sultry evening and she and Deborah went for a walk, talking about tomorrow night's party.

'The Hardacres have still got bunting from the coronation,' said Deborah, 'and they're letting us have that to decorate the bowls club. Mum was in there this afternoon with Auntie Winnie, cleaning the windows and polishing the tables.'

'It's going to be perfect,' said Sally. This party meant so much to the Grant family.

Presently they set off back to the Grants', because there was a hairstyle Deborah wanted to try out.

'Instead of just styling my hair under at the back with curlers,' she confided, bending her head towards Sally's as they walked arm in arm past Fog Lane Park, 'I want to put a proper roll in it.'

'Like Miss Newton in Housing?' asked Sally. Miss Newton had recently shown off her own neatly rounded roll and whispered that the shape had been achieved by curling her hair round a long piece of sponge that was tucked inside.

'I want a bigger roll than that. I want to look really fashionable.'

'I've heard of girls winding their hair round a stocking.'

'I told you. I want a bigger roll. I've heard of some girls using...' Deborah glanced around as if the hedges were full of eavesdroppers. She dropped her voice to a whisper to say, '... a sanitary towel.'

'A—!' Sally exclaimed, cutting herself off before she could utter the disgraceful words. Leaning her head towards her friend's so their temples were touching, she whispered, 'You can't. It isn't decent. Just imagine if your hair came undone.'

'It won't,' Deborah insisted. 'Has Miss Newton's sponge ever been seen? Anyway, I want to try it. It's all right for you. You've got thick hair. Mine's flyaway. It needs all the help it can get.'

All at once they were giggling like schoolgirls. Like sisters. Like the lifelong chums they were.

At Deborah's house, they ran upstairs. The Grants' house was laid out the same as the Whites', but the Grants lived the other way round. Mum had her parlour at the back and her dining room in the front, while the Grants lived in their front room and had the dining table in the back room, next to the kitchen. Having their parlour in the front of the house meant the Grants could see who was going past and Sally liked that, but Mum said she liked living in the back because it was more private.

Deborah closed her bedroom door and Sally helped her remove the pins that held her hair away from her face. Then, not quite believing she was doing it, Sally wound Deborah's hair round a sanitary towel and pinned the lot into position. It took a few goes to get it right.

'What do you think?' Deborah asked, turning her head this way and that in front of the mirror.

'You've certainly got a bulkier roll.'

'I'm going to wear it like this tomorrow for the party.'

'Crikey. You'd better make sure you don't dance too energetically. We don't want the ST flying merrily across the dance-floor.'

That gave them the giggles again and, once they started, they couldn't stop. The door opened and Mrs Grant looked in.

'What's so funny? Oh my goodness, it's been a few years since I saw such guilty faces. That's how you used to look when you'd been up to something when you were little. I don't think I dare ask. I just popped up to say you should keep an eye on the time, Sally love.'

'Thanks, Mrs Grant. I'd better nip home and get my things. I'll call for you at twenty past, Debs.'

Sally went home. Mum had prepared her a sandwich and a Thermos to take with her. Sally didn't need to get changed; she would do that at the mortuary. That was why she and Deborah needed to set off in good time. Their duty wouldn't start until ten o'clock, but they had to be dressed in their gas-proof suits before that. Sally and Deborah's job would be to clean any contaminated bodies that were brought in. Their work required them to wear 'light' suits, while 'heavy' gas-proof suits of oilskin jacket, trousers and gloves plus gumboots and gas-mask were the uniform of the decontamination squads who would have to work in exposed conditions.

The thought of a gas attack was terrifying. Sally and Deborah had been shocked to be allocated gas-attack work when they signed up for voluntary duty, though their shock was nothing compared to their mothers'. Sally's mum had been all for marching straight to the depot to demand other work for her daughter, but Dad had put the kibosh on that.

'If this is the job our Sally has been asked to do,' he'd said, 'then she must do it. Think of it this way. She and Deborah are good girls and any dead people they have to decontaminate will be treated respectfully, just as their loved ones would wish.'

'But they're so young,' Mum wailed.

Dad had sighed. 'Everyone has to grow up quickly in wartime.' Then he uttered the words that chilled Sally to her core. 'And if there are going to be gas-bombs, wouldn't you rather our lass was wearing a gas-proof suit?'

So far, with the phoney war already having lasted months, the two girls had never been called upon to use their training. They cycled to the wartime mortuary in good time to get changed before they went on duty at ten and they were permitted, one at a time, to grab some shut-eye if nothing happened. So far nothing had, but the bombing in Salford earlier this week had brought everyone's thoughts into a sharper focus.

At half past midnight, a wailing sound rose through the warm night air. Apprehension rattled through Sally as she and Deborah stared at one another. This was it. The real thing. Deborah's face had gone ashen and Sally was sure the same must have happened to her. Then she pulled herself together and the two of them exchanged crisp nods. They were ready.

Above them came the drone of aircraft engines, and less than a minute later the anti-aircraft guns began firing.

'It sounds as if it's right overhead,' said Deborah, her hand slipping into Sally's.

'Don't let it fool you,' said one of the mortuary men from behind them. 'Sound travels on a still night like this.'

And that must have been the case, because although the sounds continued at the same volume, and there were the *crump* sounds as bombs landed, the noises drew no closer and the building didn't shake. Sally tensed in anticipation each time she heard a vehicle nearby, but each one carried on and no bodies were brought into the mortuary.

After forty minutes, the all-clear sounded. Sally's heart thumped. Although nowhere in the immediate vicinity had copped it, tonight's raid felt like a promise of more to come.

'Should one of us try to get some sleep?' asked Deborah.

'Best not,' said Sally. 'There might be another raid.'

So they stayed up, but, as the night lengthened with no more disturbances, they took turns to sleep – though neither of them managed more than a light doze.

At six o'clock, they removed their uniforms and changed back into their own clothes to cycle home. The early morning was crisp and cool, bright with birdsong. Normally, Sally would cycle straight past Deborah's house, calling goodbye, but as they rounded the corner there was Rod outside the Grants' house. Sally braked gently and came to a halt alongside Deborah.

'Are you girls all right?' Rod asked.

'We're fine,' said Deborah, jumping off her bike. 'No bodies at all, contaminated or otherwise.'

Sally stood with one foot either side of the pedals, ready to set off again. 'I'm glad to see you in one piece,' she told Rod, aiming for a light-hearted note.

'Likewise.' Rod looked at her. 'I'll walk you down the road. Here, let me push your bike for you.'

Sally hopped over the crossbar. Was it by accident that Rod's hands landed on hers on top of the handlebar? No, it was on purpose. He pressed down on her hands, glancing at her. Sally wasn't sure what to make of that look. All she knew for certain was that Rod's eyes had changed from bright blue to dark blue.

When he failed to remove his hands from hers, she tried to pull hers away but he wouldn't let her.

Sally tried to make a joke of it. 'We can't walk down the road like this.'

'Who says?'

But then his lips twitched into a smile and his grasp lessened. Sally wriggled her hands free, leaving Rod to support her bicycle.

'I'll knock for you on my way to the bus,' she said to Deborah. Had Deborah seen? Did she know that her beloved brother sometimes held on too tightly? But she seemed oblivious.

Sally and Rod set off. Not that there was far to go. The Whites' house was only six doors down. Rod was walking her home simply as an excuse to be with her, even just for a minute or two. Sally bit her lip. Rod was handsome, good-natured and amusing. Plenty of girls would give their eye-teeth to be his girlfriend... but those girls didn't know what it was like to be held too closely.

They stopped at the garden gate and Sally opened it. She hesitated. If she laid so much as a finger on the handlebars, Rod would take possession of her hands once again.

She looked up at him. 'Thanks. I'll take the bike now.' She placed one hand lightly on the saddle, ready to whip it away if needs be. Maybe something showed in her face, because Rod laughed and handed over the bicycle, holding up his palms in surrender.

'Aren't you going to wish me happy birthday?' he asked in a low voice.

'Happy birthday.'

'I'm sure you could say it much better than that.' Rod lifted his fingers to her chin. 'Don't be shy,' he murmured, bending his head to cover her mouth with his.

Sally accepted the kiss without offering more, then gently pulled free, pressing her hand to his chest.

'You'll have all the net curtains in the street flapping as all the neighbours get an eyeful,' she said, and he laughed out loud in delight. 'I'd best go in,' she added.

She was flustered and the feeling was growing. She pushed her bike along the path at the side of their house, hardly daring to think. She just had to get through the next day or two, then Rod would go back to Barrow-in-Furness. After that she could start trying to bring Mum and Dad and the Grants round to the idea that her path through life wasn't going to be at Rod's side after all.

CHAPTER SEVEN

Betty was tired when she arrived for work at Tucker's on Saturday morning. Last night's air raid had got her all worked up and it hadn't been easy to get to sleep afterwards – well, that was the excuse she had given Grace for her tiredness. Truth be told, something bad had happened at work yesterday and it was all her fault. That was the real reason for her disturbed night.

The air raid had been scary. Thank goodness Dad had made them practise their air-raid drill over and over again. It had seemed less and less necessary as the phoney war had dragged on, but Dad had always insisted that they had regular practices.

So when the siren had sounded last night, even though she was filled with fear, Betty had known exactly what had to be done. The gas and electricity had to be turned off, as did the main stopcock. All the blackout curtains, which they took such care to put in place every evening, had to be opened wide so that, should a high explosive crash through their roof and set the house on fire on the inside, the flames would be clearly visible from without. Likewise, the buckets of water and sand that sat in the hall all the time, and frankly were a dashed nuisance, were put outside the front door in case anyone had to deal with a small fire.

Then it was a matter of filling a Thermos with tea, grabbing the nearest biscuits and collecting the air-raid box in which they stored all the important documents – birth certificates, insurance papers and what-have-you. One of Dad's rules was that they all had to be able to complete every aspect of the routine, so that, if one of them was alone in the house when the siren sounded, nothing got missed out. Last night it had been Betty and Grace, because Dad was out at work.

Tucker's opened promptly at seven o'clock every morning Monday to Saturday, though Betty didn't start work until eight o'clock and only had to arrive at quarter to. She loved working there, but the past couple of days had been uncomfortable. How could she have been so stupid as to sell that butter? But the girl had seemed so nice, so pleasant, so in need of a good turn. That was what Betty had intended it to be – a good turn. Aye, one that had come back and bitten her on the bum. And all because of a bit of butter!

Yesterday Mr Tucker had received a letter summoning him to the magistrates' court next Monday morning and he'd been instructed to bring with him the 'young female assistant' who had been on duty in the shop. Even if he'd had half a dozen assistants, there would have been no doubt as to who was meant, because the letter stated not just the date but the exact time at which the offence had occurred. Betty had been shocked and upset by the letter but, as well as that, her skin had crawled. There was something creepy about having the time written down like that. It was like being spied on – except that she hadn't been spied on, she'd been out-and-out tricked. And yes, it might have been her own stupid fault for giving in and selling the butter, but it still felt like a trick.

She had trusted that girl, had even thought how nice she looked, with her fair complexion and pretty colouring. Beneath a fetching straw hat, dark-blond hair had fallen in waves to her shoulders, and her eyes were light hazel. Betty had particularly noticed her eyes because you'd expect a blonde to have blue eyes.

But she hadn't been the friendly person Betty had taken her for. She'd been a spy from the Food Office. Now poor Mr Tucker was going to be up before the magistrate, and it was all Betty's fault. Betty hoped and prayed that the magistrate would blame her and let Mr Tucker off.

It was a strange sort of day. Mr Tucker was grouchy and sarcastic with her when it was just the two of them, but each time the door opened, setting the little brass bell jingling merrily, he would instantly turn into his usual civil self for the benefit of his customers. The moment they left, he would scowl at her again. Betty had never known him to be like this before. He had a face built for geniality, its square shape softened by ruddy cheeks and smile lines. Beneath the boater he wore along with a starched white apron as his grocer's uniform, he was bald on top, with fluffy white hair round the sides and back. Nearly all men oiled their hair to keep it flat, but Mr Tucker let his remaining hair curl naturally, saying that Mrs Tucker liked it that way.

Betty had apologised a hundred times and didn't know what else she could do other than promise never again to take a liberty with the regulations.

When she swept the floor at the end of the day, her final job before she was allowed to go home, Mr Tucker cashed up. Betty hung up her apron.

'What are you waiting for?' asked Mr Tucker.

Betty frowned. As if he didn't know! 'My wages. It's Saturday.'

'You'll have a jolly long wait, then,' Mr Tucker retorted. 'I'll be using your wages to pay the fine I'm bound to get. How could you flout the rules like that, Betty? How many times have you heard me say to customers that we play by the rules here at Tucker's? Not like Rigby's round the corner, where he keeps things under the counter and plays favourites. How could you do this to me and Mrs Tucker, Betty?'

'I'm sorry,' Betty said yet again, but at the moment she felt more scared than sorry. 'What am I to say at home? I'm meant to tip up my wages on Saturdays.'

'Say what you like – as long as it's not the truth,' ordered Mr Tucker. 'I don't want anybody outside these four walls knowing. We might yet manage to keep this quiet. The best I can hope for is that the magistrate will appreciate what an upstanding citizen I am and he'll feel sorry for me for having such a weak-willed girl in my employ. There'll still be a fine, but he might agree to instruct the newspapers not to name me.'

'Oh, I do hope so,' breathed Betty. If it came out that Tucker's had been fined for an improper sale, Mr and Mrs Tucker would be mortified. She went hot and cold at the thought.

On her way home she cooked up an excuse and, in due course, she poured out a cock-and-bull story about having left her purse at the shop. She would never normally have got away with it, but last night's air raid had got Grace worrying that there would be another tonight.

Betty tried to behave as normal. She couldn't have Dad or Grace suspecting anything. Grace would make a meal of it if she found out. A meal? Aye, a three-course dinner with double help-ings from the pudding trolley. Besides, Betty hated to think of letting Dad down. She adored her dad and he adored her – or he used to. Betty wasn't sure if he still did. Everything had changed since Grace had come along.

The then newly widowed Grace Milburn had come to live with her sister up the road a few years ago. She was a good-looking woman with conker-brown hair and light-brown eyes. Grace had soon set her sights on Mr Wainwright round the corner. The neighbours had watched with interest, but Mr Wainwright had proved too slippery. Then Betty's darling mum had died of a bad heart they didn't know she had, leaving Betty and Dad, utterly desolate, clinging together for comfort.

Next news, Grace Milburn had got her claws into Dad. Instead of shaking her off, Dad had succumbed. Betty had been astounded. Hurt too. How could he? So soon after Mum too. Dad and Grace were married eleven months after Mum was laid to rest. Not even a year.

'It's what your mum would have wanted,' Grace had told Betty, 'your dad being looked after.'

Not by you, Betty had wanted to say. Mum used to think it was a disgrace the way Grace had chased after Mr Wainwright, and now she had bagged Mum's husband. Mum wouldn't just be turning in her grave. She'd be spinning like a top.

And Grace wanted rid of Betty. Oh, she'd never said it outright, but Betty could tell. She hadn't been sure to start with, because Grace was subtle. She was overtly friendly and warm, but then there would be a quick glance and a little dig about Betty not having a boyfriend, always delivered in a charming way, of course.

'Our Betty is such a lovely girl,' Betty heard her tell the neighbours. 'It's such a shame she doesn't have a young man in tow. She'll make a wonderful wife and mother one day. Let's face it, it isn't as though she has to spend the rest of her life being the devoted daughter living at home to take care of her old dad, is it?'

And everyone would nod approvingly at Betty and agree that she would be the perfect wife and mother. Could they really not see what Grace was doing? Certainly Dad never noticed. All he wanted was for Grace and Betty to get along.

'Me and Betty get on like a house on fire,' Grace was fond of telling folk. 'That's so important with my Trevor being a police sergeant. It's a highly responsible job and he needs the peace and quiet of a trouble-free home life.'

Betty knew that somehow or other, in spite of the little stabs of anxiety that sent her stomach rolling, she must get through this weekend without seeming different and prompting awkward questions. She had to set her sights on the visit to the magistrates' court on Monday, after which everything could go back to normal.

CHAPTER EIGHT

For Rod's birthday party, Sally wore a pretty dress with short sleeves and a buckled belt. The skirt had box pleats but, as the fabric was rayon rather than something more substantial like wool or linen, the pleats moved in a subtle, floaty way. Standing in front of her mirror, she slipped her right hand inside the round neckline to straighten the shoulder pad. She wore a short necklace of blue beads that Deborah had given her for Christmas and she was going to carry the evening bag it had taken her weeks to save up for when she was in her very first job at the age of fourteen. After all this time it was a bit of an old faithful, but she loved it. It was made of satin, decorated with tiny beads, and the clasp was ivory.

She and Mum, together with Deborah, Mrs Grant and various relatives and neighbours, had spent the afternoon getting everything ready for this evening. The bowls club had been decorated with bunting and everyone had lent tablecloths. Back at home, Sally had helped Mum make a plate of meat-paste sandwiches and another of honey-and-nut tartlets. The sandwiches were in the kitchen, covered by a damp tea-towel so they didn't dry out, and the tartlets were under a fly-net.

Sally ran downstairs into the parlour, where Dad got up from his armchair and kissed her cheek.

'You look a picture,' he told her proudly and Sally gave him a hug. 'Your mum looks nice too.'

Dressed in her Sunday best, Mum looked sober and smart, as befitted someone of her age. She, Sally and Dad put their hats on and unhooked their gas-mask boxes from the hall pegs. With Sally and Mum each carrying a covered plate, they set off for the bowls club. They met others along the way and there were lots of cheery greetings.

At the bowls club, the men shook hands and chatted while the women got the food sorted out.

Sally caught hold of Deborah's arm as she went by. 'Your hair doesn't have as much of a roll as I was expecting. Did you decide against the you-know-what in the end?'

Deborah cast her gaze towards the ceiling. 'Mum came into my bedroom and caught me in the act. She was appalled. She kept on saying, "But what if your hair comes undone?" so in the end I couldn't use it.'

'Your style looks good,' Sally said loyally. 'It always does.'

Mrs Grant came up to them. 'Everything is ready,' she said to Deborah.

Deborah nipped across to the door, opened it and waved, which was the signal for Rod to make his entrance. He came in with a couple of his friends to a hearty chorus of 'Happy Birthday to You', which ended with everyone laughing and applauding. Sally glanced at Mrs Grant, whose eyes were sparkling with happiness. It wouldn't be long, though, before her son returned to his job in Barrow and then there would be tears of sorrow.

Was that the reason for the special atmosphere that evening? This wasn't just a party such as they would have enjoyed before the war. Now there was the awareness that everything had changed, that men were away fighting and goodness only knew when they would come home again. Furthermore, everyone knew that it wasn't just the servicemen who were in danger.

Mr Grant clapped his hands for silence and everyone looked at him. 'Here's what you do if the siren goes off. Everyone must go into the foyer. There's a door that leads down into the cellar and that's where we'll take shelter if we have to – but let's hope the need doesn't arise.' He raised his voice, injecting a cheerful note. 'We're here to have a party, so let's get started.'

Deborah's Auntie Maggie, double-chinned and rosebud-lipped, belted out some popular songs on the piano and everyone joined in with 'Kiss Me Goodnight, Sergeant-Major', 'Run, Rabbit, Run!' and '(We're Gonna Hang Out) the Washing on the Siegfried Line'.

'One more, Maggie,' called out Mr Grant, 'and then I'll put a gramophone record on.'

'We'll end with "The Beer Barrel Polka" in that case,' said Auntie Maggie.

'What's that when it's at home?' someone called.

'Never heard of it,' called someone else.

'Oh yes, you have,' Auntie Maggie retorted and belted out the introduction to what everyone knew as 'Roll Out the Barrel'. The song ended with a mighty cheer and then Mr Grant put on a recording of ragtime music while Mrs Grant and her helpers served the food onto plates and brought them round. Sally's mum was in charge of making tea and Auntie Maggie diluted the home-made elderflower cordial. There was another cheer when the clinking of glass announced the appearance of a crate of bottles of beer.

Everyone sat and chatted as they enjoyed the food. Then out came the cigarettes and Mr Grant stood up.

'I'm not one for making speeches, but I want to say how proud me and his mum are of our Rod and how grateful we are to have him here. So will you all please raise your glasses and your teacups and toast him. Happy birthday, Rod!'

'Happy birthday, Rod!' everyone cried, coming to their feet and raising their drinks.

'Aye, and many more birthdays to come,' called one of the neighbours.

'Hear, hear,' called some others.

'Speech!' yelled one of Deborah's uncles.

'He won't give a speech, not Rod,' Sally's mum murmured in her ear.

But as Mr Grant sat down, beaming in pride at his son, Rod crushed his Woodbine into the ashtray and stood up.

'First off,' he said, 'I want to say a huge thank you to everyone who has helped put this party together, especially Mum and Deborah.' He was interrupted by applause and waited for it to die down. 'The food was delicious and I know it was all above board, because of Deborah and Sally working in the Food Office.' There were one or two polite chuckles. 'As you all know, Sally is Deborah's best friend. She's special to me too, more special than I can say. In fact...'

There were audible gasps as he walked across the floor to her, took a ring box from his pocket and went down on one knee. A frisson of excitement ran round the room and everyone leaned forward, enchanted.

Rod took a deep breath and looked into Sally's eyes. 'I used to think of you as another little sister, but you're grown up now and I see you very differently. You're the most beautiful, caring person I know and I want to spend the rest of my life with you. Sally White, will you do me the honour of agreeing to be my wife?'

Sally sucked in a breath. She glimpsed Deborah beaming. Everyone was smiling.

'Don't look so shocked,' called a voice and there was happy laughter.

Sally's heart froze and then pounded as Rod took a ring from the little box. Then he reached for Sally's left hand, her wedding finger hand. She saw the sapphire on the gold band. If she let him put that ring on her finger, that would make it official. People were already saying 'Ahhh…' in sentimental voices. Glancing around, Sally took in the delighted, satisfied expressions on Mum and Dad's faces, on the faces of Deborah's parents. Deborah brushed away a tear and laughed at herself.

Panic speared through Sally. How could she let down all these dear people whom she loved so much? Rod too. He was important to her and everyone knew it, but they didn't know him the way she did. They knew nothing of the hands that held her too tightly.

Leaning forward, forehead to forehead, Sally gently removed her left hand, taking her wedding finger away from Rod.

'Not here,' she said softly. She had to do this as kindly as she could. 'Not in public.'

'Not in public, she says.' Rod spoke out loud and everybody laughed again. He pulled her to her feet. 'Excuse us while we go and do this in private.'

This caused yet more laughter, even some clapping. Sally couldn't look anyone in the eye. Rod took her hand firmly and led her out into the foyer. There was a floor-length blackout curtain across the door into the little vestibule. They went through, closing the door behind them. The front door was similarly blacked out. They slid behind the curtain and slipped through a crack in the door. Outside, the night was cool. It had drizzled earlier and the tang of wet grass filled Sally's senses.

It was essential that she should be the first to speak, but no words would come. Rod was about to sink down on one knee again, but she grabbed his arm.

'No, don't,' she said.

Standing, Rod pulled her close. 'You have to let me propose again before we seal it with a kiss.'

Sally tried to pull away. 'Don't,' she whispered.

'Don't what?' His arm tightened round her waist.

'Don't propose again.'

'Then let's have your answer and we can go back in and tell everyone.' Rod chuckled. He actually chuckled.

His hold relaxed and Sally extricated herself. Rod tried to take her hand, but she wouldn't let him. This elicited more chuckles.

'Steady on,' he said. 'If you wriggle, I'll drop the blessed ring. If it bounces down the steps, we might not find it until daylight.'

'Rod, you know how much I care about you,' said Sally. 'You've always been an important part of my life, but I can't do this. I'm so sorry.'

'I don't understand. I thought you'd like the birthday proposal with everyone there to celebrate with us.'

'It's lovely of you to make it special, but... I just can't.'

'Can't...? What d'you mean, can't?' Rod's voice was sharp. There was a tiny pause and then he spoke gently. 'Is it too soon? I know we only became a couple when war broke out, but that's heaps of time these days. I'll be going back to Barrow soon and I don't know when I'll get leave again. I want us to get a special licence and marry before I have to go back, but if you'd rather wait...' That sharp edge entered his voice once more.

'I'm sorry,' Sally said again. 'I can't marry you. I can't get engaged.'

'I don't understand.' Rod sounded irritated now. 'What's got into you?'

'I... I just can't. It wouldn't be the right thing for me.'

Rod raised a hand and Sally's heart delivered an almighty thump, but all he did was start to push his fingers through his hair. Then he seemed to remember he was holding the engagement ring. He pulled his hand down and stared at the ring before delving in his pocket for the box and shoving the ring inside it.

'What am I supposed to do with this now?' he demanded.

'I'm so sorry,' Sally whispered.

'Stop saying you're sorry!' Rod exclaimed. 'Well, so much for me trying to give you a proposal to be proud of. I thought that in years to come you'd tell that story to our children.' A vein pulsed at his temple.

Sally's heart felt as if it was cracking down the middle. She had never felt worse in her life. She hated to hurt Rod, yet she knew she couldn't marry him. It wasn't even because she'd met Andrew. It was because of the way her heart had thumped when Rod had lifted his hand. It was because of the way he held her hand too tightly, the way he fastened her to his side when they linked arms. His parents, especially his mother, thought the sun shone out of him and so did Deborah. The whole neighbourhood saw him as a hero because of being sent off to Barrow to work on shipbuilding. Sally admired that too and she remembered how she had looked up to Rod when she was a young lass. But since then... since then her heart had thudded when he lifted his hand, and it wasn't a shivery, happy thud. Her heart was warning her.

Silence crackled between them. Rod turned on his heel and started to make his way down the steps into the darkness.

'Aren't you going to go back inside and tell everyone?' Sally called after him.

At the bottom of the steps, Rod's feet crunched in the gravel as he turned back to look up at her. 'You're kidding. Haven't you made a big enough idiot of me already? You tell 'em.'

He marched away and was swallowed by the unrelieved blackness of the night.

Sally didn't want to be the one to tell people, but one of them had to. She slid back indoors, taking care to reinstate the blackout. As she entered the foyer once more, there was a cry from the doorway ahead of her.

'Here they come!'

This was followed by the start of a rousing chorus of 'For They Are Jolly Good Fellows'.

Sally flinched and it was all she could do to force herself to walk across the foyer and beckon to her dad from the doorway.

CHAPTER NINE

Sally didn't know how she was to get through Sunday. How could everything have gone so badly wrong? Mum and Dad, and Rod's family, couldn't understand why she didn't want to marry him. Worse, they blamed her for leading him on.

'I didn't,' Sally claimed desperately.

'Yes, you did,' said Mum. Even her own mother thought she was in the wrong. 'You sent him all those letters while he was away. You let him think you were his girl. You let us all think it.'

It was true and Sally knew it, but she hadn't done it with any evil intent. She had honestly believed herself to be Rod's girl – to start with.

On Sunday afternoon, she had the chance to talk privately with Deborah. They walked through Fog Lane Park, threading their way between the wartime allotments, where men with their sleeves rolled up were picking runner beans, sowing spring cabbages and kale, and fertilising celery with soot. Deborah was upset and hurt on her brother's behalf, but she was ready to stand by her best friend.

'I never imagined for one moment that you'd turn him down,' she said. 'I thought – everybody thought – you and him getting together was a certainty. Why else d'you think all those girls came trooping into our office with their engagement rings? It was so I could find out your ring size.'

Sally's mouth dropped open. 'You organised that?'

'I thought I was helping. All I did was help make this mess.'

'It's not your fault,' said Sally. 'It isn't anyone's fault.'

'Well, yes, it is,' said Deborah, though not in an accusing voice. Her tone suggested Sally was daft not to realise. 'It's yours. You can't deny you led him on.'

'But I didn't, I swear. I care about Rod dearly, I honestly do, but...' Sally shut her eyes for a moment.

'But what?' Deborah asked quietly.

Sally opened her eyes and looked at her best friend. Instead of her customary warm, attractive smile, Deborah's mouth was set in a firm line and her bright-blue eyes were clouded with questions.

'But what?' Deborah asked again, her tone urgent this time.

Sally could see how much Deborah wanted, needed, to understand. Speaking softly, choosing her words with care, she said, 'Rod... isn't exactly the person I thought he was.'

Deborah jerked away from her. 'What do you mean?' she demanded. Her eyes hardened and her pretty, heart-shaped face was suddenly all sharp angles. 'You're the one letting my brother down – and you're trying to make out it's *his* fault?'

Sally hadn't seen her friend like this before. The girl who used to tease her brother to his face and joke about him behind his back was all of a sudden his passionate defender. As an only child, Sally was aware she didn't understand the intricacies of sibling relationships, but it was crystal-clear to her that Deborah was in no mood to hear a word against Rod.

So instead she told a different, though equally important, truth.

'There's someone else – no, don't look like that. It's not what you're thinking.'

'Oh aye?' Deborah's blue eyes turned to ice. 'What am I thinking?'

'Whatever it is, you're wrong. I've not been carrying on behind Rod's back. I-I met somebody just a couple of days before the party.'

'You *what?*'

'Nothing happened. We just talked.'

'It must have been more than that.'

'Well, it wasn't. We talked and lost track of time, but I told him we couldn't see one another again.'

Deborah's eyes narrowed. 'So he wanted to see you again?'

'Yes, he did and I said no.'

'How come this is the first I'm hearing of it? We're meant to be best friends.'

'I couldn't tell you, could I? I couldn't tell anyone.'

'Because you were ashamed,' Deborah stated.

'Because I was confused,' said Sally.

'You're not the only one,' Deborah said bitterly. 'You've turned my brother down because of a single conversation with a stranger. Well, he must be a dazzling conversationalist, that's all I can say.'

And that wasn't the end of it. Not long after Sally arrived home, things went from bad to worse. Deborah evidently hadn't kept their conversation to herself and Rod came marching along to the Whites' house, almost hammering on the door in his urgency. Furious and humiliated, he was on the attack.

'So you've been creeping around behind my back,' he accused Sally.

They were in the front room so as to be out of Mum and Dad's way. Sally thought of Mum choosing to live in the back room away from the eyes of anyone who might pass by, and wondered if someone might glance in and see her and Rod. It was stuffy indoors, but she couldn't open the window for fear of their voices carrying.

'It wasn't like that,' said Sally.

'Then what was it like?' Rod demanded. 'From where I'm standing, it looks like you doing the dirty on me.'

'I never meant to hurt you.'

'Thanks very much,' Rod said bitterly.

'It's true,' Sally insisted. 'And I'm not seeing this other man, I promise. I went to a cafe with him once, that's all.'

'He took you to a greasy spoon? The height of romance!' Rod sneered. 'So you went out with him – and then what?'

'It was only the once.'

'Pull the other one. It's got bells on.'

'It's the truth. I-I didn't want to let you down.'

'Oh, I see. You thought you'd save that for the proposal.'

'I didn't know you were going to propose,' said Sally.

'Come off it. Don't you dare talk as if I'm some heartless love 'em and leave 'em type.'

'I know you aren't. I'm sorry.'

'Stop apologising,' Rod said forcefully. 'I don't want to hear how sorry you are. I want an explanation. Who is this bloke? How long has it been going on?'

'I've told you. Nothing's going on.'

'There must be or why are we having this conversation?'

Sally drew in a deep, shaky breath. 'I refused to see him again. It would have been unfair to you and I was trying to do the decent thing.'

Rod's lips twisted in what might have been anger or could have been pain. 'And the decent thing doesn't stretch as far as marrying me?'

'Even if I never see him again, meeting him showed me that – that it wouldn't be right to get engaged to you.'

'Well! That's me told.' There was incredulity in Rod's hard-edged stare. 'I've heard of men being dumped so the girlfriend can go off with another man. I've never heard of a girlfriend who changes her mind based on a single meeting in a greasy spoon.'

'It's not like that,' Sally protested. 'You make it sound tawdry.'

'Oh aye?' Rod taunted her. 'It looks pretty tawdry from where I'm standing.'

With a swiftness that caught her utterly unawares, he stepped forward and grasped Sally's chin, thrusting his face close.

'How could you, Sally?' Who knew that softly spoken words could contain such menace? 'I was going to give you everything. You mean the world to me and I thought you felt the same. *Every*body thought you felt the same. And you did, I know you did – until Mr Greasy Spoon stuck his oar in.'

With a deft flick of his wrist, Rod dashed her chin aside so sharply that Sally stumbled and had to regain her balance. Her heart pounded in her ears.

She laid a palm against her chin. 'There was no call for that.'

'For what exactly?'

'For holding my chin like that.' It felt important to tell him exactly what she objected to.

Rod gave a little laugh, but there was no humour in it. 'All I wanted was to look into your eyes,' he murmured, his tone so gentle that Sally questioned whether she had overreacted.

The door opened and Dad looked in. After a moment he came into the room properly.

'I think you two have had enough time to talk for now. Maybe you'd best leave, Rod,' he said, his voice steady and civil. 'Just while things settle down.'

Rod made a disbelieving noise halfway between a snort and a laugh. Head held high, he strode out, banging the front door behind him.

'Are you all right, Sally?' Dad asked.

Sally nodded. She felt drained, but there was no time to recover because Mum plunged into the room and started on her.

'What's got into you, Sally? How could you let Rod down like that? How could you let us all down?'

Sally's heart dipped. She had known that everyone had expectations of her and Rod, but she'd chosen mainly to ignore it. Now she wished she hadn't let things ride.

But these were her parents she was with. Above all, they loved her and wanted the best for her. Sally pushed her shoulders back. The moment had come to tell them.

'Mum, the thing is you don't know Rod as well as you think you do,' Sally told her. 'He – well, I think he has an unkind streak—'

'Unkind?' Mum burst out. 'Rod Grant? Give over, Sally. I've known him all his life – and that's five years longer than I've known you. Unkind, my eye!' She swung to face Dad. 'Have you ever known him to be unkind?'

The vertical lines between Dad's eyebrows deepened. 'Well, no, I can't say I have.'

Mum turned in triumph to Sally. 'There you are, then.'

'But if Sally says—' Dad began, but he got no further.

'I'm ashamed of you, Sally, trying to muddy the waters like that.' But Mum didn't look ashamed. That tightened jaw told of deep scorn. 'Do you think we're deaf? What's this about another man? We heard Rod through the wall. How could you, Sally? I didn't fetch you up to play fast and loose.'

'Now then,' said Dad, 'let the girl speak. Is it true, Sally? Is there another fellow?'

The disappointed look on his face was more than Sally could bear. It distressed her far more than his anger would have. She had always been proud of being Dad's girl.

'It's sort of true, but not the way Rod made it sound. It's not someone I'll ever see again.'

Sally braced herself for further onslaught, but the fire went out of Mum and she squished her drawn-on eyebrows together in confusion.

'Then why, Sally?' Mum's hands fluttered. 'I don't understand.'

'Did you get cold feet?' Dad asked. 'I wouldn't blame you. I thought all along that a public proposal wasn't a good idea, but nobody wanted to listen.' He shot Mum a look.

'It wasn't cold feet,' Sally said quietly. She was exhausted.

'If you've got any sense, my girl,' said Mum, 'you'll get round to their house and beg Rod to forgive your moment of madness and take you back.' And then she burst into tears.

CHAPTER TEN

Betty and Mr Tucker caught the bus on Monday morning while Mrs Tucker held the fort at the shop, no doubt with a string of lies prepared in case customers asked why she was on her own behind the counter. A few passengers on the bus yawned behind their hands. There had been another air raid last night. No bombs had fallen hereabouts, but everyone had either manned their civil defence posts or sat huddled in their shelters until the raid ended.

Betty and Mr Tucker got off the bus and made their way to the magistrates' court. They hadn't been summoned to the Salford court but to the one in Manchester.

Mrs Tucker had tried to take comfort from that. 'If you have to go into Manchester, that'll make it less likely that anyone hereabouts will get to know of it,' she'd said hopefully.

'Aye, well, we'll see,' Mr Tucker had replied. He seemed too worried and gloomy to try to buoy her up.

Mrs Tucker, with her kindly manner and her soft plumpness, had a faded prettiness. She always looked better, brighter-eyed and smoother-skinned, at the start of the day; she was rather drawn by the end of each long working day. Since the letter from the court had arrived, she'd looked drawn all the time. Another thing for Betty to feel bad about.

Alighting from the bus, Mr Tucker and Betty soon found the court building. Mr Tucker stopped and looked up at it, so Betty did as well. Poor Mr Tucker. For a moment Betty had difficulty swallowing. The Tuckers had always been good to her and how had she repaid them? By bringing shame down on their heads, that's how.

As Mr Tucker started to go up the steps, Betty followed, automatically walking quickly so as not to get left behind. Aiming to slip into the space beside Mr Tucker, she darted sideways and forward and ended up bumping into someone.

'Oh, I'm sorry,' she apologised, and turned with a smile, only to feel her lips freeze in position. It was the girl who had come into the shop. Her hazel eyes widened with shock as she recognised Betty. Heat flared across Betty's cheekbones.

'Come along, Miss White,' said a man's voice.

The girl's gaze fell away from Betty's and she hurried up the steps, leaving Betty staring. Betty wanted to run after her, grab her shoulder and spin her round so she could say – say what? Yes, the girl had landed her well and truly in the soup, but she couldn't have done it if Betty hadn't been a prize idiot.

'Miss Hughes, don't dawdle,' Mr Tucker called.

Betty caught up with him just before he could disappear indoors. Her gaze flew all around the spacious foyer in search of the girl from the shop, but there was no sign of her.

Mr Tucker asked a receptionist for directions and Betty trailed after him to a long, echoing corridor with wooden benches down one side, opposite a wall with sets of double doors in it every so often.

'Park yourself there,' Mr Tucker told Betty, indicating one of the benches before he walked off.

She sat down obediently, holding her handbag in her lap, her fingers clasped round the padded handle. She was dressed in her shop clothes. She was required to wear a white blouse and a dark skirt for work even though only the collar and sleeves showed when she wore her apron. On top of her blouse and skirt, she wore a simple edge-to-edge jacket that Mum had helped her to make, and a stylish hat with a small crown and an asymmetrical brim. There was hardly any brim on one side and lots on the other. She'd fallen in love with the hat at first sight because it looked like the sort a film star might wear.

Betty didn't feel in the slightest bit film-starry at present. She was all churned up with nerves. The corridor was full of people smoking while they waited or hurrying along looking busy. Betty didn't meet anyone's eyes. She didn't want to be asked what had brought her here.

Mr Tucker came back and stood beside her at the end of the bench. He didn't sit down and he didn't speak to her. He didn't smoke either. He just stood there, looking grim. There was a clock above the door opposite them. Betty knew they had been summoned to appear at ten and it was now nearly half past.

The doors opened and some people emerged. At the same time, a well-dressed clerk appeared and called for Mr Tucker. Betty stood up, swallowing hard, and followed him into the court-room. The magistrate sat on a raised dais, from where he had a good view of everyone in front of him.

The clerk glanced down at a piece of paper in his hand. 'Is this your shop assistant? Sit here, please, miss. Come with me, Mr Tucker. You have to stand in the dock.'

Mr Tucker stopped dead, his face suddenly grey.

'It should be me,' Betty said. 'I was the one that did it.'

The clerk eyed her. 'And the magistrate might put you in the dock – or he might not. He's a great believer that offences of this nature are the responsibility of the shopkeeper, regardless of who broke the rules.'

'But I only did it because the girl seemed so nice,' Betty

exclaimed, 'and she seemed to need the butter so much. That's not Mr Tucker's fault.'

'It is if he didn't impress upon you that you must follow the rules. That's what the magistrate will say.'

And indeed it was. The magistrate behaved as if he couldn't quite decide if Mr Tucker was a criminal or a nincompoop. To Betty's surprise, the witness against Mr Tucker wasn't the girl who had come into the shop, but a man called Mr Morland, who described how his clerk, Miss White, had purchased butter from Mr Tucker's grocery shop. Betty looked round – and there she was, the butter-girl herself. The butter-wouldn't-melt girl, more like. Betty caught her eye and glared at her, which forced her to look away.

The magistrate delivered a lecture on the purpose of rationing before delivering his verdict.

'Fined five guineas,' he declared.

Five guineas! *Five.* An educated man with a good job might earn as much as thirty pounds a month. To a humble grocer like Mr Tucker, five guineas was a small fortune. Not just pounds either, but guineas. Five pounds and five shillings. Mr Tucker had kept back Betty's wages to cover any fine, but one week's pay was only twenty-five bob. That left four quid, four whole pounds, that Betty would have to repay.

'Did you bring the errant shop assistant with you?' asked the magistrate. 'Good. A two-pound fine for her. Next case, please.'

Two pounds? Two whole pounds – on top of Mr Tucker's fine. Betty felt as if all the breath had been sucked from her body.

Sally's heart had swollen in sympathy when she saw the grocery shop assistant in the courtroom, but then the girl had looked daggers at her and Sally had felt like hauling her to one side to say, 'If only you knew! I realise this is bad for you, but I'm having a crummy time too.'

Usually she didn't like having to trail to court in Mr Morland's wake. The Food Office clerks who conducted the tests and caught out shopkeepers were supposed to give their own evidence to the magistrate, but Mr Morland was a bit too fond of the sound of his own voice to permit that. Nevertheless, his clerks had to be present in case the magistrate had a question for them – which never happened.

Today, though, Sally had been grateful to get out of the office and escape to court. After all the upset of Saturday night and Sunday, having to sit opposite Deborah in the office was just too much for either her or her erstwhile best friend. It stunned her to think of the barrier that now existed between them. They'd been pals all their lives. Might their friendship really be over? Sally's heartbeat was heavy and sluggish in her chest. The thought of losing Deborah was in some ways worse than what had happened with Rod.

Sally and Mr Morland spent the whole morning in court before returning to Albert Square, in the middle of which was the statue of the Prince Consort himself on a plinth within a medieval-looking structure with a tall tower supported by four columns. They headed for the Gothic-style Town Hall with its splendid clock tower. The lowest parts of the Town Hall were now hidden behind thick walls of sandbags.

In the foyer, Mr Morland stopped to speak to a colleague. Sally went straight to the canteen, but stopped dead in the doorway at the sight of Deborah at a table with half a dozen other girls. One of them caught sight of her and they all turned round to look. Sally's face felt impossibly hot. For a moment she considered brazening it out – but only for a moment. Why go looking for trouble? Things were bad enough already.

Instead Sally went to the Community Feeding Centre. What a horrid name! It made the people who ate there sound like charity cases from Victorian times, when really the Feeding Centres were restaurants that had been set up all over the country so that people had access to nutritious meals at reasonable prices.

The folk at the tables around Sally were enjoying their meals, but Sally had to force down her Lancashire hotpot. She would have given anything not to have to return to the office, but she had no choice.

She had expected the afternoon to be difficult, but she had never imagined walking into the office to find her desk had been moved. Instead of her desk and Deborah's being pushed up together so they faced one another as they worked, Sally's was now shoved into a corner. She went cold with shock, then heat flushed through her body. It was tempting to heave her desk back into its rightful place, but what for? At least if she was tucked away in the corner, she could get on with her work undisturbed.

How could her best friend treat her in this way?

Mr Tucker said barely a word on the way back to the shop. Betty didn't blame him. He must feel every bit as shocked as she did. Mr Tucker had had to pay the fine before they'd left the magistrates' court. He had brought his chequebook with him just in case. He'd had to pay Betty's fine too, because she couldn't possibly have paid it on the spot.

'I'll pay you back, Mr Tucker,' she had said humbly. The two fines put together made a stomach-churning total of seven pounds five shillings. Where was the money to come from? And all because of a bit of butter. Oh, glory.

When they got off the bus, Mr Tucker walked back to the shop with such a long stride that Betty had to take little running steps to keep up – or maybe he would rather leave her behind. Her gas-mask box bumped against her as she hurried.

Reaching the shop, Mr Tucker turned the sign to CLOSED and faced Mrs Tucker.

'Five guineas,' he announced without preamble.

Mrs Tucker uttered an exclamation and pressed a hand to her mouth.

'And it'll be in the *Manchester Evening News* and the *Salford City Reporter,*' Mr Tucker added. 'The magistrate...' His words dried up and he had to clear his throat. 'The magistrate refused to keep my name out of the papers.'

The couple both cast accusing looks in Betty's direction. She wanted to sink through the floor.

'I've never been so ashamed in my life,' said Mr Tucker.

'There, dear, it wasn't your fault,' said his wife.

'I'm well aware of that, thank you,' said Mr Tucker. 'We all know who's to blame. I can never trust you again after this, Betty. I can't even stand to look at you. You'll have to go – and don't come back. You're sacked.'

Normally Sally and Deborah would have left the office together and caught the bus home to Withington, chattering all the way. They never ran out of things to talk about. Today, though, Sally pretended not to have finished some paperwork, keeping her head down to hide her burning cheeks as Deborah tidied her desk, took her jacket and hat from the coatstand and picked up her gas-mask box and handbag.

'Good evening, Mr Morland,' she said clearly.

The legs of Mr Morland's chair scraped as he stood. Sally looked up.

'I don't know what's going on between you two young ladies,' said Mr Morland, 'and I don't want to know, but I'll tell you this. I will not tolerate this atmosphere. This is a place of work, not the school playground. If you don't sort out your silly quarrel, I'll do it for you.'

With that, he left the office.

Sally looked at Deborah. 'If we could just talk—'

'Don't kid yourself that I'm going to kiss and make up just

because old Morland says so,' Deborah retorted. 'It'll take a lot more than that.'

With a toss of her head, she marched out. Sally flopped back in her seat, exhausted. Then she sat up and straightened her desk. As she gathered her possessions ready to go home, she fought against tears. She walked down the stairs more slowly than usual, anxious not to catch up with Deborah. If she sat on a bench in Albert Square for a few minutes, she could be certain of getting a different bus.

As she headed for a bench, she was dimly aware of a movement diagonally behind her.

'Miss White – Sally.'

Her pulse was racing even before she turned to face Andrew Henshaw. She drank in the sight of him as if she hadn't seen him in years, the kind brown eyes, the sensitive mouth, his athletic grace.

She gazed at him, feeling dazzled and tearful and warm and *safe*.

Andrew removed his cloth cap, holding it in both hands. 'I don't want to be pushy – well, actually I do. I couldn't leave things as they were. I've been hanging around outside the Town Hall, hoping you'd appear. I know you said you didn't want us to meet again, but I couldn't leave it like that. I don't want to sound as if I don't respect your wishes, and if you tell me again that you don't want to see me, I swear I'll go away. But I had to give it one more chance.' He took a step closer. 'I had to give *us* one more chance. I'm sorry,' he added anxiously. 'I never intended to make you cry.'

Sally swiped a hand across her eyes. 'It's not your fault. It's just – everything.'

'Can we go somewhere and talk?' asked Andrew.

'We might as well sit here.' Sally nodded towards the bench. 'If we go to the Worker Bee, there'll be people nearby on other tables. At least here, no one can listen in without hovering right beside us.'

Andrew donned his cap and escorted her to the bench. They sat angled towards one another, with a gap between them. There was no suggestion of touching, of intimacy, yet Sally had never felt closer to anyone in her life.

She poured out her story.

'I was sort of promised to this other man. I've known him all my life. No actual promises were exchanged, but we've been writing to one another and my parents approved and so did his, and he's my best friend's brother. I'd been having serious doubts, but I never said anything. So I knew I couldn't see you again. I had to deal with the other situation first.'

'You were trying to do the right thing,' Andrew said. 'And here I am chasing after you. I'm sorry if that puts you in a difficult position. It's just that this feels very much like the right thing to me.'

'Does it?' Sally asked softly.

'Oh yes, without question.'

'Rod proposed at the weekend,' said Sally, 'and I turned him down. Now both families, not to mention all the neighbours, think I'm a flighty piece of work who led him up the garden path.'

Andrew's hand moved as if seeking hers, then fell back. 'I'm glad you didn't accept him. Dare I ask, am I the reason?'

The flicker of anxiety in his brown eyes told Sally he wasn't taking anything for granted. 'You're one of the reasons. I've known for some time he wasn't the person for me. Meeting you helped me to make a stand.'

Now Andrew did take her hand, sending sparks of happiness cascading through her. 'Whatever happens next, we'll face it together.'

CHAPTER ELEVEN

It was the oddest feeling. Betty felt dislocated from her old life, her real life. On Thursday night at about eleven, a single aircraft was heard in the skies over Salford. Instead of bombs being dropped, what fell from the sky were bundles that burst open during their descent, scattering masses of pamphlets. Pamphlets! Herr Hitler had sent a message to the general population called 'A Last Appeal to Reason'. What a cheek! Outrage sent the determination to defeat the enemy soaring to new heights. Betty knew she needed a hefty dose of that determination in her own life to help her face what came next.

Her stomach knotted every time she thought of how her life had changed. It wasn't just her life either. Things had changed for the Tuckers too. Mr Tucker had been so proud of his reputation and now it was mud. His customers would never forget what had happened. Years after the war ended, he would be remembered as the local man who had flouted the strict rules of rationing.

Things were difficult for Dad and Grace too. Betty having lost her job, she now had to be supported. Before she had left the shop for the final time after she was sacked, she had grasped her courage in both hands and asked Mr Tucker if he would give her a reference. At first he had nearly bitten her head off. Then he said she was welcome to a reference – but, before relief could consume her, he had added that it would include specific details of how she'd come to lose her position. In other words, it wouldn't help her get a new post.

'How am I to get a new job without a reference?' she said now at home.

Grace tossed her head, setting her conker-brown waves shimmering. 'You should have thought of that before you broke the law.'

'I'm sorry,' said Betty, 'but everyone makes mistakes – don't they, Dad?' she added desperately. 'Isn't that what you've always said when you've helped keep a young lad on the straight and narrow?'

'Aye, love,' Dad agreed, rubbing his moustache, 'but that was lads who kicked a ball through someone's window and ran away or bunked off school regularly or kept getting into fights. What you did, our Betty – I can hardly believe it. My own daughter.'

Grace laid a comforting hand on his arm. 'There, there, Trevor. Don't take on. She's a good lass at heart.'

'A good lass with a magistrate's fine under her belt. That's not the sort of thing that goes away.'

Betty burst into tears and ran from the room. She hated herself for letting everyone down.

Later, after Dad had set off to do his night shift, Grace had a word with her.

'You do realise, don't you, that you can't stop here under this roof now?'

Betty blinked. Grace's voice was soft and kind, yet her words were anything but.

'It wouldn't be fair to your dad, would it?' Grace continued reasonably. 'You must see that. He's a police sergeant, with all those constables looking up to him. How can he harbour a criminal under his roof?'

Betty gasped. 'I'm not a criminal.'

'What else d'you call it when you've got a police record?'

'It was only a fine, not a prison sentence.'

'And that's something we have to be deeply thankful for, because the magistrate could have sent you to prison if he'd wanted. You have to face it, Betty. You're damaged goods, and it's not just your reputation that's in tatters. So is poor Mr Tucker's. And, leaving aside the shame you've brought on this house, your dad has had to dig into his life savings to reimburse Mr Tucker for the fines he had to pay because of you. You'll never be able to repay your dad, not that much. It's a small fortune.'

'I will pay it back, no matter how long it takes.' Betty's voice was quiet but fierce. 'Dad knows I will.'

'And how do you propose to do it?' asked Grace. 'Nobody round here will want to employ you.'

Betty shook her head. What could she say?

'Anyroad,' said Grace, 'the money is less important than the shame. You've tainted your dad's good name, Betty, so now it's up to you to do the decent thing and you know what that is, don't you?'

Betty looked at her. Grace smiled and then smothered it, but not before Betty had seen it.

'You have to move out,' said Grace. 'For keeps.'

Sally's days were a heady mixture of the wonderful and the unbearable. Things were hard at home.

'You're the talk of the street,' said Mum, her hazel eyes dull and weary.

'Your gran, God rest her soul, would have called it being the talk of the wash-house,' Dad said in a humorous tone.

Mum scowled. 'Don't be common – and don't make light of the situation.'

Every time she set foot outside, Sally was aware of the neighbours glancing her way and murmuring to one another, but Mum had no sympathy.

'If all you'd done— all!' Mum said with a bitter laugh. 'If all you'd done was turn Rod down, the talk would have stopped by now. It's because you two-timed him with this new man.'

It didn't matter how many times Sally swore she hadn't started going out with Andrew until after Rod's ill-fated proposal.

'I feel as if nobody believes me,' she told Dad.

'That's what worries me,' Dad said gently. 'With everyone against you, it's bound to push you towards this new chap. Are you sure what you feel for him is real?'

The breath hitched in Sally's throat. 'Of course I'm sure. I've never felt this way about anybody before.'

'Then I'd like to meet him,' said Dad.

'Mum wouldn't let him through the front door.'

'Leave your mum to me,' said Dad.

Sally hugged him, but she couldn't help feeling apprehensive. Later, she sat on the stairs earwigging.

'I won't have him in this house,' said Mum. 'It's not even been a fortnight since Rod's party. What would people say?'

'Who cares?' Dad replied. 'It's our lass that matters. If you take against this new man without so much as meeting him, you risk pushing Sally away.'

Later, Mum talked to Sally about it.

'You don't know what it's like,' said Mum. 'You have no idea how precious you are. Nobody ever wanted to marry me when I was young, when I was the right age, when I could have had a family. Look at me compared to Deborah's mum. I could be Mrs Grant's mother. Then I met your father and we fell in love and got wed. Everyone told me I was too old to have children. I...' She stopped, her cheeks reddening.

'I know about the babies you... ended up not having.' It was a clumsy way of saying it, but Sally couldn't bring herself to utter the word 'miscarried'. Mum would probably be shocked that she even knew it.

'People were kind enough each time it happened,' said Mum, 'but there was also a strong feeling of "Well, what did you expect at your age?" even if no one said it out loud in front of me, not to start with, anyway. They were right, of course. I was far too old. I should have been preparing to be a grandmother, not desperately hoping for a baby of my own. I felt ashamed of hoping.'

'Why?' breathed Sally.

'Because of my age. It didn't seem respectable.'

'Well, I'm glad you had me.'

'Oh, so am I. I thought I would burst with happiness when you were born. I've always wanted you to have everything I didn't have. I wanted you to marry young, like girls are supposed to, and have several children while you still had the energy. It's jolly tiring taking care of a child, though I always tried not to let it show, because it underlined how old I was. I always thought you'd marry Rod. It seemed so right, with you and Deborah being best friends and him the older brother. I waited and waited for you and Rod to see one another in a different light. Then the war came. Plenty of couples rushed into marriage, but I never worried about that with the two of you. If you did rush, what of it? You were right for one another and it was only a matter of time. And now you've thrown it all away – and for what? For a stranger.'

'He doesn't feel like a stranger,' said Sally. 'It feels like I've always known him.'

'That just goes to show what madness this is,' said Mum.

'It's not madness, Mum.' Sally kept her voice quiet and polite, but she felt irked.

'Don't get that look on your face. That's your obstinate look.'

'I'm not a child,' said Sally.

'You're behaving like one. I've never known you to be so giddy and reckless.' Mum clicked her tongue, casting her gaze up to the ceiling for a moment. 'I shouldn't have said that. Your father said I have to be nice to you or we might end up losing you.'

'You'll never lose me,' Sally assured her – or was conciliation perhaps not the best response? She needed to stand up for herself. 'But I do want you to meet Andrew. He's a good man.'

Mum sighed heavily. It sounded dramatic, but there was nothing put-on about the bleakness in her eyes. 'But think of all the damage you meeting him has already caused.'

So far, when Sally and Andrew had gone out together they met up somewhere, but Andrew felt bad about not collecting Sally from her house. To Sally, meeting him elsewhere felt like the only way. It saved trouble. She was very aware of the Grants living just up the road. But she also hated feeling the need to avoid her own territory. People might think she was ashamed, when really she was trying to keep the peace.

Sally and Andrew both had war duty on various nights, which meant they couldn't get together as often as they longed to. When they were free at the same time, they went for walks or to the pictures, sitting in the dark, watching the Pathé Newsreel followed by the big film, all of it seen through a haze of the tobacco smoke that hung in the air.

After seeing Errol Flynn and Olivia de Havilland in *Dodge City*, they stood alongside everybody else for the national anthem, then joined the shuffling lines of people heading for the exit. Sally slipped her gas-mask box onto her shoulder and hooked her handbag over her arm. As they came downstairs, people around her took out their torches, ready for heading into the blackout.

Andrew took her arm to guide her. Over to their left somewhere, a man's voice said, 'Oh, excuse me. I didn't see you,' and then burst out laughing. It was a common thing to happen. You said sorry for bumping into somebody only to find you had apologised to a pillar box or a lamp-post.

'Did you enjoy the film?' asked Andrew.

'Very much. I love Errol Flynn.'

'If he's the competition, I don't stand a chance.'

'He's the one who doesn't stand a chance.' Sally laughed and squeezed his arm. 'I love going to the pictures, but I also love coming outside afterwards, because it means we can concentrate on one another.'

Andrew said lightly, 'How about concentrating on meeting my mother?'

'You've told her about us?'

'Of course. Not that I needed to say anything. She could see for herself that I've been walking around in a happy daze.'

'And she doesn't mind?' Sally asked.

'Mind? She's delighted. Will you come to our house? She'd love it and so would I.'

Sally was so used to the turmoil that her relationship with Andrew had caused that the simplicity of the welcome she looked set to receive made her feel as if she could float away.

'Of course I'll come,' she said happily. 'I'd love it too.'

The moment she knew that Sally was going to meet Mrs Henshaw, Mum changed her mind about inviting Andrew to her house. She wanted to meet him before Mrs Henshaw met Sally.

Sally was pleased and relieved, but she felt nervous too, and not without cause as it turned out.

Mum wore her Sunday best and prevailed upon Dad to change out of the comfy old tweed jacket he wore around the house and put on his suit. They looked as if the King was coming to tea, not their daughter's new boyfriend.

Sally would have liked to meet Andrew off the bus, but Mum wouldn't have it. The Whites sat and waited for their guest to arrive. Mum's starchiness seemed to affect them all. Instead of whiling away the time pleasantly, Dad cleared his throat now and then and Mum kept smoothing her skirt. Sally wished they would behave as normal. Why had Mum seen fit to impose a layer of formality on the occasion?

The doorbell rang and Sally jumped up eagerly and hurried to answer the door, her heart soaring as she welcomed Andrew. His gaze was as clear-eyed as ever but there was a trace of nervousness in his smile. He carried two bunches of snapdragons in pink and yellow.

'These are for you,' he said, offering Sally one of the small bouquets, 'and these are for your mother.'

'Thank you,' said Sally. 'They're lovely. I love them and Mum will too. It's a treat to have flowers in the house. Come in. Mum and Dad are looking forward to meeting you.'

Mum and Dad were on their feet when Sally took Andrew in. She performed the introductions. This mattered so much. Greetings and handshakes were exchanged and Andrew presented Mum with her flowers.

'Oh, how delaightful,' said Mum. 'They really are quaite lovely.'

Sally was almost too stunned to speak. What on earth did Mum think she was doing, putting on a posh voice like that?

'Look, I've got some too,' said Sally. 'Do you want to put both bunches in water, Mum? Then you can choose which vase you'd like.'

'That's quaite all right, Sally,' Mum replied. 'I'll let you choose.'

And Sally was despatched to the scullery, leaving Mum and Dad to start on Andrew. She attended to the snapdragons as swiftly as she could. Leaving her own vase behind, intending to take it upstairs to her bedroom later, she carried Mum's flowers into the parlour. Please let Mum have dropped the refined voice. Instead Sally walked in to find Dad laughing in a jolly way that wasn't like him at all. Usually he was a quietly spoken man with a warm chuckle, yet here he was sounding overcome with mirth.

Sally's discomfort increased. Whatever had got into him?

Well, she knew the answer to that: Mum's starchy attitude, that's what. It was extraordinary. Her parents had always been natural and friendly towards Rod. Why couldn't they be the same with Andrew? Had Sally's new relationship really caused them such a huge upheaval?

Mum and Dad grilled Andrew. Dad's questions were kindly to start with, as Sally would have expected of him, but they then became more pointed after Dad found out that Andrew was a teacher.

'What are you doing in the school holidays?' Dad asked.

'Running a youth group.'

'That hardly counts towards the war effort.'

'It's important to keep youngsters busy,' Andrew said mildly. 'There's plenty for them to do. Some of them are training to be ARP messengers and they're learning to recognise planes by their silhouettes.'

'Leave that to the leaders of the Boy Scout troops,' said Dad. 'It's not a fitting job for you. Believe me, I know what I'm talking about. I never fought in the Great War. When they first brought in conscription, I was above the age. It wasn't until the age went up to fifty-one that I was called up and given a post in the stores. I was presented with a white feather more than once. Do you know what that means? An accusation of cowardice, that's what it means.'

'And Dad was never a coward,' said Sally.

'I'm sorry that happened to you, sir.' Andrew spoke softly and with respect.

'I'll never forget those determined-faced women marching up to me and thrusting the feathers into my hand. I feel the shame of it to this day. Never mind teaching. Take my advice and enlist. Staying safely at home isn't worth it. Not that staying at home will be safe this time round, what with the bombings, but you get my meaning. You have to be able to live with yourself afterwards.'

Later, Sally tackled Dad. 'Did Mum put you up to that? Are you trying to separate Andrew and me?'

'Those were my own true thoughts,' said Dad, 'and I'm hurt that you would think otherwise. I've never said anything of the kind before. I've never admitted to my shame, but it's there all the time, just under the surface. I said what I said in the spirit of trying to help that young man. I did it for *you*, Sally, so you can be proud of him.' He uttered a bitter laugh. 'And you think I did it to appease your mother. That pains me, that does. I wish I hadn't bothered.'

Andrew lived in a modest red-brick house with old sash windows. Mrs Henshaw came bustling out of the parlour the moment she heard the front door, unlike Mum, who had waited for Andrew to be shown in and introduced. Mrs Henshaw had faded brown hair with a smattering of grey. She wore it scraped back from her face in a mass of tiny curls with a dead-straight side parting. It wasn't a flattering style, but maybe she had only just taken out her rollers. Clever eyes and a straight nose, together with an air of capability, made her look severe, but then she smiled and her whole demeanour changed, became softer, more amenable. Something inside Sally sagged in relief.

'This is my mother,' Andrew started to say.

'Don't be silly,' Mrs Henshaw said good-humouredly. 'She knows who I am – and I know who she is.'

'I'm pleased to meet you,' said Sally.

She held out her hand, only to find it wrapped inside both of Mrs Henshaw's while that lady looked at her in frank appraisal.

'So you're the girl who's stolen my boy's heart.' Mrs Henshaw made it sound as if this was the best thing that had ever happened.

'Mum!' Andrew exclaimed, but he laughed as he said it.

Sally laughed too. She ought to feel embarrassed, but she didn't. She liked Mrs Henshaw right away.

'Come along in,' said Mrs Henshaw, leading the way into the parlour.

Sally looked round, eager to see Andrew's home. The walls were plain cream with a narrow wallpaper border of cabbage roses beneath the picture rail. A mirror hung above the brown-tiled fireplace and a large modern radiogram stood on a table in one of the alcoves that flanked the chimney-breast. In the other alcove was a wooden bookcase on which one shelf was devoted to ornaments, and on the opposite wall stood an upright piano and a glass-fronted china cabinet in which one of the shelves was empty.

'My late husband made that cabinet,' Mrs Henshaw said proudly, 'and Andrew made this small table and that bookcase.'

They chatted for a while, exchanging information about their voluntary night-time war work. Without going into detail, Sally explained that she was trained to decontaminate people who had died of being gassed. Andrew worked with a light rescue squad and his mother was with the WVS.

When Mrs Henshaw got up to put the kettle on, Sally felt sufficiently comfortable to offer to help.

Mrs Henshaw gave her a wide smile. 'You can help next time, but this time you're a guest.'

When she returned with a tray of tea things and a plate of scones, Andrew held the door open for her.

'Mum has brought out the best china for you,' he said to Sally, glancing at the empty shelf in the cabinet.

Sally smiled. Mrs Henshaw was so welcoming. She felt warm and accepted.

'These are carrot scones,' said Mrs Henshaw. 'You wait. We'll be making everything with carrots before long – but I shouldn't be telling you that, should I? You must know all about it.'

Sally talked about her job and Mrs Henshaw offered to gather recipes for her. She asked lots of questions about Sally's family and her life in general, but not in a nosy way. She seemed warm and interested. Sally felt it as a wrench when it was time to go.

'I'm very pleased to have met you,' Mrs Henshaw told her. She waited a moment for Andrew to pop out into the hall to fetch Sally's jacket and her gas-mask box, then, in a quieter voice, asked, 'You won't hurt my boy, will you? I know you've thrown over another man for him. I would hate to think you've made a mistake.'

'I promise you I haven't,' Sally answered.

Mrs Henshaw looked into her face. Then she smiled and nodded. 'I do believe you're right.'

CHAPTER TWELVE

Betty was sick to death of doing the housework. She was happy to help out, but Grace was taking advantage. Not that Betty was in a position to say anything, especially when Grace made such a point of telling Dad what a good girl Betty was.

Frankly, Betty felt like the maid. Her days now started with raking out the old-fashioned kitchen range and clearing up after breakfast. Grace even had her cleaning the front step!

'You're only doing what I do every single day,' said Grace.

As well as her daily tasks, today Betty had to do the ironing and turn out the kitchen cupboards. While Betty was busy, Grace donned her felt hat with the rosette on the side and went out. Later, she came home looking pleased.

'I've been to the Labour Exchange on your behalf,' she announced. 'I talked to a very nice lady about you needing a new job.' She dropped her voice into a confidential tone. 'I explained about you not being viewed as fit to get a job round here.'

Betty stiffened, but why should she be shocked? Grace had made it clear this was her intention. Had Betty been foolish not to try harder to get a new job sorted out for herself? But she had wanted to hide away at home. She remembered all too well how the neighbourhood used to keep one eye on Grace back in the days when she was chasing after Mr Wainwright. Now that same critical eye was ready to home in on Betty after her transgression and the disgrace she had brought on the Tuckers.

She swallowed. 'Did the Labour Exchange lady give you any ideas?'

Grace gave a tinkling laugh. 'Better than that. We've found you a job. You're going to work in salvage. Apparently, there's a depot in Chorlton-cum-Hardy.'

'Chorlton-cum-Hardy?' Betty's heart gave a thump. 'That's miles away. It's the far south side of Manchester. If you went any further, you'd be in Cheshire.'

'Exactly.' Grace beamed, her light-brown eyes gleaming with pleasure. 'It'll be a fresh start for you. The lady gave me an appointment with the billeting officer tomorrow, so you'll soon be fixed up with somewhere to live. Won't that be grand?'

The worst place for Sally was the office. She'd tried to make her peace with Deborah, but it couldn't be done. Deborah simply couldn't forgive her.

Taking advantage of Mr Morland's absence from the office, Sally tried to discuss it.

'I know how much I hurt Rod—'

'Do you?' Deborah interrupted her. 'No, you don't, because if you did, you'd never have done it.'

Sally pressed her lips together. Should she have tried harder to make Deborah see what Rod was really like? But it was too late now. Everyone believed she had ditched Rod because of Andrew.

She settled for, 'You can't marry somebody just because they want you to.'

'True, but you can keep your distance and not write to them and not let them and everybody else think you're keen when really you're not. It doesn't matter what you say, Sally. You can't make this right. Rod's gone back to Barrow now – alone. We all thought you'd be going back with him as his wife.'

Deborah was close to tears. Sally rose from her desk, her heart tugging her towards her friend. She wanted to touch Deborah, to hug her, but Deborah gave her a look that stopped her in her tracks.

'When Rod went away at the start of the war,' she said, 'and the two of you said you'd write to one another, Mum and I were thrilled to bits. We were so happy we danced around the kitchen. I wanted you to be my sister. I couldn't think of anything better than my best friend marrying my brother. Mum said we mustn't be obvious about what we were thinking. We certainly mustn't say anything. "We have to let nature take its course." That was what she said.' Deborah made a sound that couldn't be called a laugh because it was full of bitterness. 'It did that all right.'

'I'm sorry for hurting everyone,' said Sally.

Deborah released an angry sigh. Sally decided she wasn't going to apologise again after this. How many times had she said she was sorry? And it hadn't made any difference. She was deeply sorry for the upheaval she had caused, but she could never be sorry for meeting Andrew. That was the best thing that had ever happened to her – and yet nobody else thought so, except possibly for Andrew's mother.

One person who tried to see matters from Sally's point of view was Dad, but even he had his doubts.

'Be careful,' he warned Sally. 'I've told you before, but you didn't seem in the mood to listen. I'm worried that all this upset is making you think you're fonder of Andrew than you really are.'

'I'm a lot more than fond, Dad,' Sally said.

'But are you?' he asked seriously. His blue eyes were tender and worried. 'It's a very emotional time. It would be all too easy to get carried away.'

Sally's heart sank. She felt she was locked in battle with everyone except for Andrew and Mrs Henshaw. Even Dad wasn't completely on her side. Her parents had always made a fuss of her, relishing every moment with their one and only child, and it was unsettling to be out of favour.

Something else that was difficult was spending her war work nights alongside Deborah at the mortuary. The Sunday night leading into the last week of August brought an air raid. Sally felt the hairs lift on her arms as they waited for the bodies to arrive. The drone of aircraft engines filled the night as bright beams of light criss-crossed the dark skies in search of the enemy. The sound of the powerful ack-ack guns attempting to bring down the Luftwaffe planes competed with the spine-chilling whistling as strings of high explosives dropped to earth, bringing death and destruction.

Anxiety tied a knot in Sally's stomach. She hoped Mum was safe in their Anderson shelter. She thought of Dad too, out on ARP duty. Was he even now digging through the wreckage of what had once been someone's much-loved family home, trying desperately to reach people trapped in the cellar? It was difficult to know how far away the bombs had fallen. They all sounded close even though some of the fires that lit up the night were a fair distance away.

Sally couldn't bear to think of her darling dad out in this, and with no more protection than a tin hat and an ARP armband could provide. But she knew too that he wouldn't want to be anywhere else. After admitting to the shame that had dogged him since the last war, Dad was more determined than ever to do his bit this time round.

There was a flurry of activity as two ambulances drew up outside the mortuary. Sally exchanged glances with Deborah. She saw the fear in Deborah's eyes and was sure her own eyes expressed the same. Was this it? The moment the first gas deaths arrived? They pulled on their gas-masks and adjusted them, ready to perform their duty to the best of their ability. For the first time since refusing Rod's proposal, Sally sensed their old friendship and felt bolstered by it.

There were no gas-attack victims that night or on the following night.

'Don't kid yourselves it won't happen,' Mr Warren, one of the mortuary workers, warned the girls after two bodies had been brought in, neither of them the victims of a gas attack. 'Jerry won't stop at anything – including gassing innocent civilians.'

'I know,' said Deborah. 'My uncle was gassed in the Great War and he died young because of it. My nan never got over losing him.'

And then, as if Mr Warren's words had conjured up the very scene he had described, a skinny messenger, aged thirteen or fourteen, came tumbling through the front door, eyes brimming with excitement and importance in his cheeky, freckled face.

'Gas attack!' he cried. 'Over at Christie's Fields.'

'That's not in the Withington area,' said Deborah.

'It's near enough,' said Mr Warren, 'and we're a heck of a lot nearer than the Chorlton mortuary is.' He asked the lad, 'What's your name, son?'

'Noakes, sir.'

'Have you been sent to give us advance notice, Noakes?'

'No. One of the wardens said that if there are as many gas-dead as he fears, then it'd be best to have one of your gas attendants on site. That way the ambulances will only have to deal with the injured.'

Deborah began to say, 'There's nothing we can do at the scene—'

'I'll go.' Sally turned to Deborah. 'I can't wash them and decontaminate them, but I can wrap them in shrouds and maybe get details of names and addresses. I can – I can keep them separate from the other corpses.'

'I'll come with you,' Deborah said.

'No,' said Mr Warren. 'You can't both go. You must stay here and get the room prepared, Miss Grant.'

'If a bomb falls while we're on our way,' Noakes told Sally, 'dismount and lie in the gutter, then get going again.'

Almost before she knew it, Sally was on her way with her gas-mask box in her bicycle basket and a haversack with rolled-up shrouds on her back. Noakes raced ahead of her. Sally was amazed by his courage. Personally, she had never been more frightened in her life. The darkness was packed with noise – the drone of aircraft engines, the clatter of the ack-ack guns, the prolonged whistling as strings of high explosives plunged to earth, the deep boom and ground-shaking explosions as bombs found their targets. The air was alive with movement. At one point, Barlow Moor Road vibrated and Sally's bike wobbled dangerously, making her skin go clammy.

Christie's Fields belonged to the famous cancer hospital and were playing fields, used by their medical staff as well as by the local football league. A large public air-raid shelter had been built there in anticipation of war. As well as being a surface shelter, it also had an underground level.

Sally slowed her bicycle and came to a halt, stepping off it and leaning it against a tree on the edge of the plot of land before retrieving her gas-mask. The air was sickly with the small of gas and Sally felt confused. It smelled like household gas to her, not like any of the telltale aromas that were said to signal deadly gas.

Before she could so much as look round and identify the man in charge, a middle-aged man appeared beside her. He had a squarish face and a large nose and his armband proclaimed him to be with the ARP. He stared at Sally and she realised that her gas-proof clobber had taken him by surprise.

'I've come from the mortuary to see to the people killed in the gas attack,' she told him.

'You what?'

'We had a message,' said Sally.

'I took it, Mr Donovan,' piped up Noakes. 'Mr Ambrose sent me.'

'Oh, he did, did he?' said Mr Donovan. 'It's not his job to send messages, especially not wrong ones. You had no business going on his say-so, Noakes. There's been no gas attack here. That's the mains you can smell.'

'Sorry, sir,' said Noakes.

'I'd best get back to the mortuary,' said Sally.

'Aye, love. Your services aren't needed today. Pray God they never will be. A high explosive landed beside the shelter and took one side off. We've got a light rescue squad here. They've fetched people out, but there are still some left below ground. What we really need,' and his face twisted in anxiety, 'is for the gas men to come and deal with the ruptured mains. If we don't get sealed off, the whole lot could go up.'

'Good luck,' said Sally.

She was on her way to fetch her bicycle when her name was called.

'Sally! Sally White!'

Her brain couldn't tell which direction the voice came from, but her heart knew and it told her which way to turn. Andrew! Andrew Henshaw came towards her. His clothes and skin were caked in grime and brick dust and his gas-mask dangled from his hand.

'Sally, what are you doing here?' Andrew's clear-eyed gaze fixed on her face.

'False alarm.' Sally moved a hand, indicating what she was wearing. 'I'm here in case of gas-attack victims.'

'None of those, thank heaven,' said Andrew.

'And thank heaven this is just light rescue,' Sally added.

'It's borderline heavy rescue. It's a devil trying to get down to the lower level. The whole place is damaged, right down to the foundations. We've sent for the heavy rescue chaps, but we can't afford to wait. With that ruptured gas main, we need to get everyone out pronto.'

'Henshaw!' came a yell. 'Get over here. You're needed.'

'Go,' said Sally.

Andrew nodded, his gaze locking with hers one last time before he turned away. Sally watched him jog towards the building. He was slim but muscular and he carried himself with confidence. The people he rescued must feel they were in safe, trustworthy hands.

Even though she knew she really should head straight back to the mortuary, Sally lingered. Rescued people coughed and gulped as first-aiders checked them over before encouraging them to put on their gas-masks. WVS ladies took care of the walking wounded, providing blankets and tea from a mobile canteen standing at a distance. Ambulances were stationed at a distance too and the hairs lifted on Sally's arms as she fully realised why.

Of course. Because of the damaged gas main and the danger of an explosion, only the rescuers were allowed near the building. Sally's shoulders tightened as she saw Andrew climb over the heap of rubble and vanish from view.

Sally stayed where she was, gazing intently at what remained of the building above ground. How could she leave while Andrew was still inside? He meant so much to her. He meant everything. This was what he did in every air raid. He entered unstable buildings and got people out. He saved lives – but at what risk to his own? Everyone outdoors in an air raid risked their lives – ARP, rescuers, engineers, even the WVS ladies with their tea urns – and they did it willingly, with determination and with more thought for those in need of help than for themselves.

Sally's heart beat hard. Then the ground moved, actually moved. Everyone froze. After a moment, the earth settled but what remained of the building dropped – just dropped. It didn't tumble and scatter. It dropped dead straight, to the ground, flinging up a vast cloud of filth. At the same time, the largest heap of rubble shifted and spread out.

'Get down!' yelled a man's voice. 'The gas might go.'

Everyone threw themselves down, covering their heads. A heavy weight of dread filled Sally's chest, but her dread wasn't on her own account. It was for Andrew, still inside the shelter's cellar. If the gas main ignited...

Long seconds dragged by, then a voice shouted, 'Everyone move further away – beyond that corner.'

The first-aiders and the WVS started shepherding their charges away. Sally didn't want to leave but it was more than time for her to go back to the mortuary. That was where her duty lay – though her heart remained with Andrew.

A pair of rescuers heaved a gas-masked man out from what remained of what had been the building above the ground. Even before he pulled off the gas-mask, Sally recognised him. That slim body that told of physical fitness, those strong shoulders. Andrew! It took all her resolve to stay put as a number of the men, including Mr Donovan, had a quiet but urgent talk.

One of the men yelled, 'Noakes! Where's that boy?'

Mr Donovan spoke sharply. 'He's not doing it. He's a messenger boy. He's only thirteen and I'm not letting you send him in there.'

'But we need someone small,' said another voice, 'or those still in there will cop it.'

Sally stepped forward. 'I'll do it. I'm smaller than any of you. What do I need to do?'

'Sally...' Andrew said and then stopped. He drew in a breath and nodded, accepting the situation, respecting her determination. 'You'll have to wear your gas-mask. The stench in there is awful and getting worse. We need to get a sack of gas-masks in there. Some of the people in there left their houses in such a hurry that they didn't bring their own. The problem is that an interior wall collapsed when everything shifted and there are people stuck behind it. There's a small hole. You'll have to squeeze yourself into it and pass the sack through, then get yourself back here.'

Sally removed her gas-contamination gloves. She couldn't afford to get them damaged. As she pulled on her gas-mask, a feeling of unreality came over her. It was her first time of wearing her gas-mask in a real situation, even though the gas wasn't the German poison everyone lived in fear of.

'I'll take you down there as far as I can,' said Andrew, 'but then you'll be on your own. You'll need a torch. Be careful, my darling.'

Before he could put on his gas-mask, another man intervened. 'Henshaw, we need you over there. I'll take the young lady in.'

Feeling surprisingly calm, Sally lowered herself through the jagged-edged hole, her feet feeling around for the floor or what remained of it. As she moved forward, she felt a sort of thump in the air behind her as her guide followed her in. He carried a sack over his shoulder and held a flashlight aloft in his other hand. He went past her, leading the way. Sally followed with care. Around her, the building creaked and groaned. The floor beneath her feet shifted as she walked, threatening to snap her ankle, fling her onto her back or toss her flat on her face.

Her guide pointed to a slender horizontal aperture and handed Sally the flashlight. Her heartbeat raced as she slid through, grateful for the beam of light. When she made it to the other side, fear swooped through her at finding herself in a confined space just three feet high. An empty sack was pushed through after her, followed by the gas-masks one by one. Sally put them into the sack.

Shining the light around, she saw where she needed to go. She was surrounded by timber and rubble on all sides and there was just one gap. Sally slithered towards it, dragging the sack, then pulled herself up on her knees, shoulders hunched and head bent.

She shone the beam of light through the gap as a sign of hope to those trapped on the other side, then scrabbled to remove a gas-mask from the sack and pushed it through the hole. It jerked as someone took hold of it.

When she'd sent all the gas-masks through, Sally yelled, 'Don't worry. The men will soon get you out.' Her voice was loud inside her gas-mask, though she knew it would be muffled to the listeners, supposing they could hear her at all.

She crawled back the way she'd come, fighting panic when she couldn't make out the gap she had squeezed through. Then she saw it and her whole body went weak with relief. She pushed herself through, feeling as if she had entered a vast cavern when she emerged on the other side.

Her guide took the sack and the flashlight and they commenced their journey back. When they reached the bottom of the hole that led to the surface, Sally braced herself against the edge, preparing herself for the climb. A sharp pain ripped across her right palm and she jerked back her hand, uttering an involuntary cry that must have travelled because the guide pulled her hand to him, shining the light onto it.

Sally stared in dismay at the bloody gash. The wound stung.

Her guide patted his pockets and produced a handkerchief, but it was as filthy as the rest of his garments and he stuffed it back in his pocket.

Sally didn't wait any longer. She scrambled up through the hole and hands reached out to lift her free. She pulled off her gas-mask and then wondered if she should have left it on. The air smelled foul.

'What have you done to your hand?' asked Mr Donovan.

'It's nothing,' she answered.

'It looks nasty,' said Mr Donovan. 'You might need stitches.'

'It needs a good clean,' said another man. 'It might get infected.'

'Do you think she needs to go to hospital?' asked another voice.

'Where's Andrew Henshaw?' That was what Sally most wanted to know.

'Who? Oh, he's gone. All the light rescue blokes have. We've got heavy rescue here now. They've just been waiting for you to come out before they go in.'

'Well done, love. You taking those gas-masks down was a big help. Now get gone. You need to be well away in case the whole show goes up.'

Sally went over to the first-aiders. A girl of about her own age cleaned her hand, applied a liberal dose of iodine and dressed the wound.

'Any sign of infection and you must go straight to your doctor.'

Sally thanked her and cycled back to the mortuary, proud and also rather shocked that she had taken part in a rescue. How she wished Andrew had been there when she had emerged from the remains of the building. Not so she could show off, but just so she could see him, so they could have had a moment together, so that they could each have seen that the other was safe and sound.

That was what life meant in wartime. You could only know for certain that someone was safe when you were together. At other times, all you had was hope.

CHAPTER THIRTEEN

Just as she had on the other mornings following a night on duty, Sally went home, had a wash and did her hair, ate her breakfast and headed off for work, the same as everyone else. It didn't matter how tired anyone was. This was how it was going to be for the duration. She made light of the dressing on her hand. There wasn't time to tell everything that had happened. Besides, she didn't want Mum panicking because she had contributed towards a rescue.

Sally took her gas booklet to work with her so she could revise during her tea break. Last night's brush with the possibility of a real gas attack had left her feeling unsettled.

'I'm scared of forgetting what I've learned,' she told Deborah.

'There have been no gas-bombs so far,' said Deborah, adding fervently, 'Thank goodness.'

Their old closeness hovered between them. Sally looked down at her booklet, reading about the difference between blister gases and non-blister gases.

'My dad reckons mustard gas is the worst one,' said Deborah, 'because, unless it gets in your eyes and stings, you might not even realise it's there.'

Sally shivered. 'It's horrible to think of being exposed to some-thing so harmful and not realising until it's too late.'

'It was mustard gas that did for my uncle,' said Deborah.

Sally was grateful for the chance of a civilised conversation with Deborah, even if it had taken long, frightening nights of air raids to bring it about. Dinnertime was approaching. Sally half-hoped Deborah would suggest eating together in the staff canteen, but she was also wary of anything that might jeopardise this new fragile link between them.

The house telephone rang. There were two black telephones in the office, one connected to the switchboard for making and receiving external calls, the other for speaking to colleagues inside the building.

Deborah picked up the receiver. 'Food Office. Miss Grant speaking.' She listened and her expression hardened. 'Thank you.' Replacing the receiver in its cradle, she looked at Sally. 'That was the reception desk downstairs. Lover boy's here.'

In an instant the atmosphere in the office snapped from quiet and reflective to ice-cold. Sally dropped her gaze from Deborah's, then wished she hadn't because she didn't want to appear ashamed. She looked up again and met Deborah's bright-blue eyes – or was that a mistake? Did it make her appear brazen? Oh, she was fed up of second-guessing what everyone else was thinking and feeling. It was about time others thought about her feelings and treated her with more respect.

Deborah looked at the clock on the wall. 'You might as well go early.' Her voice was flat and cool. 'I'll cover for you if Mr Morland comes back.'

'Thank you,' said Sally.

Deborah cast a brief, scornful glance at Sally before bending over her work once more, saying in an offhand voice, 'Far be it from me to separate you from lover boy.'

Sally didn't dignify that with an answer. She gathered her things and left without a word.

As she ran downstairs, her pulse quickened and she felt breathless, neither of which owed anything to her hurry. She saw Andrew before he saw her. His face was drawn and tired, like everyone's at the moment. Then he looked up and his eyes shone at the sight of her, making her heart swell in response. No matter what difficulties she might face in other parts of her life, it was all worth it because of this, because of Andrew Henshaw, because of the sheer delight that radiated through her body. Rod had never made her feel like that, not even remotely.

Reaching the foot of the staircase, Sally made herself stop and walk sedately across the black-and-white-tiled foyer. Otherwise she would have run straight into Andrew's arms. She smiled up at him, drinking in every detail of his face, his warm brown eyes, the straight nose, the narrow, firm jawline. Tears sprang into her eyes at the memory of Andrew's features covered in grime last night.

'You're all right,' he said.

'Yes.'

'You're safe.'

Sally nodded, remembering how last night she had wanted to see him, just to see him.

Andrew jerked his head away for a moment, but not before Sally glimpsed a bright telltale sheen in his eyes. He blinked a time or two, then returned his gaze to hers.

'You aren't injured,' he breathed.

'No, I'm not. Well' – Sally smiled ruefully as she lifted her right hand – 'just this. It's nothing, though I do smell rather unromantically of iodine.'

Andrew swallowed and his Adam's apple bobbed. 'I managed to dash back to Christie's Fields after the next rescue. I wanted to make sure you were all right, but I was told you'd been injured and had been taken to hospital.'

'Hospital? It was mentioned, but it wasn't necessary. Honestly, I'm fine.'

'As soon as my shift ended, I went to Withington Hospital and Manchester Royal Infirmary.'

Sally's breath caught in her throat. 'You did that? For me?'

'I wanted to find you,' said Andrew. 'But you know what? Even if you'd been admitted somewhere, they wouldn't have given me any details of how you were because I'm not family. Your parents would have been informed, but I wouldn't be entitled to be told anything.'

Sally didn't know what to say. It was true. Next of kin were informed. Should she give Dad Andrew's address?

'I know it doesn't seem the most romantic thing to say,' Andrew continued, 'but knowing the hospital staff wouldn't talk to me made me realise how much you mean to me. I love you, Sally White.' Without removing his gaze from her face, he sank onto one knee. 'I love you with all my heart and I always will. Will you marry me – soon? Immediately?'

Emotion hitched inside Sally's chest but, no matter how over-whelmed she felt, there was no doubt whatsoever in her mind or her heart. She wanted to say 'Yes,' but she couldn't speak. All she could do was nod as the happy tears started to fall.

Andrew rose to his feet and drew her into his arms. Sally was dimly aware of exclamations and scattered clapping around them. It didn't matter to her that they were in a public place. This was the most precious and perfect moment of her life.

CHAPTER FOURTEEN

Sally and Andrew went to the Worker Bee for a meal of liver, mashed potato and cauliflower with sauce, followed by rhubarb fool. They were too busy smiling and laughing and holding hands to pay much attention to what they ate, though afterwards Andrew roundly declared it was the best meal he'd ever had.

'We should have it every year on our wedding anniversary,' he said.

Delight rippled through Sally. Their wedding anniversary. They were engaged. Engaged!

'It's happening so fast,' she said. 'I feel I'm being swept along.'

'Is it too fast?' Andrew asked at once. 'I don't want to push you into anything.'

'I didn't mean it that way. It's perfect.'

Sally knew that other people might not view it as perfect, but she shoved those thoughts aside for now. Nothing would be allowed to spoil these special moments.

'We'll have to choose you a ring,' said Andrew. 'I want you to have whatever you want, but in the meantime...'

Delving in his jacket pocket, he brought out a ring box and opened it to reveal a dainty gold band with a sapphire flanked on either side by a small diamond. Sally took one look and fell in love.

'It's my grandmother's ring,' said Andrew. 'I thought – that is, I hoped you might wear it until we can get you a ring of your own.'

Sally was about to slip the ring onto her finger, but then she blushed and handed it to Andrew, splaying her fingers. Taking the ring, Andrew slid it on. Sally felt as if her heart might burst.

'I love you, Sally,' he whispered.

'I love you too – and I love this ring. I don't suppose I could have it instead of a new one, could I? It's so pretty.'

'It suits you. It's my late father's mother's ring. My mum has always said I should give it to my wife one day.' Andrew smiled and said softly, 'I never thought you might want it as your engagement ring.'

'It's a bit big,' said Sally. 'It will need altering – but not yet. Let me wear it for a few days first. I promise not to wear it on mortuary duty.'

Andrew walked her back to the Town Hall. On her way up to the office, she removed her ring, then changed her mind and put it on again. She refused to behave as if she felt ashamed. She would tell Deborah her news as gently as she could and hope that her tact would be rewarded by a show of graciousness.

No such luck. Deborah already knew. After the public proposal in the foyer, word had evidently spread like wildfire around the building, and Deborah had had ample time to work herself into a state of anger, but it wasn't a heated emotion. She was ice-cold.

'You couldn't wait, could you?' she said. 'You couldn't do it privately at home. You had to do it in public with the world and his wife watching.'

Before Sally could respond, Mr Morland walked in with a smile on his face.

'I hear congratulations are in order, Miss White.'

'Yes, Mr Morland.'

'I wish you all the very best, my dear, and I hope that you and your intended will be as happy as my good lady wife and I have been for nearly thirty years.'

'Thank you.'

'When do you hope to marry?' Mr Morland asked.

'Soon,' said Sally.

'Will she have to leave when she gets married, Mr Morland?' Deborah asked pointedly.

'Of course not,' was the reply. 'Not in wartime. The usual rule has been suspended for the duration.'

Deborah looked Sally straight in the eyes. 'Shame,' she said.

Deborah left the office shortly before four o'clock to administer tests in Longsight, from where she would go straight home. Sally was relieved to see her go. She busied herself making out fresh ration cards to replace ones lost in air raids. Would there be another raid tonight? She kept stopping to admire her beautiful ring, feeling a little surge of happiness when she did. She turned it back each time it slid round on her finger.

'I hope that ring won't prove to be too much of a distraction, Miss White,' said Mr Morland.

Sally couldn't wait to get home to tell Mum and Dad. Would they be pleased? Would this make Mum realise that she and Andrew were serious about their relationship? And if Mum accepted Andrew, would that remove Dad's doubts? A picture flashed unbidden into Sally's mind of how thrilled everyone would have been if she had got engaged to Rod. That was how getting engaged was supposed to be, the way everyone imagined it, with joy and pride and hugs all round. But she didn't feel any regret for how things were with her and Andrew. The lack of fairytale perfection simply proved how deep their feelings were for one another.

But when Sally got home, Mum and Dad already knew.

Deborah had got home first and told her mother and then Mrs Grant had told the neighbours.

'We should have heard it from you, Sally,' Mum said in a voice full of reproach.

'Yes, you should and it's not my fault you didn't,' said Sally. 'Deborah had no business telling anybody.'

How had word got around so quickly anyway? By rights, Deborah ought to have arrived home at approximately the same time as Sally... unless she had bunked off early from the Longsight tests.

'Please be happy for me, Mum,' said Sally. 'It matters so much to me what you think.'

'Of course we're happy,' said Dad, but his blue eyes were clouded with concern. 'Everything is happening so fast, that's all.'

'Does being quick matter when it's right?' Sally asked gently.

'It has to be a long engagement,' Mum decreed. 'You need time to get to know one another.'

'No!' Sally exclaimed in dismay.

'If it's true love, you won't mind waiting,' said Mum. 'You'll be proud to prove it's the real thing.'

'We're at war,' Sally said desperately. 'Couples aren't waiting.'

'Well, you'll have to,' Mum said firmly. 'You're under twenty-one and can't marry without parental permission. I'm telling you here and now that I refuse to give my consent.'

Sally came downstairs wearing a pretty rayon dress with padded shoulders, short sleeves and a buckle belt. The dress was blue and she had a blue scarf to tie loosely round the crown of her straw hat. Her cardigan was in pale blue, chosen not just to tone in but also because Mum had knitted it. Wearing it was a kind of peace offering.

As always before she went out, Sally showed her parents what she looked like. They were in the parlour. The sweet scent of

Dad's pipe tobacco hung in the air. Mum looked up from her copy of *Woman's Illustrated*.

'Are you off out?' Dad asked.

Sally nodded. She moved her arms slightly outwards, putting herself on display. 'What do you think? Too much blue?'

'I suppose you want to wear it to go with your sapphire ring,' said Mum.

'Are you seeing Andrew?' asked Dad.

'Yes,' Sally told him.

Mum lifted her chin. 'Are you going to tell him about not having permission?'

'Of course she is,' said Dad. 'You wouldn't expect her not to.'

Sally decided to tell the truth. 'We'd arranged for Andrew to come round here this evening, but now I don't think that's a good idea. I'd rather go and meet him off the bus.'

'Is this you punishing your mum, Sally?' Dad sounded sad and stern at the same time.

'No,' Sally answered at once. She perched on the arm of Mum's chair and took her hand. 'Not having permission is a horrible blow and I won't pretend otherwise. Part of me wants to be furious with you, but I know you're doing what you think is right, what you believe is best for me.'

'You get lots of whirlwind romances in wartime,' said Mum, 'and plenty of them turn out to be whirlwind mistakes.'

'Ours won't,' Sally said staunchly. 'Ours is the real thing. I wish you could see that.'

'It isn't five minutes since you were writing to Rod Grant,' said Mum, 'and we all hoped—'

'Best not bring that up again,' Dad put in mildly. 'You could bring Andrew here, you know, Sally.'

'I will bring him here again,' she replied, 'just not this evening. We got engaged today. It's meant to be happy and exciting. I never thought for one moment... Anyway, we'll go somewhere and have a good time. You understand, don't you?'

'Of course we do,' said Dad. 'Now off you pop.'

Sally kissed them. Putting on her white jacket, she picked up her handbag and gas-mask box. It was impossible not to feel elated as she anticipated being with Andrew – being with her fiancé.

The bus drew up and Andrew alighted, chucking his spent cigarette onto the pavement and grinding the stub beneath his heel before taking her unashamedly in his arms.

'Good evening, Mrs Henshaw-to-be. Have you come to walk me to your house?'

'Not exactly.' Sally drew away, looking up into his face. 'There's bad news, I'm afraid. We can't have parental consent. We have to wait until I'm twenty-one. That's not until next April.'

Andrew's face fell. 'I never expected that. Lots of couples are tying the knot at the moment.'

'Mum thinks we don't know one another well enough.'

'I'll tell you how well I know you, Sally White,' said Andrew. 'I know you well enough to know I want you to be my wife and that I will love you and look after you for the rest of my days.'

Sally's heart overflowed. It was a mistake for Mum to keep them apart.

Andrew planted a smile on his face. 'So my job this evening is to talk your parents round, is it?'

'No. I want us to have a happy evening – and that means...' Her throat suddenly clogged with disappointment and hurt. She went on doggedly, 'That means we can't go home.'

'Well, your parents might not be keen,' Andrew said lightly, 'but my mother is thrilled to bits.'

'Is she really?' Hope fluttered inside Sally.

'With bells on.' Andrew took her hand. 'Let's catch the next bus back to Chorlton and treat ourselves to a healthy dose of motherly approval.'

Sally laughed as they ran hand in hand across the road to the bus stop. She wanted to share their happiness with someone who would join in with a will, and that was exactly what Mrs Henshaw did from the moment they arrived – in fact, from before they arrived, because she saw them from the window and came hurrying outside before they could get as far as the front door. Sally allowed herself one moment to wish that Mum could have greeted the news with hugs and kisses, then she entered into the moment wholeheartedly.

'Let me see the ring,' said Mrs Henshaw once they were indoors. 'Oh, doesn't it suit you? Andrew said how lovely it looks on you and he was right.'

She produced a bottle of sherry from the sideboard and toasted the health of the young couple. Then she went round and fetched some of her neighbours 'to make a party of it'. Everyone shook Andrew's hand and made a fuss of Sally, while Mrs Henshaw poured sherry with a generous hand.

'When are you getting wed?' they were asked.

'We haven't set a date yet,' said Andrew.

'Give them a chance,' said Mrs Henshaw. 'They only got engaged today.'

Sally was called upon to describe the proposal and all the women sighed when she said that Andrew had gone down on one knee.

Mrs Henshaw gave Andrew the bottle to top up everyone's glasses. There was laughter when the bottle was emptied. Cigarettes were offered and a smoky haze filled the room. Mrs Henshaw sat at the piano and played popular tunes that everyone could sing along to: 'South of the Border (Down Mexico Way)', 'Little Sir Echo', 'Wish Me Luck (as You Wave Me Goodbye)' and, loveliest of all, 'We'll Meet Again,' which made gratitude expand in Sally's chest. She was so very lucky to have Andrew at home in a reserved occupation.

'Are you having a good evening?' Andrew quietly asked Sally later on while everyone was chatting and laughing.

'The best possible,' Sally answered truthfully. She would never have believed when Mum dropped her bombshell that the evening would develop into such a happy occasion.

Andrew shot back his cuff to look at his wristwatch. 'It's nearly half ten. I'd better take you home before your parents start worrying.'

Sally gave Mrs Henshaw a warm hug. 'Thank you. This has been perfect.'

They said goodbye to the neighbours, collecting yet more good wishes as they went round the group. Just as they were ready to leave, the siren started to wail.

CHAPTER FIFTEEN

Betty couldn't believe this was happening. She was leaving home; she was actually leaving home. Like most girls, she had always assumed she would stay here until the day came for Dad to walk her up the aisle. A mad, silly, little-girl part of her hoped that Dad might put his foot down and refuse to part with her, but he didn't.

'We both know it's for the best,' he said sadly.

And Betty cursed herself all over again. She also secretly cursed Grace, who, she was sure, must have ever so gently and ever so regretfully made Dad see why Betty couldn't stay here any longer.

'Chin up, our Betty,' Dad said cheerily before he left for work. 'This is a big opportunity. It's proper war work, something to be proud of. The chances are your days at Tucker's would have been numbered anyway. You're young and single. Believe me, all single girls will end up being called up this time round to do war work and probably the married ladies as well, except for those with babies.'

For her father's sake, Betty plastered a smile on her face and gave him a big hug. She never wanted to let him go. She didn't want him to let her go, but he unwound her arms, ending the embrace with a kiss on her cheek, his moustache rasping softly against her skin. Blinking back tears, Betty locked her smile in position and nodded.

When Dad left, she stripped her bed and finished packing. Grace had borrowed a suitcase from next door. They had a spare one. Everyone had suitcases in their air-raid shelters in case they had to leave in a hurry if there was an invasion. Mr Abbott's was a proper leather case, not a cardboard one. It had leather straps with buckles to fasten round it after it was clicked shut. It even had a little keyhole, though Mr Abbott hadn't lent the key.

Betty heaved the case downstairs and stood it in their narrow hallway in line behind the buckets of water and sand that had to be placed outside in the event of an air raid. The past few nights had been scary. Although Betty didn't want to leave home, the raids had made her feel glad that she would be doing what Dad called proper war work instead of standing behind the counter in a grocer's. Not that salvage sounded like real war work, but at least it was something that contributed to the war effort. Everybody had to do their bit if the country was going to win and Betty had the feeling her bit was going to be very small indeed, but at least she'd be making a contribution.

After Grace had done her facial exercises to stop her neck from sagging, the two of them set off for the bus stop. Grace carried Betty's emergency carpet bag from their Anderson shelter and Betty carried Mr Abbott's suitcase. The suitcase wasn't heavy but it was unwieldy and pulled at Betty's arm. They passed some of the neighbours heading out with their shopping baskets. Everyone said goodbye and wished Betty luck, but she chewed the inside of her cheek at the thought of what they would say about her once she was out of earshot. Grace smiled brightly at all and sundry. Did others imagine she was putting on a brave face at having to send away her errant stepdaughter? Betty knew different. Nothing had been said, but Betty knew in her bones that

Grace would be delighted to see the back of her and have Dad to herself from now on.

They caught a bus into the middle of Manchester, where they had to get another bus out to Chorlton-cum-Hardy.

'You can't go wrong,' a helpful ticket inspector told them. 'You go all the way to the terminus at the other end. Ask for Chorlton Office.'

They thanked him and found the correct stop for the Chorlton bus.

'I can manage,' said Betty. 'You don't have to come with me.'

'Yes, I do.' Grace laughed. 'I have to fetch Mr Abbott's suitcase back to him. Besides, your dad will want to hear all about where you're staying. It's called Star House. Doesn't that sound lovely?'

It seemed to take a long time to reach Chorlton, because the bus had to make a detour to avoid bomb craters in a couple of roads. Finally, it swung round in a hairpin manoeuvre into the terminus.

'It's just a few minutes' walk from here, apparently,' said Grace.

Two clippies were standing together, smoking and chatting. One was young and trim, the other middle-aged and full-figured. Each of them wore the jacket, skirt and peaked cap, together with a small ticket machine worn on a strap across the body, that marked them out as bus conductresses. Grace asked them for directions and they set off, Betty lugging the suitcase, switching it from hand to hand.

'This is Beech Road,' said Grace. 'We have to walk down here, past the rec, then Wilton Road is on the right.'

The recreation ground was surrounded by hedges and the scent of privet lifted brightly into the air as they went by before turning the corner into Wilton Road. All along the other side of the road, and all down this side beyond the rec, were long lines of red-brick houses, each with a big bay window downstairs beside the front door. Under each bay window could be seen the top of another window belonging to the cellar beneath. Star House was one of those that faced the recreation ground. It had two glass panels in the upper half of its door, above which was a decorative semicircular window with a star etched in its centre. Which had come first? The name or the star?

Before Grace could knock, the door opened to reveal a woman of a similar sort of age. Her blue eyes and fair skin were completely at odds with her jet-black hair, which she wore scooped away from her face, with fashionable waves to her shoulders. Beside her high heels, a chestnut-brown dachshund appeared. It yapped spiritedly at the newcomers.

'Now then, Minnie.' The lady of the house stooped in a fluid movement accompanied by a creak of corsets. She scooped the little dog comfortably under one arm. 'We don't bark at guests, do we? Good morning.' She smiled at Betty and Grace, her eyes quick and assessing. 'Miss Hughes?'

'I'm Mrs Hughes,' said Grace. 'Betty's stepmother.'

'How do you do? I'm Mrs Beaumont. That's B, E, A U, not B, O, W. Welcome to Star House. I'll show you to your room first, Miss Hughes, then we can talk about what's what. You're in Marie Lloyd.'

'Beg pardon?' said Betty.

'Marie Lloyd,' said Mrs Beaumont. She trilled, '"*My old man said, 'Follow the van and don't dilly-dally on the way.'*"' That was always one of Mr Beaumont's favourites,' she went on, switching straight back into her speaking voice without pausing for breath. 'All my rooms are named after stars of the music hall. Come in. We'll go straight upstairs. I'll just put Minnie in here. In you go, angel.' She opened a door and popped the dachshund inside.

Betty and Grace entered the hallway, along which stretched a runner of dark green. A runner of the same hue went up the stairs. Along the hall walls and the staircase wall were framed photographs, all of them signed.

'Florrie Forde,' Grace whispered to Betty, impressed. 'And look – Vesta Tilley as Burlington Bertie.'

Betty had heard of the great ladies of the music hall. She recognised the pictures of some newer performers. Robb Wilton in his policeman's uniform, with his trademark mannerism of placing a palm to his cheek. Arthur Askey with his round-rimmed glasses and Richard Murdoch looking clever and handsome, from the *Band Waggon* comedy programme on the wireless.

There was no time for questions. Mrs Beaumont was already at the top of the stairs. She threw open a door and waited for them to join her.

'You're at the front of the house, Betty,' said Grace. 'Very nice.' She walked straight across to the window.

Betty followed her inside, plonking down her suitcase as soon as she was in the room. A small linen chest stood at the foot of the bed and there was a washstand in one corner, its lower half hidden behind a gingham curtain. There was also a narrow hanging-cupboard and a set of drawers. The room was clean and pleasant, attractive even. It struck Betty that she would be perfectly happy to have it as a hotel room for a week's holiday by the sea. It was strange to think of being here for the foreseeable future.

She joined Grace at the window. The curtains and matching pelmet were beige with flowers in muted blue and pink, their long curving stems in a dull green. Propped in the corner was a lightweight frame covered in blackout fabric, which could be fitted over the window before dusk.

'You can see into the rec from here,' said Grace.

The recreation ground, like so many public spaces, had been turned over to allotments. Behind the privet hedge were rows of vegetables, some topped by a wigwam of sticks with beans growing up it, the stems dotted with tiny scarlet flowers. Here and there stood cold frames, their glass catching the sunshine and giving off little sparkles.

'I'll leave you to settle in,' said Mrs Beaumont. 'Come downstairs when you're ready and I'll tell you the rules.'

When the door closed behind Betty's new landlady, Grace turned to her. Her eyes were bright and Betty expected her to say something like, 'What a lovely room,' but what she said was, 'My goodness – that *hair!* Straight out of a bottle.'

Grace moved to stand in front of the mirror and patted the conker-brown hair that fluffed out beneath her felt hat.

'There's no need for you to hang about,' said Betty. 'You'll want to get home.'

Grace turned to her with a tinkling laugh. 'Don't be silly. I can't leave without the suitcase, can I? What would Mr Abbott say?'

They unpacked. The drawers were lined with newspaper to deter moths and each drawer also contained a small muslin sachet.

Grace picked one up and sniffed. 'Lavender.'

Betty opened the hanging-cupboard and took her summer dress from the suitcase. She had two dresses for this time of year, the light-green shirtwaister she was wearing and a lilac dress with white flowers printed on it. Beneath the lilac dress in the suitcase were her winter clothes, underlining the permanence of this move.

'Is that everything put away?' Grace looked round. 'Let's go downstairs and hear the rules, shall we?' She paused, looking at Betty.

'What is it?' Betty asked.

'Take your hat off,' said Grace. 'This is your home now.'

Lifting her hands, Betty removed her asymmetrical 'film-star' hat and placed it on the shelf in the top of the hanging-cupboard.

Grace fastened the empty case. A tiny smile played upon her lips. Was she thinking that, without a suitcase, Betty wouldn't be able to come running back to Salford?

'Time to go down,' said Grace.

She opened the door, leaving Betty to pick up the case. As

they went down, Mrs Beaumont appeared at the foot of the stairs, with Minnie at her ankles.

'There you are. Good. This is the sitting room at the front. The dining room is behind.'

She led them into the sitting room, where a carpet with a faded maroon and dark-blue pattern covered much of the floor. An upright piano stood against the wall and there was a tall cabinet with drawers below and glassed-in shelves above. A standard lamp with a tasselled shade stood beside one of the armchairs and there was a matching settee. Beside the hearth stood a wicker dog basket lined with a tartan blanket, with a ruby-red cushion on top with a gold tassel at each corner.

When Betty and Grace were seated, Mrs Beaumont disappeared to put the kettle on, followed by Minnie. The landlady returned shortly with a tray. She handed round the cups and saucers while the little dog sat on her red cushion, her bright eyes taking everything in.

Mrs Beaumont talked about her house.

'I am a theatrical landlady – hence the name of the house. A great many important names have rested their heads under my roof – Vesta Tilley, Vesta Victoria, Harry Champion.' Mrs Beaumont paused for a moment. Was she about to burst into a rousing chorus of 'Any Old Iron'? But she carried on talking. 'And newer stars too. You saw the photographs of Stinker Murdoch and Big-hearted Arthur in the hall, of course.'

'Indeed we did,' Grace murmured.

'Oh, they've all stayed here,' said Mrs Beaumont as if she had served tea and crumpets to Gracie Fields only last week. She took a moment to insert a cigarette into a long holder, sucking daintily on the end as she lit up. Betty thought it was the most sophisticated thing she'd ever seen.

Catching her looking, Mrs Beaumont said, 'I use a holder of ten inches. Theatre-length. Never opera-length. Some of those are a foot and a half. Ridiculous! As a theatrical landlady, I prefer theatre-length. Naturally.'

'Naturally,' Betty murmured, enchanted.

'When you're a theatrical landlady,' said Mrs Beaumont, 'you can't have ordinary guests, you know. Theatricals keep such particular hours. They work late and don't come home until all hours, and then they need to sleep in. You couldn't mix them with commercial travellers.'

'I suppose not,' said Grace, 'when you put it like that.'

'Then the war came,' said Mrs Beaumont, 'and the government shut all the places of entertainment. Well, I thought, how am I supposed to make my living now? So I offered Star House to the billeting officer and started taking war people.'

'All the theatres and cinemas are open again now,' said Grace. 'They have been for ages.'

'I was thrilled when that happened,' said Mrs Beaumont, 'but the trouble with the billeting people is that once they've got their teeth into you, they don't let go, so I'm stuck with providing billets for the duration.'

'I'm sorry,' said Betty. It seemed the right thing to say.

'I'll give you a rent book,' said Mrs Beaumont. 'Your rent will be eleven and six a week, which covers your room and breakfast. I can provide a high tea or an evening meal for an extra charge. You'll find the necessary at the end of the garden beyond the Anderson shelter, but I do have an actual bathroom upstairs.' She preened, sucking in her cheeks to prevent her face breaking into a proud smile. 'The rent includes two baths a week.'

Not just a bathroom but an *actual* bathroom, Betty noted. Grace caught her eye, looking amused, but it was a superior sort of amusement. Betty was amused too, but in a warm way. She liked her new landlady.

'I only make beds for stars,' Mrs Beaumont continued, 'so you'll have to make your own. That means making it properly with everything tucked in, not just flinging the covers over. I will check. And I allow no gentlemen in the bedrooms, not even brothers.'

'I haven't got any brothers,' said Betty.

'Good. I had one young lady a while back who said a gentleman was her brother. I walked in on them and all I can say is that if they were closely related, they should have been arrested for kissing one another in that way.' Mrs Beaumont gave a delicate shudder.

'My Betty is a good girl,' said Grace.

Betty looked at her. This was the first time she had ever been Grace's girl. Was it just an expression of Grace's resolution to get shot of her?

'There's one more rule you need to know about,' said Mrs Beaumont. 'It's one I invented when I knew you were coming here.'

Betty's cheeks felt red-hot. Had her new landlady somehow heard about how she had let the Tuckers down? Was Mrs Beaumont afraid that she might bring disgrace on Star House as well?

'I've got three other girls here,' Mrs Beaumont went on. 'They all work at the munitions factory in Trafford Park, so they work together as well as live together.'

'That's nice for them,' Grace commented.

'It is,' said Mrs Beaumont, 'and I won't have anybody feeling left out.' She looked at Betty. 'So I've told them that from now on I'll be using their first names and I expect you and them to be on first name terms too. I don't want you feeling they're a clique and you're the outsider. They're called Stella, Lottie and Mary.'

'And I'm Betty.' She said it quickly in case Grace stuck her oar in with an objection. Mind you, Grace would probably agree to anything as long as it involved Betty not going home with her.

'When do you start you new job, Betty?' asked Mrs Beaumont.

'Tomorrow.'

Mrs Beaumont laughed and frowned at the same time as she

addressed Grace. 'Do you remember the days when folk started a new job on a Monday? Here's your lass with a new home on Thursday and a new job on Friday. But that's the war for you.'

Soon after that, Grace stood up to leave. She shook hands with Mrs Beaumont.

'I feel I'm leaving Betty in capable hands,' she said.

'Rest assured she will be safe with me,' Mrs Beaumont answered.

Honestly, they were talking about her as if she was six years old!

Grace gave Betty a peck on the cheek. 'Good luck in your new job.'

'Thanks. Give my love to Dad.'

'Don't be silly. You make it sound as if you've moved hundreds of miles away.'

Just then, that was exactly how it felt. Betty drew in a breath to sigh, but then felt a small stirring of – surely it couldn't be excitement. But it was. Before the war, no girl would have left home except to get married, not unless she was a nurse who was expected to live in the nurses' home, or something of the kind. But now single girls were leaving home and it was respectable for them to do so. More than that, it was patriotic. And yes, there was something exciting about it. So far, Betty had felt crushed by Grace's smiling determination to get rid of her, but in that moment she vowed she was going to make a success of this. And let Grace put that in her pipe and smoke it.

CHAPTER SIXTEEN

It was probably going to be hot later, but at this time in the morning the air was bright and fresh and full of birdsong. Betty always took it as a sign of hope that there could be birdsong in the morning after a night of air raids. She had spent four hours in Mrs Beaumont's Anderson shelter last night, staggering to bed shortly before three. Tired as she had been, it had taken a while to get to sleep because she was nervous of starting work today.

She walked along Beech Road in the opposite direction to the bus terminus. The salvage depot was down here. She had found it yesterday, not even five minutes from Star House. This end of Beech Road was well served with shops. There was a confectioner on each side of the road, one with F PARKER over the door, the other with P PARKER. Rival brothers, perhaps? There were two grocers as well, though with different surnames, plus two newsagents, a chemist and an ironmonger. The police station was along here too.

Betty had been told to report for duty at half past six, which had come as a bit of a shock to the system, and not just because of last night's air raid. At Tucker's, she'd hadn't had to arrive until quarter to eight. At least it was only a hop and a skip from Star

House to the salvage depot. She had worried in case it was too early to expect breakfast, but Mrs Beaumont hadn't batted an eyelid.

'The munitions girls work all kinds of hours,' she said. 'I don't suppose you'll be doing night shifts, will you?'

The thought hadn't occurred to Betty before, but surely salvage didn't involve working through the night? It was only gathering together all the things that could be reused or put to use in a different way. It wasn't something that had to be done round the clock like building munitions.

She arrived at the depot. That word, 'depot', had made it sound enormous and sprawling and even a bit scary, before she had come here yesterday and seen for herself what a small place it was compared to the factory-sized unit of her imaginings. She couldn't see inside the premises because of brick walls to either side and a tall wooden fence along the front, with double gates big enough to drive a van through.

There was a single door in the fence too. It had a keyhole, but someone had already unlocked it and it opened when Betty raised the latch. She had to lift her feet to step over an upright plank across the bottom.

Shutting the door behind her, she looked round, getting her bearings. Straight ahead at the far end, filling the plot from edge to edge, was a building. Mrs Beaumont had told her it used to be a small warehouse. Presumably it still was a warehouse, but with a different purpose in wartime. The building was flat-roofed and no taller than a two-storey house and was maybe a little wider than a pair of semis. In front of the building lay the yard, one side of which was covered over by a simple frame with a flat roof, like a bike shed would be.

The whole yard, both in the open and under cover, was filled with piles and crates of salvage, some covered in tarpaulin. There were sacks of salvage too, all higgledy-piggledy. Over in one corner was a gigantic mound of household metal objects – it had probably started off just in the corner, but by now it had expanded across the ground.

'Saucepans for Spitfires,' said a man's voice.

Betty nearly jumped out of her skin. She'd been so busy gazing around that she hadn't noticed him approach. He was an older man, round-faced, with an old-fashioned wing-collar. His jacket and waistcoat stretched across an ample tummy. He looked too old to be working, but lots of folk had come out of retirement to do their bit, many of them stepping into the shoes of lads who had gone off to fight. Women were doing men's jobs too, working on the buses and the railways, in factories and workshops. Some men seemed surprised that women were able to cope with whatever was asked of them, an attitude that made Betty seem to hear her mum clicking her tongue in annoyance.

She looked now at the vast heap of aluminium objects in the Saucepans for Spitfires heap, not just pots and pans but all kinds of kitchen objects, as well as coat hangers and the tubes off vacuum cleaners. Back in July, an appeal had been launched to persuade housewives to part with all the aluminium items they possibly could in order to provide metal to build propellers and other equipment for the RAF. The women of Britain hadn't needed much persuasion. The RAF was engaged in fighting Goering's Luftwaffe for superiority in the air in what Mr Churchill called the Battle of Britain. Housewives the country over had donated their kitchen implements and other items. Betty had given a cake-slice that had belonged to Mum, feeling that she was donating it for the pair of them, her throat aching as she pictured how proud Mum would have been.

This vast sprawling heap in the depot was obviously part of Chorlton's contribution to the war effort.

Betty looked at the man. He must work here. Did he run the depot? A welcoming smile would have been nice, but was apparently too much to hope for. In fact, bushy eyebrows over deep-set eyes and his downturned mouth made him look positively grumpy.

'Miss Elizabeth Hughes?' he asked.

'Betty.'

'You'll be Miss Hughes to me. I'm Mr Overton and I'm in charge here, for my sins.'

He sounded so gloomy that Betty dared to say, 'You don't sound pleased about it.'

'Pleased?' The word came out as a bark, gloom replaced by disgust. 'I've never been more humiliated in my life.'

To Betty's profound relief, it wasn't just her and the grumpy Mr Overton at the salvage depot. There was also a girl called Pamela Stanwick. She was long-limbed with a narrow, high-cheekboned face and hair the colour of treacle, though the only bit of it on show was an inch or so of fringe peeping out from beneath her turban.

'You might want to wear a turban,' Pamela told Betty, 'or at least a snood to keep your hair tidy and out of the way. This isn't the cleanest job you'll ever have.'

Pamela wore dungarees, which emphasised her tall, slender frame. Betty hadn't realised before that trousers could be so flattering.

'There are dungarees you can have,' said Pamela, 'but they're really men's things, so you'll have to do some altering and they're a right nuisance to sew, being such sturdy fabric.'

'I'll manage,' said Betty. She would manage very happily if she could end up looking as trim as Pamela. And there would be no Grace to tell how lovely she looked and then go and whisper in Dad's ear what a shame it was, because girls wearing trousers wasn't the done thing at all.

'You have to wear your own clothes to come to work and to go home again,' Pamela added. 'Mr Overton won't let you come and go wearing dungarees. He says it would lower the tone.' She pulled a face. 'Because, as we all know, sorting out salvage is a really high-class job. There's a changing room upstairs. Come along. I'll show you.'

Pamela led the way into the building at the end of the yard and Betty followed her upstairs, their footsteps clattering on the bare wooden treads. The changing room turned out to be less of a room and more of a glorified cupboard. There were hooks on the wall and a few shelves as well as a bank of small cupboards with keys in the locks.

'Bag one of those for yourself and hang on to the key,' said Pamela, and Betty stowed her handbag inside one. 'Now then, in here are the dungarees.'

Pamela opened a tall, narrow cupboard. Betty expected to see garments hanging up but instead they were scrunched onto tight shelves.

'Here, get changed into this and we'll roll up the legs for now,' said Pamela.

Far from being transformed into a shapely war worker, Betty felt more like a sack of potatoes. 'They swamp me.'

'You'll soon get them altered,' said Pamela, kneeling to turn up the legs for her. She sat back on her heels and grinned up at Betty. 'I'm glad you're here. I've been on my own for the past fortnight. There was another girl, but she left to join the WAAF. I'm leaving too,' she added, sending Betty's stomach plummeting to the floor. 'I'm going to be a land girl up in West-morland.'

'When do you finish?' Betty asked.

'Next Friday,' Pamela said cheerfully. 'That's plenty of time for me to pass the baton, as it were. Don't look so worried. They'll find another girl to replace me, though I don't know when.'

'So I'll be here on my own,' Betty almost squeaked. She cleared her throat and pinned on a smile, not wanting to look feeble.

'You'll be fine,' Pamela said dismissively. 'And you won't be on your own, will you? Mr Overton's here.'

That reminded Betty. Dropping her voice, she said, 'He told me it was humiliating for him to be here.'

Coming to her feet, Pamela nodded. 'Salvage is women's work, you see. It's done in the home by housewives and the WVS do lots of the general organising and collecting. Strictly speaking, collecting salvage is the responsibility of the local corporation, but many of the refuse lorries are busy helping clear away rubble and so forth following air raids at the mo, so when stuff is removed from here it's often as not the WVS that organises it.'

'And Mr Overton doesn't like that?'

'He doesn't have a problem at all with salvage as such. It's important for the war effort. He just hates it being his job. He used to be a bank manager and everyone looked up to him. He came out of retirement and offered himself for war work, only to get landed with this. It's a real comedown for him and he's taken it hard.' Pamela clapped her hands together. 'Right-o. Let's get started, shall we? Bring your gas-mask with you. We'll start inside. Not that there's much to see. I'll show you the way up to the roof.'

'Why do we go up there?' asked Betty.

'We don't, but the fire-watchers do. It's the only interesting thing about the building.'

'Will I be a fire-watcher?' Betty asked.

'No, love. You're a girlie and Mr Overton thinks men do a better job. It's one of the reasons I'm glad to be leaving, actually. Mr Overton's attitude gets jolly annoying after a while. I signed up for war work to do my bit for my country and to – to honour my brother. He was a merchant seaman and his ship was torpedoed.'

'I'm sorry to hear that,' Betty murmured.

'And doing my bit doesn't include being made to feel that women aren't as good as men. My sister has been taught to operate a crane – and here am I, shunting salvage around and being told men are above such things. So I'm going to be a land girl and help grow crops and look after the animals and keep the country fed. That's what my brother was doing when he died – bringing food here.'

'So you're going to carry on his work, but in a different way,' Betty said, realising. She realised too what an easy war she'd had thus far.

Pamela tossed her head, but not before Betty had glimpsed the sheen of tears in her eyes.

'These stairs go up to the attic,' said Pamela. 'Don't breathe too deeply or your lungs will get coated in dust.'

The stairway was narrow and enclosed. At the top was a long attic that looked like it stretched across the whole building.

'Mind you only step on the joists,' Pamela warned. 'The in-between bits are just wattle and daub. Stand on that and your foot will go straight through. We're heading for that ladder up to the skylight.'

Bent over so as not to crack her head on the roof timbers, Betty trod carefully in Pamela's confident wake. What was the point of this if Mr Overton wouldn't trust girls to be fire-watchers? She reached the foot of the ladder as Pamela was climbing up. Pamela disappeared through the skylight, then her face popped back into view.

'Up you come.'

Betty made her way up, clinging on tightly. She didn't like heights and she didn't like the thought of falling off and plunging between the joists straight through the wattle and daub. Little as she liked the ladder, she was reluctant to let go at the top to reach for the edges of the skylight. Taking a deep breath, she hauled herself through. Pamela grabbed her arm and helped her onto the roof, giving her a moment to steady herself before stepping away and giving her a big smile.

About to demand what the point was of dragging her up here, Betty first glanced around – and the indignant words died on her lips. From here there was a view across the rooftops of Chorlton.

'From here, we are queens of all we survey,' said Pamela. 'I bring my tuck-box up here sometimes and eat my dinner. Believe me, I don't want to sit inside with Mr Overton. He's not exactly comedy material. You can't see it from here, but over that way are the main post office and the station. If you're up here at the right time, you can see smoke or steam or whatever it is puffing up into the air out of a train's funnel. Over that way is Chorlton Park, which has a school next to it.' Pamela turned further round. 'That way is Chorlton Green and the meadows. And that way is Stretford and, if you keep going, you get to Trafford Park.'

'Is that where the munitions factory is?' asked Betty, remembering Mrs Beaumont's mention of it. 'There are munitions girls billeted in the same house as me.'

'I don't envy them,' said Pamela. 'I'd much rather be out in the fresh air.'

Betty noticed a couple of piles of sandbags on the roof.

'For the fire-watchers,' said Pamela. 'They come on duty at ten at night and stay until six. They have to leave the yard unlocked all night in case there's a fire and others need to get into the yard toot sweet to help. The fire-watchers have keys and they lock up when they leave at six and the place stays locked up for a whole half-hour until we arrive at six thirty. There are buckets of water in the yard that have to be kept topped up and there's a pile of sand as well.'

They went downstairs and outside. Pamela hung up her gas-mask box on a hook attached to one of the wooden posts that held up the roof over one half of the depot's yard, indicating to Betty that she should do the same. There was no need for her to explain. Everyone knew the importance of keeping their gas-masks close at hand.

'We store all the different types of salvage,' said Pamela.

'Paper, rags, string, rubber. Over there on that shelf is a box for empty cotton reels.'

'What are they needed for?' Betty asked.

Pamela shrugged. 'No idea. We've just been told to collect them. And over here, of course, we have our grand heap of aluminium.'

'It's impressive,' Betty commented, gazing at the sprawling pile of pots and pans and other assorted metal items.

'It's our second pile,' said Pamela, not without a hint of pride. 'We've already loaded up one and sent it on its merry way. Not bad for a small place like Chorlton, wouldn't you say?'

A yawn took Betty by surprise and she clapped her hand over her mouth. 'Excuse me. It was an early start for me this morning.'

'You'll get used to it,' said Pamela. 'You do realise it's a twelve-hour shift, don't you? That includes compulsory overtime.'

Betty nodded. Everyone engaged in war work was doing compulsory overtime.

'I'm not saying the number of hours will drop when the big drive for aluminium comes to an end shortly,' Pamela told her, 'but the hideously early start will finish – apparently,' she added. 'The depot is open six days a week, Monday to Saturday.'

'Do we get a day off in the week when we work Saturday?' Betty asked. She quite liked the sound of that.

Pamela looked at her as if she was mad. 'Certainly not. You work five days one week and six days the next. You'll be working tomorrow and you'll also have to work on Saturday next week because I'm leaving on Friday. Then you'll work every Saturday until they appoint a new girl.'

Betty started to protest at the thought of being left alone to cope, but Pamela was already talking about something else.

'Before we make a start, there's one thing I have to show you. It's the gas rules. I know you know them, but I have to show you anyway, so if you get gassed to death you can't say you didn't know.' She grinned. 'You know what I mean.' Leading the way back to the building, she opened a door, indicating the posters on the wall inside. 'The gas rules. If you haven't done so already, commit them to memory.'

Betty scanned the familiar information and instructions that were designed to keep people safe in the event of the much-dreaded gas attacks. At the top, the warning signal and all-clear signals were printed in red, respectively hand-rattles and hand-bells. This was followed by the unsettling information about the different forms that gases could take. Some were like mist, but others were invisible; some could take liquid form, which always made Betty wonder how they could be counted as gas. Smells to beware of were listed – bleaching powder, onions, mustard, horse-radish – and then came the physical effects – running eyes, irritation in the nose and throat, pain in the chest or mouth, blisters on the skin. It was horrifying to think that the terrible weapon that had destroyed so many lives in the Great War trenches could now be inflicted on ordinary civilians going about their business. Last of all was the ACTION section, beginning with *Immediately put on your Gas-Mask. Put on your hat, coat and gloves.* Even though she had seen the information before on many occasions, Betty reread it, knowing it could be essential to keeping her alive.

'All done?' asked Pamela. 'Let's make a start on some work, then. A lot of what we do is sort salvage into different piles. Not very thrilling, I grant you, but it has to be done. We have to make sure that, when a collection van arrives, it doesn't matter what they've come to collect. They can just load it up and get on their way.'

'So our job is to sort out the various types of salvage?' Betty tried not to sound as dubious as she felt. It didn't sound interesting – which was a polite way of wondering if she was doomed to die of boredom.

Pamela nodded. 'Yep. Mostly it's obvious what's what, but some of it can be fiddly, though it's easy when you get the hang of it. F'rinstance rope, string and twine all have to be kept separate from one another. And if someone tries to hand in empty tubes – you know, ointment tubes, shaving-cream tubes – they really ought to take them to the chemist, though we can accept them here. They're made of metal, you see, but they have to be kept separate from the other metal things. Jewellery counts as metal as well and we put that in a box indoors.'

Betty nodded.

'I'd get gloves, if I were you,' Pamela advised. 'Not nice ones. Gardening gloves, if you can find them these days. Not everything is as clean as it might be.' There was that grin again. 'I'll take pity on you as it's your first day. You can go through the paper and remove any paperclips, treasury tags or staples. They play havoc with the machinery in the paper mill, so I've been told. And hang on to the paperclips and treasury tags.'

'For salvage?'

'For fastening things together,' said Pamela. 'Lots of things have already vanished from the shops, paperclips among them. I'll make a start on those sacks. They have all kinds of salvage jumbled up inside them. Lots of sorting to do.'

Pamela left Betty to it and Betty tried not to let her heart sink as she viewed the boxes of paper she had to work her way through. Searching for paperclips and so forth wasn't the most dazzling task she had ever been given, but it was up to her to make the best of things. Her main concern, though, was the thought of Pamela leaving on Friday next week. She liked her and didn't want her to go. Quite honestly, even if she hadn't liked Pamela, she still wouldn't have wanted her to leave, because the idea of being stuck here with nobody but Mr Overton wasn't exactly appealing. When would a new girl be appointed? And when she did arrive, she would expect Betty to know everything.

That settled it. Betty needed to learn as much as she could by Pamela's last day this time next week.

CHAPTER SEVENTEEN

Deborah had been out of the office all Friday morning, conducting food tests on shopkeepers, while Sally had been working at her desk.

'I'm afraid this is how it has to be,' Mr Morland had told her. 'The atmosphere in here when you and Miss Grant are together is not conducive to concentration.'

'I'm sorry, Mr Morland,' Sally answered.

'So you should be. It's highly inconvenient having to take two silly, squabbling girls into account when drawing up the timetable. There is a war on, you know.'

After dinner, Sally returned to the office to collect some files. She was running an advice session that afternoon here in the Town Hall. Deborah, now back at her desk, looked up as Sally entered the office, then bent her head again and carried on writing up her tests without a word. Sally was vexed. This was ridiculous. She wanted to say something, but what good would it do?

Besides, Deborah was the least of her problems. Mum was still adamant about refusing permission for Sally to wed and, although she understood it in her head, her heart ached when she thought of just how far away next April was. She hadn't said a word at work about Mum's decision. After she had said in front of Deborah that she and Andrew intended to marry soon, word had rushed round the building. Eventually, Sally would be forced to admit that the 'soon' was actually some considerable time away, but she wasn't going to say that until she was forced to.

Fortunately, Mum had never been one for gossiping about her own business, so the neighbours, including the Grants, didn't know as yet. Sally sighed. It was all so very different to how she had always imagined getting engaged.

She and Deborah had decided when they were children that one day they would be each other's bridesmaids. That wasn't going to happen now. Sadness swelled in Sally's chest. The loss of their lifelong friendship was profoundly upsetting, but Andrew was her soul-mate. It was a rotten shame she'd had her head turned by Rod before she knew any better. She was sorry if she had hurt him, but she'd done the right thing. She was sorry to have hurt everybody. Would they all come round in the end? She smiled wryly to herself. Maybe they would admit she'd been right and forgive her and Andrew about the time of their tenth wedding anniversary.

She set aside personal matters to concentrate on giving the correct information during her advice session.

One woman came to see her purely to complain. 'It's a disgrace putting tea on the ration.' She shifted her shoulders indignantly, making her fox-fur wriggle. 'How am I to manage?'

'The Ministry of Food advice is one spoon per person and none for the pot,' Sally told her.

'I've always added one for the pot. It's the correct way to make tea.'

'I know,' said Sally, 'but you really need to change for the duration or you'll run out.'

The next question came from a pretty girl of no more than twenty, who had come for a green ration book. Sally congratulated her and explained what she was now entitled to, such as additional meats and eggs.

'You can also have milk at the reduced price of tuppence a pint,' she said. 'Once the baby is born, you give back your green ration book and Baby gets a ration book of his own.'

Sally's mum found it frankly shocking that Sally, an unmarried girl, should deal with ladies who were expecting happy events, but she enjoyed it. It proved that life went on, no matter how difficult the circumstances.

At the end of the session, she gathered up her pamphlets and returned to the office. Remembering what Mr Morland had said earlier, she pinned a smile on her face before she went in.

'How did your advice session go, Miss White?' asked Mr Morland.

'It went well, thank you. I dealt with quite a few enquiries and a couple of ladies gave me new recipes. I'll get my mother to try them at home and if they're good I'll type them up and add them to our collection.'

'Strictly speaking,' said Mr Morland, 'it's not up to us to provide recipes above and beyond what the Ministry of Food supplies.'

Sally wondered if Mrs Morland would agree in these days of shortages and rationing, but she couldn't ask. Not so long ago, she and Deborah would have shared a secret smile at this point, but not any more.

Mr Morland stood up. 'Ladies, I have something to say to the pair of you. As you know, I am not happy with the way you have brought your private quarrels into the workplace. The atmosphere of quiet industry has been replaced by one of tension and I don't care for it. Miss White, you are due to marry shortly. In peacetime, this would have solved the problem because you would have left your job, but that no longer applies. Therefore I have taken the liberty of securing a new position for you.'

Sally caught her breath in surprise. Her startled gaze fell on

Deborah, who looked pleased – and something more than pleased. She knew something.

'I am aware that,' Mr Morland continued, 'your fiancé, Miss White, resides in Chorlton-cum-Hardy, and hence that is where I have found you a position.' He beamed. 'Consider it my wedding present to you.'

'What job is it?' asked Sally.

Deborah piped up. 'You're going to be a pig-swill girl.'

Sally opened the front door and walked inside, hanging up her gas-mask box on its hook and removing her hat and jacket, calling hello to Mum and Dad as she did so. They were in the parlour, just as they always were when Sally arrived home from work. Mum was darning Dad's socks and he was working on the cross-word, his pipe sticking out from the side of his mouth.

'I'll have this finished in a minute,' said Mum. 'Then I'll go and do the tea. I've got some pilchards.'

'I've got something to tell you first.' Sitting down, Sally explained about her new job in Chorlton.

'Well!' Mum exclaimed. 'That's a turn-up for the books.' She gave Sally a sharp look. 'Are you sure this new job is Mr Morland's idea and not yours? Only it's a bit of a coincidence, the job being in Chorlton.'

'No, it's not,' said Sally. 'It's in Chorlton because that's where Andrew lives and Mr Morland thinks we're getting married right away.'

'And who gave him that idea?' Mum asked.

'I'm the one who told him about Chorlton, but it was before you said no to the wedding.'

'You'll have to set him straight, then, won't you?'

'The job is all arranged, Mum. I start in the middle of September – not this coming Monday, the Monday after.'

Dad stepped in. 'Salvage work, eh? What will you be doing?

Going door to door collecting old newspapers and bundles of rags?'

You're going to be a pig-swill girl.

'I don't know the details,' Sally said.

'Only it doesn't sound much of a job,' said Dad.

'I'm sure there's more to it than that.'

My goodness, she certainly hoped so. She loved her job in the Food Office. It knocked spots off being in the typing pool. She loved helping people and, if it didn't sound big-headed, she loved the thought that she had specialist knowledge. She enjoyed collecting the extra recipes too. It might not be required of her, but she felt it was useful and, well, it made her feel good about herself. It made her feel she was good at her job.

She was about to lose all that now – and for what? To collect materials for salvage door to door like Dad suggested? For a moment her disappointment was so intense that she couldn't breathe.

She forced herself to cheer up. After two nights off from mortuary duty, during both of which there had been air raids, she was to return to the mortuary tonight. Deborah would be there too. Not for worlds would Sally show how upset she was at losing her beloved position in the Food Office – and for grotty old salvage work, of all things. What a comedown – or was that unpatriotic of her? Everybody had to do their bit and, if Sally White's bit involved collecting old rags and string and pieces of rubber, then so be it.

She was still reeling from being told about her new job when she got another shock within minutes of arriving at the mortuary.

'Ah, there you are, Miss White,' said Mr Johnson, who was in charge of the duty rosters. 'At the start of this week, Miss Grant asked if the two of you could be moved onto opposite rosters, but now she says there's no need because you're leaving. Is that correct?'

Sally didn't know which piece of information to deal with

first, that Deborah had asked not to work with her any longer or that she had blabbed about Sally's move to Chorlton. For a moment, she felt as if her life was running out of control and she couldn't keep up with it.

'You really ought to have told me,' Mr Johnson was saying. 'I don't appreciate hearing it from a third party.'

The injustice stung Sally.

To Deborah, when they were alone, she said, 'Kindly leave me to make my own arrangements. It's nothing to do with you when I'm leaving.'

'On the contrary, it's everything to do with me,' Deborah retorted. 'It's bad enough having to see you in the office without having to be on duty with you here too.'

'Look, I don't know how many times I have to say it, but I'm sorry I hurt Rod,' said Sally. 'I truly am. If you weren't so angry, you'd know that. We've been friends all our lives. Doesn't that count for anything? Don't you – don't you miss me?'

For half a second, something flickered inside Deborah's bright-blue eyes. Sally wasn't sure what it was, but she gently bit her lip as she felt a little burst of hope.

Then Deborah said, 'Someone's got a high opinion of herself,' and turned away.

Sally wanted to shake her, but then, to her surprise, Deborah swung back to face her.

'It's as if you don't realise.' Deborah's voice was thick with emotion. 'You haven't just hurt Rod. You've hurt our whole family. You've been one of us for so long and all we wanted was for you to marry Rod and make it official that you were one of us. It isn't just the way you've let Rod down, although that's bad enough. It's like you've turned your back on all of us.'

Was this the moment to try again to tell Deborah about Rod's behaviour? Not that Deborah had been in any mood to listen last time – any more than Mum had when Sally had tried to tell her.

Before Sally could decide whether to say something, the siren sounded. She looked at the clock. Twenty-five past ten. The raids last night and the night before had started at half past ten.

'They're early tonight,' Deborah said flippantly.

Sally's shoulders tightened. Would tonight be the night? That was what she asked herself each time she came on duty. Would tonight see the first gas attack? Would she and Deborah be called upon to put their training into practice? Not that she wanted anybody to die in such an agonising and horrible way, but there was an anxious part of her that needed to get her first gas-attack victim over and done with. She needed to know that she could cope with the thorough cleaning that would decontaminate the body.

Was it nasty and vicious of her to think such a thing? Once upon a time, she could have whispered it to Deborah and maybe she would have had the comfort of finding that Deborah felt the same. But she couldn't possibly confide in her now for fear of her old friend holding it against her.

The raid dragged on for over four hours. No bodies were brought in. There was something surreal about waiting for such a lengthy period, feeling all wound up ready but not actually being called upon. Meanwhile, fire-watchers risked their lives on roofs; gas and electricity men made places safe when the mains were ruptured; the ARP wardens and light rescue men dug through rubble to uncover the injured while the heavy rescue teams tackled the hardest, most dangerous rescues; and ambulance men and women drove their casualties along streets that might at any moment take a direct hit.

All of that was going on outside, maybe not in the immediate vicinity but certainly not very many miles away.

Sally thought of Andrew, working in his light rescue squad. As the all-clear sounded, she shut her eyes and prayed for his safety. Had she really only met him on the first of this month? She couldn't imagine her life without him.

CHAPTER EIGHTEEN

In common with other office workers, Sally worked until one o'clock on Saturdays. As she walked up the stairs to the office, she overheard others talking about last night's raid. Swinton and Pendlebury had both been bombed.

'And did you hear about the Palace Theatre?'

Sally couldn't help herself. She turned round to ask, 'Please tell me the Palace wasn't hit.' She had been to so many shows there over the years, including some wonderful pantomimes when she was a child.

'It's fine as far as I know,' the middle-aged lady with horn-rimmed spectacles told her. 'Some high explosives fell on a warehouse behind it, and you know what people are like. It started a rumour that the Palace had taken a direct hit and lots of folk had copped it.'

'But it didn't happen,' her companion added earnestly.

'I'm pleased to hear it,' said Sally, relieved. 'Sorry to barge in on your conversation.'

She carried on up the stairs. Mr Morland had arranged for Deborah to spend most of the morning testing shopkeepers, so Sally was happy enough to go to the office. She smiled wryly to herself. The shopkeepers of Manchester were going to have an easier time after she left the Food Office and Mr Morland didn't feel the need to keep Deborah out of the way so much of the time.

Anyway, she didn't mind whether Deborah was there or not this morning. Andrew was going to meet her outside just after one o'clock and that meant she could cope with anything. The thought of seeing him so soon made her want to hug herself for joy.

No matter how happy she was, Sally wasn't the sort to daydream her time away. She was proud of her job and soon immersed herself in her work. She might not be here for much longer, but that was no reason to start slacking.

At last the morning ended and she ran downstairs and out of the front doors to where Andrew was waiting for her. His face lit up when he saw her, his brown eyes glowing with love. Sally ran to him. He caught her in his arms and swung her round, making her laugh.

'I couldn't wait to see you,' Sally declared as he put her down, holding her for an extra moment to make sure she had found her feet.

'Because I'm the love of your life?' he enquired with a twinkle.

Sally laughed. 'That, too, of course, but also so I can share my news.'

Linking his arm and lovingly huddling close to him as they crossed Albert Square, Sally explained about her new position in salvage.

'I know where the depot is,' said Andrew. 'Down the end of Beech Road.' He smiled broadly. 'You'll be working in Chorlton. I like the sound of that.'

'But I'll still be living at home,' Sally pointed out. 'Mum has made that very clear.'

'I know I ought to say, "It's only until you're twenty-one," but I hate the thought of waiting.'

'I know,' Sally agreed. 'It's so hard being made to hang on when we're both sure of what we want.' She squeezed the arm she was linking. 'Let's not be grumpy. The last thing I want is to spoil our time together. All we can do is hope that my parents will see for themselves how serious we are and that it will bring them round to our way of thinking.'

It was what she longed for more than anything else.

On Monday Sally received a letter through the internal post confirming her new appointment at the salvage depot and requiring her to report for duty at half past six on her first morning.

'Half past six!' Mum exclaimed that evening when Sally told her. 'That's an early start.'

'I'll have to move to Chorlton,' said Sally.

'You can't,' Mum said at once.

'But it makes sense,' Sally protested. 'Just think what time I'd have to get up if I carry on living here. It would be tricky enough if the buses are running normally, but with craters in the roads and all the disruption after every air raid, it'd be even harder.'

'Well, I don't know.' Mum sounded tetchy. 'I don't like the sound of it at all.'

'Lots of girls live away from home now, Mum, because of war work. It's not as though I'd be going to the other end of the earth,' Sally added, trying to introduce a note of levity.

She left it at that, hoping Mum would get used to the idea. Dad hadn't really said anything and Sally knew he too was waiting to see what Mum said.

Then something new was thrown into the mix.

When Andrew told his mother about Sally's future early starts, Mrs Henshaw immediately offered Sally a roof over her head. She even travelled over to Withington on the bus to meet Sally's parents in an attempt to set their minds at rest.

'Your Sally can have Andrew's room and I can turn the front parlour into a bedroom for him. I can assure you that Sally will be as safe under my roof as she is under yours, if you know what I mean.'

Everyone knew precisely what she meant. Dad mumbled something and practically stuck his face inside his teacup. Mum went scarlet. Sally turned scarlet too, but not entirely with embarrassment. The thought of sleeping with Andrew made her skin tingle all over.

Mum refused to commit herself one way or the other.

Later Sally said gently to her, 'It's barmy for me to live here and work there with such an early start. You can see that, can't you?'

'I don't want you living with that woman.' Mum's mouth set in a stubborn line.

'She's not "that woman". She's Andrew's mother,' Sally replied at once. 'And why wouldn't you want me to live with her? She's kind and sensible and she's been perfectly sweet to me.'

It wasn't what Mum wanted to hear. They seemed to have reached a stalemate.

It was Dad who broke it. When Sally came in from work the next evening, he pointed to the sofa with his pipe in a silent instruction to sit down. Sally obeyed. Mum looked subdued, though her hands worked like lightning, her knitting needles clicking at top speed. She kept glancing at the pattern, something she didn't normally do.

'Mum and me have been talking about you moving in with Mrs Henshaw, Sally,' Dad began, 'and we've decided it's the best option. We can't have you traipsing over to Chorlton for such an early start every morning, and what if we have another bad winter like the last one? All that snow: who knows how long the journey would take?'

'Oh, Dad,' breathed Sally. Tactfully she looked at her hands in her lap in case her eyes were sparkling. She didn't want to make this worse for Mum.

'I went over to Chorlton this afternoon and had a long talk

with Mrs Henshaw,' said Dad. 'She showed me the room you'll have. She also showed me what will be Andrew's room. One of the neighbours is going to lend them a bed for him.'

'It sounds as if it's all arranged.' Sally hardly dared to believe it.

'Aye, well, not until Mum has been over to see it. She'll do that tomorrow – won't you, love?'

Mum jerked her chin, but Sally knew she would do as Dad wanted. Most of the time Dad sat back and let Mum be in charge, but, when he made up his mind, Mum and Sally both knew that was that.

'Before I went round to the Henshaws', I went to the billeting office to see about getting you fixed up that way, Sally,' Dad went on, 'but you'd have to go on a list and there wouldn't be a choice. Some places only take girl lodgers but some take men as well and I wouldn't feel comfortable about you living alongside strange men. You could have had a bed-sitting room right away, but I'm not having my daughter fending for herself like that. I want you living in a proper home where there's a mother figure to take care of you. If it can't be your own mum, then who better than your future mother-in-law?'

For one breathless, wonderful moment, Sally thought Dad was about to say she and Andrew could get married, but he didn't.

'So, Mum will come with me tomorrow to see Mrs Henshaw's house and talk things over.'

Sally jumped up, intending to hug Dad, but upon seeing her mother's face, she knelt beside Mum's chair instead.

'Thanks, Mum,' she said.

'I haven't said yes yet,' was the stiff reply.

But they both knew she would.

CHAPTER NINETEEN

On Sunday, the day before Betty's stint on her own in the salvage depot started, the munitions girls who shared her billet at Star House took her out for a walk.

'It'll do you good,' said Stella, a tall redhead. 'Blow away the cobwebs.'

'And give you something else to think about instead of next week,' Mary added. She was a little dumpling of a girl with blue eyes and a generous heart.

'I am a bit nervous about it,' Betty admitted. That was something of an understatement, but she didn't want to appear feeble.

'It's hard work at the munitions,' said sandy-haired Lottie, 'but there's a lot to be said for having plenty of other girls all around you for company.'

They took Minnie the dachshund with them. She had a red leather collar with a metal name-disc dangling from it, with STAR HOUSE, WILTON ROAD engraved on one side and MINNIE and a star on the other.

'Can she walk far?' Betty asked. 'She's only little.'

'You'd be surprised,' said Mrs Beaumont. 'She loves the meadows. Now off you go, girls. You'll be a good girl for them, won't you, my little angel?'

As they left Star House, Stella said, 'Have you been to the meadows before, Betty? It's a long stretch of meadowland that runs alongside the River Mersey on both sides. There are parts that you can't get access to because of gun emplacements, but most of it is unspoilt.'

'It's rather lovely,' said Lottie, 'like being in the countryside.'

Betty enjoyed the walk. It was a big improvement on stewing over what next week would be like. She appreciated the company too. The three munitions girls had welcomed her into her new billet with cheerful jokes about having another girl to share clothes with. An only child, Betty found she liked the others' company. It was fun sharing bedtime drinks and talking about their favourite film stars. Mind you, she was grateful she didn't have to put in the working hours the others did. The munitions factory kept going for twenty-four hours a day and everyone had to do their share of night shifts.

That was one good thing about the salvage depot: it was only open during the day. Betty hadn't minded it when Pamela was there. How was she going to find it when she was on her own?

Betty was filled with resolve on Monday as she set off. Above all, she didn't want to make a chump of herself by fumbling over not knowing what to do. She'd paid close attention to everything Pamela had told her, so, even if Mr Overton didn't provide much guidance, she hoped she would know enough to get by.

At the depot, she changed into her dungarees. Pamela had been right; it definitely hadn't been easy to work with the sturdy material to make the necessary alterations, but Mrs Beaumont had been a big help.

'I was always good at sewing,' she'd told Betty. 'I fancied myself as a wardrobe mistress at one time, but alas it wasn't to be.'

To Betty's surprise, simply making the garment shorter in the leg and the body hadn't been enough for Mrs Beaumont. She had insisted on adding some shaping as well.

'You've got a nice figure,' she said.

Betty remembered that each time she stepped into the dungarees, and it gave her a boost. Mum used to pay her little compliments about her appearance.

Drawing her shoulders back, she went downstairs with her gas-mask box over her shoulder to face the day alone. Endlessly sorting through the salvaged materials wasn't an appealing prospect, but if that was what was required...

She drew on the pair of old gardening gloves she had found in the second-hand shop last week and set to work on the sacks of mixed salvage. If she could empty all the sacks and distribute the contents into the right places, that would, she hoped, give her a sense of achievement. The yard's big gates stood open, as they did all day. If she angled herself so that she was facing the outside world, a passer-by might stop for a chat.

'Good morning, Miss Hughes. Keeping busy?'

Betty turned round. 'Morning, Mr Overton. I'm sorting out what's in these sacks.' As if the old duffer couldn't see that for himself! She hid the thought behind a polite smile. If he was a better boss, this would be a pleasanter place to work.

A van pulled up on the road outside. Betty glanced across, watching for the men to get out. Instead, a woman climbed down on the driver's side, followed by another woman who slid across from the middle of the bench seat. A third woman climbed down at the other side. Well, and that was a lesson she should have learned by this time, Betty acknowledged. Women were every bit as capable as men and could do anything that men could.

Mr Overton took one look and skedaddled, leaving Betty to deal with them.

Betty smiled a greeting. All three women were middle-aged and wore the dark-green uniform of the Women's Voluntary

Service; or at least, the woman who had been sitting in the middle of the seat wore the whole lot – the two-piece herringbone-tweed suit, the smart hat, even the scarf and the handbag. Imagine having a handbag as part of a uniform! The other two women wore single items from the uniform. You often saw that. Women bought what they could afford. These three all wore the shallow-crowned felt hat with the WVS badge on the front. Lots of women just purchased the hat. Even so, there was, according to Grace, talk of adding a beret as a cheaper option. There was also talk of a suit with fewer buttons that would be less costly.

The lady in full uniform headed for Betty with the sort of confidence that proclaimed her to be in charge. She was middle-aged with grey eyes that were cool and keen and looked as if they missed nothing. She walked with energy and confidence, shoulders back and head up, as if everyone's attention was upon her and it was her duty to set a good example to the plebs.

She stopped in front of Betty and made a show of looking all around.

'Where is Miss Stanwick?'

The question, uttered in a voice Betty labelled as 'posh', suggested that Miss Stanwick jolly well ought to be here on parade and ready to drop her best curtsey.

And good morning to you too, thought Betty. She said, 'She's gone to join the land army.'

'Indeed?' The lady's eyebrows climbed up her broad fore-head. 'She didn't inform me.'

'Was she supposed to?' Betty asked. She couldn't imagine Pamela neglecting her duty.

'Naturally,' the lady said as if Betty was a fool not to know that. 'How am I supposed to organise salvage matters efficiently if information is withheld from me?' She shook her head as if ridding herself of the thought of Pamela's shortcomings, then breathed in sharply. 'I take it you're my new girl.'

My new girl? 'Betty Hughes.' Betty extended her hand

politely, then realised she was wearing her grotty work gloves so withdrew it again, with a laugh that went unshared.

'Well, Miss Hughes – I assume it's Miss? I hope you'll be more reliable at keeping me informed than your predecessor was. I am Mrs Lockwood from the WVS, as you can see, and I have special responsibility for salvage.' With a flourish, she indicated the band on her sleeve, which read SALVAGE OFFICER.

Betty was confused. 'I thought Mr Overton was in charge.'

'He oversees the day-to-day running of this depot. What are you doing?'

'Sorting through the salvage in these sacks.'

Mrs Lockwood snorted. 'Call that sorting? Picking and choosing, more like. Here, give me that.'

She grabbed the sack from Betty's hands and upended it onto the ground. Out came paper, string, bits of wood, some metal blades and an inner tube.

'There. Now you can see what's what. Don't stand there gawping, girl. Get on with your work. You'll never get finished at this rate. I don't tolerate slackers and the sooner you learn that the better.' With that, Mrs Lockwood turned to her companions. 'Load up the paper, ladies. We're expected at the paper mill.' She turned back to Betty. 'I trust you've removed all the staples and what-not.'

'As far as I know,' said Betty.

'What sort of attitude is that, young lady? "As far as I know," indeed! You should be able to say, "Yes, Mrs Lockwood," without a shadow of doubt in your mind that you have done your job properly.' The formidable Mrs Lockwood looked Betty up and down, her mouth twisting slightly as if she wasn't impressed. 'I can see I'm going to have to keep a firm eye on you, Miss Hughes.'

* * *

After the WVS women had loaded up the paper and driven away, Mr Overton reappeared. He asked Betty if she intended to join the WVS.

'It's what young ladies ought to do,' he said.

Betty thought of all the 'young ladies' who were currently building bombs, operating cranes and steam-hammers, driving lorries and ploughing the land. All she said was, 'I'll think about it.'

'Only think about it?' Mr Overton frowned. 'That doesn't sound very patriotic.'

Betty bridled. She admired the WVS, but she'd been pushed into this salvage job by Grace and she didn't intend to be pushed into the WVS just because Mr Overton deemed it suitable.

She carried on working her way through the contents of the sacks before she finally picked up the things Mrs Lockwood had tipped onto the ground. For two pins she would jolly well leave them there, but then she would get into trouble with Mr Overton.

'Hello, love. Do you work here? Can you do me a favour?' A headscarfed housewife approached her, carrying a wicker basket from which she produced a metal fish-slice. She held it out with a gap-toothed smile. 'I'm Mrs Archer from Reynard Road. I've handed over nearly all the metal I've got, and was glad to do it an' all, but I kept back a couple of bits, obviously. Well, you have to, don't you? Nobody can manage without a saucepan, can they? The point is, I kept this here fish-slice and really and truly I can manage without it.'

'So you've come to hand it in,' said Betty.

'Actually, I've come to see if you'll do a swap. You see, if push comes to shove, anyone can get by without a fish-slice, but you try cooking without a colander.'

'I see what you mean.'

'So can I do a swap, then, love? I'm not asking for summat for nowt.'

Where was the harm? Betty cheerfully agreed, helping Mrs

Archer to sort through the most accessible parts of the metal heap. They chatted as they sorted and Betty enjoyed the company. They found a colander and Mrs Archer departed, looking pleased.

Betty felt pleased too. She'd always enjoyed helping folk, and assisting the housewife had made her feel the way that working at Tucker's used to make her feel. Oh, this job was going to suit her down to the ground.

All in all, the week didn't go too badly. She made up her mind not to let the loneliness get her down. Yes, the work was dull, but she was doing her bit and that was what counted.

On Wednesday a lady came into the depot bringing, of all things, an artificial leg.

'It's made of aluminium,' she explained. 'My dad passed away last month and I'm sorting out his stuff. He'd like to think of his leg being made into a Spitfire.'

Betty thanked her and expressed her condolences, thinking at the same time that this would make a fine tale to tell at Star House. It would give them all a good chuckle.

Another little incident that lifted her spirits occurred when a girl of about twenty came into the yard. She was a pretty thing with brown eyes that were awash with tears. Betty went straight over to her, concerned.

'Oh, please can you help me?' the girl asked. 'It's my mum's...' And she dissolved into tears. She fished inside her handbag, produced an embroidered hanky and performed a dainty mopping-up operation. 'I'm sorry to make a show of myself, but it's my mum's brooch.'

'What about it?' Betty asked encouragingly.

The girl sniffed and blinked a couple of times, pulling herself together. 'I think it got put in with the salvage. I'm so sorry to trouble you. I need to get it back before Mum realises it's gone. We were bombed out and that brooch is all she has left from things Dad gave her.' She looked despairingly at the massive pile of metal. 'Would it be in among all that?'

Betty smiled warmly. If the girl hadn't been so upset, she might have been tempted to indulge in a little gentle teasing about having to search through the heap. As it was, she took the girl's arm and squeezed it.

'Come with me and we'll see if we can find it, shall we? We keep all the jewellery in a special box. What's your name?'

'Jenny Baxter.'

'I'm Betty Hughes.'

Sure enough, when Jenny had rifled through the contents of the box she lifted out a circular brooch set with a ring of purple stones round a milky-white stone with subtle dashes of colour in it. Betty would have liked a closer look, but Jenny was so thrilled she clasped it tight, beaming at Betty.

'Honest to God, you've saved my life. I can never thank you enough.'

'You're welcome,' said Betty.

'I'd best leave you to get on with your job,' said Jenny, 'I'm sure it's very important. Thanks for taking the time to help me.'

'It was my pleasure,' said Betty, but she was talking to thin air. She laughed, feeling satisfied as she returned to work. Maybe this job wasn't so boring after all.

Best of all, Mr Overton sought her out to tell her that a new girl would be starting with her on Monday.

'Monday?' Betty repeated. 'This coming Monday?'

She couldn't believe her luck.

CHAPTER TWENTY

All through that first week of September, Sally was sure she had never felt happier in her whole life. She was going to live under the same roof as the man she adored. True, it wasn't as good as moving in with him as his wife, but it would be wonderful all the same. Imagine spending all that time together. It would be good for Mum and Dad too. It would show them how perfect Sally and Andrew were as a couple.

In other ways it was a difficult week, with raids every night as well as the first daylight raid, which was truly frightening. On Tuesday night, Chorlton-cum-Hardy was attacked and some houses were destroyed, though to Sally's profound relief this happened nowhere near the Henshaws' house. More unsettling, because she knew where in Chorlton it was, was that the gas main on the junction of Nell Lane and Mauldeth Road West was ruptured. It brought to mind that night at Christie's Fields.

Sally couldn't wait to move in with the Henshaws. She'd had to come clean at work during the week; there had been so many questions, all based on the assumption that she must be getting married soon, that she had told the truth about having to wait. Besides, if she hadn't confessed, Deborah would undoubtedly have done it for her, because Dad had insisted that Mum must be open with the neighbours about Sally's move so that the Whites would have control over what was said and the neighbours would see that everything was above board and respectable.

Now it was Friday, Sally's last day at work in the Food Office. It was strange to think that she was doing everything for the final time, but she was too happy about her future to feel sad that she was leaving.

Deborah made herself scarce after dinner. The other girls came into the office in a chattering group, bringing with them a waft of tobacco smoke mingled with Evening in Paris perfume.

'We've come to say goodbye and good luck,' said Miss Greening from Housing. Her bubbly good nature seemed to have infected the others and they were all smiling.

'Thanks,' said Sally.

'Are you sad to leave?' asked Miss Brelland. She turned her head to blow out a stream of smoke, her reddish-gold hair catching the sunshine that poured through the window between the strips of anti-blast tape.

'I've loved working here,' said Sally, 'but in wartime, you go where you're sent.'

Miss Jameson laughed. A dark-haired girl with roses in her cheeks, she worked in Welfare. 'And it's sending you to your fiancé's house.'

Everyone laughed and a frisson of excitement skittered around the group.

'As you know,' said Sally, 'I'm not allowed to marry until I'm twenty-one, so this is the next best thing.'

There was a chorus of 'Ahh' followed by requests to see the ring. Sally explained to those who didn't already know about Andrew's grandmother's ring and how he'd had it made smaller to be the perfect fit on her finger. As she spoke, Sally couldn't help but be aware of Miss Greening and the other engaged girls whom

Deborah had brought into their office to parade their rings so as to ascertain the correct size of Sally's finger.

Soon the group started to disperse, everyone wishing Sally well. She hummed to herself as she settled back to work. The afternoon went on. Just when she was starting to think of tidying her desk for the final time, the door burst open and Deborah flew in. She came to a breathless halt in front of Sally.

'I don't know if I should be here,' she blurted out.

'It depends,' Sally said crisply. 'Are you going to be nice to me? I won't put up with any nastiness, not on my last day. The least you can do is be polite.'

Deborah's face crumpled, her blue eyes no longer bright blue but clouded with distress. 'How did it come to this? We've been friends since we were babes in arms.'

'Please don't say it's my fault because of meeting Andrew.'

'I'd never have thought it possible for us to fall out.'

'Me neither,' Sally agreed softly.

'I feel torn in two,' said Deborah. 'I can't be disloyal to Rod. He's my brother.'

'I know how much you care about him,' said Sally.

'And Mum's heartbroken over what's happened. I can't bear to think of Rod being so hurt. They're both angry with you.'

'You were angry too.'

Colour flared in Deborah's cheeks. 'I know and I meant it at the time, but now you're leaving and, and—' Her words choked off and she pressed a hand to her throat. 'It's brought it all home to me. I wasn't angry with you just because of what you did to Rod. It's because of what's happened to us, to our friendship.'

'We can still be friends,' said Sally. 'I'm willing. I never wanted it to stop.'

'But how can I?' cried Deborah. 'How? Rod would think I'd turned against him.'

'He knows you better than that.'

'That's easy for you to say. Mum would think I'd turned

against him as well – and that would hurt her. She's distraught over what's happened to him. I can't do that to my family.'

Sally released a sigh straight from her heart. What a mess this was. Making up her mind, she said quietly, 'I can see this is hard on you and I understand. You don't have to decide anything now while everything feels so raw, but if ever you want to be friends again, I won't ever turn you away.'

Stepping forward, Sally pulled Deborah into a hug. Deborah stood stiffly, not responding.

Then she whispered, 'Thanks.'

After three solid weeks during which there had been at least one raid virtually every night, on the night before Sally was to move to Chorlton there were no raids. She woke early on Saturday morning, refreshed and excited. Stretching luxuriously, she wriggled her toes. She was part of a new generation, the war generation, and they knew the importance of making the most of every single moment.

She got dressed and went downstairs for breakfast, marvelling at the thought that this time tomorrow she would be getting up in Andrew's house. Credit where it was due, Mum put on a cheerful face. Was she under orders from Dad? It didn't matter if she was. She was trying her best and Sally appreciated it.

The plan was to get packed, then Andrew was coming here later this morning. He and Sally would take the luggage by taxi to Chorlton. There had been some discussion as to who should pay for the taxi. Andrew said he should because he was taking Sally to her new home, but Dad wanted to because it was his duty to see Sally safely on her way. In the end Sally had stepped in and said she would pay because she was perfectly capable of standing on her own two feet.

She already had her ration book in her handbag. Mum had deregistered her from the local shops yesterday. Handing over your ration book to your new landlady was the wartime symbol of moving digs. To Sally it felt like a symbol of independence too.

While Dad went to the tobacconist's, Mum helped Sally empty her drawers and the hanging-cupboard and produced paper bags for her trinkets and pieces of jewellery. Sally had taken her library books back yesterday evening and handed in her tickets. The next time she borrowed books, it would be in Chorlton. Dad had written a letter for her to show the librarian as proof of her change of address.

'It feels as if every single detail of my life is altering,' Sally told Mum.

'It's a big thing, leaving home,' said Mum. 'I was at home until I was in my thirties because of not marrying until later in life.'

'You make it sound as if you were ancient.'

'I was, by marriage standards.' Mum's face crumpled and she dashed away a tear. 'This is a big change for Dad and me as well, our only child leaving home. The house is going to feel empty without you. I'm not saying that to make you feel bad,' she added.

'I know,' Sally said softly. 'There's one thing that won't change. How much I love you.'

'Oh, Sally.'

Tears brimmed in Mum's hazel eyes but her cheeks glowed with pleasure. Sally was about to hug her when there was a loud knock at the front door.

'I'll go,' said Sally. 'It's a bit early for Andrew.'

But maybe he couldn't wait any longer. She ran downstairs, opened the front door – and stared incredulously at Rod.

'Is it true?' he demanded, his bright-blue eyes flashing. 'Are you moving in with that bloke?'

'Not in the way you make it sound,' said Sally.

'Oh aye? You won't be living in sin, then?' Rod gave a harsh laugh. 'Who d'you think you're trying to kid?'

Shocked though she was, Sally was determined to stand her

ground. She spoke quietly. 'We'll have separate bedrooms – not that it's any of your business. Now if that's all you came to say...'

She took a step backward, starting to close the door, but Rod shoved it open wide with a single sweep of a powerful arm. He planted his feet wide apart, thrusting out his chest. His eyes were cold and hard, their colour pure flint.

Behind him came a voice from the gate – Deborah, sounding anxious.

'Rod! What are you doing? Come home – please.'

At the same time, Mum appeared behind Sally.

'Sally, what's going on? Rod! I didn't know you'd come home. You can't come round here shouting like this.'

'Oh, can't I? The way I see it, I've got every reason.' Fixing his gaze on Sally, Rod jabbed a finger in her face. 'You led me right up the garden path, you did, and don't deny it. I'd have given you everything, but you threw it back in my face – and for what? For a dirty bugger who isn't even going to give you a wedding ring before he gets inside your knickers.'

'Rod!' Deborah cried, flinching at the crude words.

'Rod!' came another distressed voice and this time it was Mrs Grant's. She pressed a hand over her mouth to hold in a cry. Above the hand, her eyes were filled with shame as she glanced around – which made Sally look round too. The neighbours were out in force, all the road's women in their pinnies, drawn outside by Rod's raised voice. They watched in shock and fascination, mouths straight, eyes dark with censure – but the censure was for Rod, not for Sally.

'I think you should go,' Sally told Rod.

Once again she made to shut the door, but Rod pounced, hauling her outside. Sally cried out in surprise, the sound erupting from her lungs as she twisted free of him.

'You don't shut that door on me, Sally White,' Rod said fiercely. 'You stop where you are until I say otherwise.'

Sally felt the colour drain from her face. Rod had made her

feel uncomfortable in the past by exerting his physical strength in small ways, but she had never seen him lose his rag before. She was scared, but she had to meet this situation, and she knew that some of her resolve was derived from the presence of the other women. With nearly all the men away fighting, female unity and camaraderie were more important than ever and would help them through.

'Go home, Rod,' she said. 'You aren't wanted here. *I* don't want you here.'

'You *what?*' Rod bellowed.

He made another grab for her, clamping his fingers round her arm before she could dart away. Behind her, Mum gave a shriek. Rod yanked hard, bringing Sally right up close to him. Her heart was racing, nearly exploding. She remembered how Rod used to make her feel clamped to his side when they linked arms. This behaviour now, this strong-arming, was the truth of what she'd have had to live with if she had married him.

Rejecting the instinct urging her to try to pull free, Sally stood tall, thrusting her face towards his, meeting his furious gaze.

'What next, Rod?' Her voice was calm and clear. 'Are you going to wallop me one?'

He stared back at her, the whites of his eyes on show around irises that were black with rage. Cords stood out on his neck and his lips curled back, baring his teeth. Then he glanced left and right, his gaze ping-ponging between Sally and the neighbours. Breathing hard, he dropped her arm – cast it aside, more like – as he stepped away.

'You haven't heard the last of this,' he muttered.

Sally made a show of leaning forward, tilting her head. 'I didn't quite catch that, Rod. Can you say it again? Louder? For everyone's benefit?'

'What's happening?' It was Dad's voice now.

With a growl, Rod turned on his heel and marched off, shouldering his way past Dad and stalking up the road. His mother followed, wringing her hands. Deborah flung Sally a wet-eyed look of shame before she too followed her brother.

'What was all that about?' Dad asked.

'Rod Grant was yelling blue murder at your Sally,' said Mrs O'Keefe from next door.

'Manhandling her an' all,' added Mrs Evans from over the road.

'He what?' Dad's mouth slackened in disbelief.

'It's true.' Mum looked dazed. 'I've never seen the like. Who'd have thought it?'

'Are you all right, Sally love?' asked Mrs O'Keefe.

'Yes, thanks. A bit shaken, that's all.'

'Ha! "All," she says.' Mrs Griffin from two doors down joined in. 'I reckon we're all shaken up – and more than a bit.'

'I had no idea Rod Grant had that in him,' said Mrs O'Keefe.

'What a good job you never got engaged to him, Sally,' Mrs Evans said with a shudder and a murmur of agreement ran up and down the road.

'You had a lucky escape,' said Mrs Lloyd, jiggling her baby on her hip.

It was old Mrs Uttley who got to the heart of the matter. Edging closer, leaning on her walking-stick, she asked Sally, 'Has he done this to you before, lass? Is that why you never got engaged to him?'

In spite of the number of people present, the world suddenly went very still. With all eyes upon her, Sally nodded.

She quickly added, 'It was never as bad as this – nothing like. But...'

'But you knew.' Mrs Uttley nodded her head. 'You sensed it.'

'I had no idea,' said Mum.

'None of us did,' said Dad.

Mum gave a small gasp. 'You tried to tell me, didn't you, Sally? And I didn't listen. I was too busy blaming you for going off with Andrew.' Her chin trembled and she hugged herself.

Sally slipped an arm round her. 'It's all right, Mum.'

A movement along the road made everybody look round. Tears of relief welled behind Sally's eyelids as Andrew came hurrying along the pavement, concern pulling his brows together.

'Is something wrong?' he asked.

'Aye, lad,' said Mrs Evans. 'We've all seen Rod Grant for the bully he really is, that's what.'

'And to think we all took his side when Sally let him down,' said Mrs O'Keefe.

Andrew went straight to Sally. Leaving an arm round Mum, she gave him her free hand. Instead of the usual tingling she felt at his touch, what she felt now was confidence and safety, gratitude and happiness. She had given her heart to a good man, an honourable man, a man who was worthy of her trust and her parents' trust.

'Did he hurt you?' Andrew asked.

Sally shook her head. 'I'm glad you're here.'

'I wish I'd been here a few minutes ago to protect you.'

'Sally stood up for herself like a good 'un,' said Mrs Uttley. 'Not like a fishwife,' she added. 'I don't mean that. She carried herself well is what I mean.'

'I'm proud of you,' Andrew told Sally, 'but I'm sorry you had to face that on your own.'

'I wasn't on my own.' Sally looked around at her neighbours. 'I had plenty of witnesses and their presence helped more than I can say.'

'Nay, lass, we didn't do anything,' said Mrs Evans.

'You did,' Sally assured her. 'You gave me strength.'

'I should have paid attention when you tried to tell me,' said Mum.

'That's water under the bridge,' said Dad. 'What matters now is that our daughter has got a kind, loving man by her side.' He stuck out his hand to shake Andrew's. 'Welcome to the family.'

·   ·   ·

The taxi waited outside. Dad and Andrew carried out Sally's things, Mum and Sally following. Some of the neighbours came out to see Sally on her way – neighbours who, if Rod hadn't shown his true colours, would have watched her departure from behind their net curtains.

Mum nudged Sally. 'Look who it is.'

Along the road, outside the Grants' house, stood Deborah, biting her lip and looking uncertain – as well she might, with critical gazes directed at her from all sides.

Sally started to go to her, then stopped.

'Where's Rod?' she asked.

'Gone,' said Deborah.

They met halfway.

Deborah's fair-skinned cheeks burned. She dropped her chin to her chest, then drew in a breath before she lifted her face to meet Sally's eyes.

'I'm so sorry,' Deborah whispered. 'I had no idea that would happen. I-I was the one who wrote and told him you were moving in with your boyfriend and his mother.'

'Deborah!' Sally exclaimed.

'I honestly didn't intend to cause trouble,' Deborah was quick to explain. 'I thought – I hoped it would make Rod see there was no point in carrying a torch for you any longer. I-I honestly believed I was helping.'

Her voice cracked and she gulped but didn't let the tears fall. Sally's heart reached out to her, but she still had an important question.

'Did you know he was on his way here from Barrow?'

Deborah's eyes widened. 'No, absolutely not, I swear. He just turned up. I was never more surprised in my life than when he marched through the front door.' Her hands locked into fists. 'Actually, that's not true. The most surprising thing that ever happened, the most shocking, was when... when he confronted you that way. I've never seen him like that. Neither has Mum.

When Dad gets in from work, he isn't going to believe it. Me and Mum are so sorry.'

'It wasn't your fault,' said Sally.

'Has Rod...? Have you seen him like that before?'

'I've had glimpses,' Sally admitted. 'It was instinct more than anything else. Even if I'd never met Andrew, I knew I didn't want to spend my life with Rod, but it was difficult with everyone seeing us as the perfect couple and him as a hero for working in shipbuilding.'

'I wish you'd told me,' said Deborah.

'There was nothing to tell,' said Sally, 'nothing that wouldn't have made me sound silly. Besides—' She stopped. She cared for Deborah too much to rub her nose in it.

But Deborah caught the unspoken words. 'You did try to say something, didn't you? I remember now. You said he wasn't the person you thought he was and I thought you were trying to blame him for your own shortcomings. I can't tell you how sorry I am.'

'It's over now,' said Sally.

'Mum can't stop crying. She says it's bad enough that it happened, but for it to happen in front of the whole street...'

'I know.' Sally spoke gently. The moral support that had helped her when she most needed it would already have turned into dark criticism of the Grant family. It would be some time before equilibrium was restored.

'Mum says she doesn't know how she'll face anyone again.' Deborah glanced along the road, her gaze brushing across the neighbours, who all looked steadily at the two girls.

Sally made up her mind. 'I know what might help.'

'What?' Deborah asked.

'This,' said Sally.

Stepping closer, she put her arms round Deborah in a warm hug, showing everybody who was lapping up the scene that, whatever Rod Grant had done, she bore no ill-will towards his family.

CHAPTER TWENTY-ONE

'You're chirpy this morning,' Mrs Beaumont said to Betty as she served breakfast in the dining room. The landlady wore a wrap-around apron, but, whereas every other such pinny Betty had ever seen in her life had been plain, Mrs Beaumont's was patterned with a vivid array of colourful flowers – peonies, roses and huge daisies against a background of foliage in apple green and forest green. It must be because of her being a theatrical landlady.

Betty beamed at her. 'Yes, I feel chirpy. There's a new girl starting at the depot today, so I shan't be on my own any more – and I'll have this coming Saturday off.'

What a treat that would be. She'd only been allowed one Saturday off per quarter at Tucker's and now she was due to have a free Saturday every other week.

She got ready to go to work, bending down to fuss Minnie before she set off. The early mornings were noticeably cooler now that they were halfway through September. The sun was already bright in a periwinkle-blue sky, promising a fine day ahead. Betty caught hold of that thought and hung on to it. It wasn't going to feel like a fine day for a lot of people. There had been raids in the early hours of Sunday morning and then a four-hour raid on Sunday night. How many had lost their homes and their precious possessions, built up over years of family life? Worse, had there been injuries? Deaths?

Betty had set off in plenty of time, wanting to open up the depot and be ready to welcome her new colleague, but as she passed the local shops she saw a girl up ahead, hanging about outside the depot's high fence.

Betty put on a spurt. The girl was facing away from her and Betty could see that, beneath her straw hat, dark-blond hair sat in a plump roll at collar length. Mum always said you could tell a lot about a person from their hair.

'Hair and shoes. A good haircut, neatly styled, and polished shoes. That's how to create a good first impression.'

The girl turned round. All set to utter words of welcome, Betty stared, the words freezing on her lips.

'You!' The word burst out of her.

She couldn't believe her eyes. It couldn't be – but it was. The butter-wouldn't-melt girl herself – here!

The girl had recognised her too.

'Oh.' Her cheeks coloured. 'I remember you.'

'Oh aye?' snapped Betty. 'Remember all of the idiots who fell for your act, do you? Or am I memorable because I was so easy to fool? I lost my job because of you.'

'I'm truly sorry to hear that.'

'You shouldn't be. Thanks to you, there's one less person out there daring to flout the rules and help a fellow human being in need.'

'I was just doing my job.'

'Well, that's all right, then,' Betty retorted.

'I hated doing it, but it was one of my duties.'

'You tell yourself that, love, if it makes you feel better.'

So much for Betty's chirpy spirits. It was time to get rid of this girl and pin on her best smile ready for when her new colleague arrived.

'What brings you here, anyroad?' Betty challenged. 'I suppose you've come to do the dirty— oh, I beg your pardon, I mean to *do your duty* at the grocer's. Maybe I'll pop along and warn them to beware of a girl with a sob story.'

'You'd be wasting your time. I don't work for the Food Office any more.' The girl's light-hazel eyes flicked a glance towards the depot's fence. 'I'm starting here today. I'm a bit early and I'm waiting to be let in.' She stepped aside as if to let Betty go past. 'Don't let me keep you.'

Betty's mouth dropped open and she gawped. 'Shut your mouth, Betty,' Mum used to say, 'or you'll let the flies in.'

'You?' Betty said again, but, instead of an explosion of shock, this time it came out as a breathless croak of disbelief. 'You – here? Working here?'

The girl's face fell. 'You don't mean you work here too?' She drew in a breath and gave Betty a tentative smile. 'Look, shall we start again? I'm Sally White.'

She held out her right hand and what could Betty do other than shake it?

'And your name?' Miss White prompted gently.

'Betty Hughes.' Betty felt winded. Winded and wrong-footed and overwhelmed with disappointment. The chummy morning of her imaginings evaporated like morning mist.

Pulling herself together, she took out her key and unlocked the door.

'Mind your step,' she said, lifting her feet over the plank running along the bottom of the doorway.

Miss White followed her into the yard, looking around with bright-eyed interest.

'It's a bit of a mess,' said Betty, 'but I'm in the process of sorting it out.'

When planning her new colleague's first day, she had originally intended to say this cheerfully, but now she heard herself sounding defensive. Miss Butter-Wouldn't-Melt probably thought she should have got it sorted out already.

'How long have you worked here, Miss Hughes?' Good grief, now she sounded like she was interviewing Betty.

'I started at the end of August,' said Betty. There she went, sounding defensive again.

'So this is your third full week,' said Miss White.

Betty had planned to make a joke out of the short time she'd been here so as to show the new girl she didn't have much experience. She'd intended to say something like, 'So we'll be learning together,' but now, faced with Miss Butter-Wouldn't-Melt, her lack of experience felt like a huge disadvantage. She wished she'd made more of an impression on the depot. Her heart sank as she seemed to see it through Miss White's eyes. What a mess.

But there was one way she could assert herself.

'Your clothes won't do,' she said. 'You need dungarees. They really ought to warn people in advance.'

'Are there any going spare?'

'This way,' said Betty. 'But I warn you, they're men's and they're huge. They're also a so-and-so to alter. I spent hours on mine – well, me and my landlady did.'

'I'm sure my fiancé's mother will help me.'

Betty looked at her. 'You're engaged?'

'Yes.' Miss White's eyes sparkled. 'My old boss at the Food Office knew my fiancé lives in Chorlton, so he got me this job.'

The mention of the Food Office reminded Betty to be vexed, though it wouldn't do to go all stroppy. That would just put her in the wrong.

Aiming for an impersonal tone, she said, 'Here's the changing room. It's a bit of a squeeze. You can have one of those cupboards for your handbag. Keep the key safe.' She opened the cupboard that held the dungarees. 'Take your pick. You can roll up the legs for today.'

'I might as well take the top one if they're all going to need altering.' Miss White held the dark-blue dungarees against herself. 'Actually, these don't look too bad for size.'

Betty realised. 'They were Pamela's, so they've been altered already.'

'Pamela? My predecessor?'

'Yes. She went off to join the land army.'

They got changed. Betty took off her hat and tied a scarf over her head and under the back of her hair, checking her appearance in the tiny mirror.

'You hair is a beautiful colour,' said Miss White. 'Golden.'

'If you're asking if it comes out of a bottle, it doesn't.'

'I didn't mean that.'

Betty was shocked at herself. 'Sorry. I shouldn't have snapped at you. It's just thrown me having you here.'

'I never expected to see you again either.'

'Anyroad, we're stuck with one another now,' said Betty.

'I really only meant to pay you a compliment about your hair,' said Miss White. 'I wasn't trying to get round you.'

'I like your hair too,' Betty admitted. 'I noticed it when you came into the shop. It's fair but not ordinary fair. Dark blond.'

'I like that.' Miss White looked chuffed. 'My mum calls it dirty blond. I'll think of myself as dark blond in future.'

How come they were talking about hair, as if they were pals? Betty chewed the inside of her cheek. The jury was still out as far as Miss Butter-Wouldn't-Melt White was concerned.

Returning to the impersonal, she said, 'We'd best get started.'

As they left the changing room, their gas-masks slung over their shoulders, Betty hesitated at the foot of the stairs to the loft. Should she? But no. Miss White didn't deserve to be shown the view from the roof.

Betty led the way downstairs and started to point things out. Mr Overton appeared. Normally Betty would have left it to the boss to introduce himself, but today it felt important to assert herself.

'Mr Overton, this is our new girl.'

'How do?' said Mr Overton, shaking hands. 'Miss White, I believe? Miss Hughes will show you everything.' To Betty he said, 'The ladies will be along later to pick up rags, rubber and paper.'

When he walked away, Miss White asked, 'The ladies?'

'The WVS. They take the salvage to wherever it goes.'

'So we don't take it?'

'I just said, didn't I?' Betty was starting to feel tetchy again.

'Where does it go?'

Forget tetchy. What she felt now was a moment of panic as her mind went blank. It was like being back at school. What did Miss White think she was playing at, asking all these questions? Pushy so-and-so. Betty was annoyed with herself as well. Why hadn't she asked these questions of Pamela when she had the chance? But she'd never been bursting with initiative.

'The paper goes to the paper mill,' she said, neatly sidestepping her ignorance about where other things went by giving the instruction about removing the paperclips and so on. She wanted to sound knowledgeable but all she felt was inadequate, especially with Miss White listening so closely. But she seemed to have fallen for Betty's act. Before she could start asking penetrating questions about rubber and rags, Betty continued the tour. What else could she sound knowledgeable about?

'While I think of it,' she began. That was good. It made it sound like a throwaway remark. 'If anyone brings us old ointment tubes or toothpaste tubes, those are supposed to be taken to the chemist.'

'Really?' Miss White sounded interested. 'Why's that?'

A flush crept across Betty's cheeks. 'That's just where they're meant to go, though we can accept them here.'

She could have kicked herself. Why hadn't she asked Pamela for details? But no, that was her all over. She just accepted what she was told. She didn't ask questions. Blundering around in her mind for something she could say to make up for her ignorance, she saw... the front gates.

'As well as the door we came in through when we arrived, we also have that big gateway for deliveries and collections.' An almost hysterical voice in her head asked what precisely she thought she was doing, explaining what the gates were for. 'Let's get them open, shall we?'

As they pulled the gates open, half a dozen headscarfed women came hurrying into the yard, carrying cloth bags over their arms.

'You're open at last.' The speaker was in her thirties, with a smattering of freckles across the bridge of her nose. 'We're on our way home from the night shift at the munitions and we've come to swap our kitchen things.'

'You've what?' Betty didn't know what was going on. Noticing Miss White looking at her enquiringly, she felt even less in control.

'We're all from Reynard Road, love,' said one of the others. She had apples in her cheeks, but the rest of her skin was grey with tiredness. 'Someone here at the depot helped our neighbour, Mrs Archer. Was it you? Anyroad, she told us we could have metal things from you as long as we do a fair swap.'

'So we've all brought summat.' A thin-faced wisp of a woman dug inside her bag and pulled out a tin nutmeg grater. 'I've got this and I want to swap it for a milk pan.'

'I want a milk pan an' all,' said the freckled woman. 'I've brought this.' She fought to draw a coal shovel out of her cloth bag. 'Who do we need to speak to?'

Betty gulped. When she'd helped Mrs Archer, she'd never imagined that lady spreading the word among her neighbours. Was every housewife in Chorlton going to descend on the depot, intent upon ransacking the metals heap?

'Miss Hughes,' came Mr Overton's voice.

Betty swallowed before turning round. 'Yes, Mr Overton?'

'When you've finished dealing with these ladies, I'd like to speak to you.'

'It's Mr Overton from the bank,' one of the women said in a stage whisper.

'He's the one to ask,' said the one with apples in her cheeks. 'He's in charge here.'

'Ask me what?' said Mr Overton.

Before the freckled woman had finished explaining, Mr Overton had turned to regard Betty through narrowed eyes.

'Is this your doing, Miss Hughes?'

Oh, the temptation to drop the absent Pamela in the soup! But honesty compelled Betty to admit, 'Yes, sir. I saw no harm in it.'

'No harm?' Mr Overton's voice might be quiet but it vibrated with displeasure. 'We're collecting for the war effort, not running a bring-and-buy stall, you foolish girl. Get rid of these women.'

Turning smartly on his heel, he stalked away across the yard. The breath caught in Betty's throat. Although she'd had to deal with the occasional tricky customer at the shop, she'd never had to handle any truly difficult situations, because Mr Tucker had always stepped in. Looking at the women's expectant expressions, she went hot and cold.

'I'm, er, I'm really sorry about this, but, er, well...'

Betty's mind went blank and she dried up. Before she could pull herself together, Miss White stepped forward.

'I'm sorry, ladies. I'm afraid there has been a misunderstanding. When your neighbour was allowed to exchange an item, that was an oversight and it shouldn't have happened.'

'D'you mean we can't swap our stuff?' demanded the wisp of a woman, all at once appearing considerably less wispy.

'That's exactly what I mean.' For all Miss White's politeness, there could be no doubting her firmness. 'Isn't that so, Miss Hughes? I apologise on behalf of the depot and I hope it won't put you off collecting and donating salvage. In fact,' she added with a smile, 'if those items you've brought are unwanted...'

Betty's mouth dropped open as Sally flaming White charmed the women into parting with what they'd brought before they set off for home.

'I hope you didn't mind my stepping in,' said Miss White, 'only you seemed a little at a loss.'

Mind? Of course she minded! Miss White had made her look a complete twerp. Not only that, but Miss White thought she'd done Betty a favour and probably expected her to be grateful. Before Betty could think how to respond, Mr Overton returned. He was carrying the box they used for the salvaged jewellery. Betty perked up. At least this was something she knew about.

'A brooch that I had particularly noticed because of its elegant design is missing,' said Mr Overton. 'Do you know anything about it?'

He didn't actually utter the words, 'Have you pinched it?' but he might as well have done. Betty could have crowned him for speaking to her like that in front of Miss White.

She said calmly, 'Do you mean the brooch with the purple stones and the milky-white stone in the middle? Its owner, or rather her daughter, came to find it. It had been handed over by mistake.'

'And you permitted her to take it?' Mr Overton enquired. 'Tell me, Miss Hughes, did this lady describe the brooch to you? Before she set eyes on it, I mean?'

'Well – no...'

'So you simply handed over the box and invited her to paw through the contents, did you? And she *recognised* her mother's brooch?'

'It wasn't anything special,' said Betty. 'Well, except for its sentimental value. It was the sort of brooch old ladies wear on their hats. You know, a bit big and showy.'

'A bit big and showy?' Mr Overton closed his eyes. 'Give me strength,' he muttered before continuing in a piercingly clear voice, 'That brooch was a large opal surrounded by amethysts, Miss Hughes. Amethysts! An opal!'

Betty's mouth had gone dry, robbing her of the power of speech. Not that she had anything to say in her own defence.

'The woman was a confidence trickster,' declared Mr Overton, 'and you, Miss Hughes, are an unutterable fool.'

CHAPTER TWENTY-TWO

Sally was glad to get home at the end of her first day. She was tired, not so much physically as emotionally. It was surprisingly arduous feeling uncomfortable in another person's company. Her spirits lifted as she approached her new home. *Home*. She felt content but excited too, because it was all new. On Saturday morning she had still been living at home with her parents. Now she was living alongside the man she adored. She had only met Andrew at the beginning of August and now, just weeks later, she was his mother's lodger – except that she was more than a lodger. She was a member of the family.

She let herself in. The scent of baking hung tantalisingly in the air. Mrs Henshaw came out of the kitchen, wiping her hands on her apron. She came along the hallway and kissed Sally's cheek.

'How was your first day? We want to hear all about it.'

'That's my line.' Andrew appeared from the parlour. 'And the hello kiss is my job.' His lips brushed Sally's cheek.

'Something smells good,' Sally said.

'That'll be the pastry,' said Mrs Henshaw. 'We're having veg pie with potato pastry. It'll be on the table in twenty minutes.'

As Mrs Henshaw returned to the kitchen, Sally turned to her fiancé, wanting to get the bad news over with as soon as possible so she could concentrate on enjoying the evening. Quickly she told him about having to work this Saturday.

'I'm sorry. I know we had plans for a day out, but the other girl has worked two Saturdays in a row.'

'That's fine.' Andrew gave her a hug. 'We have a lifetime of Saturdays ahead of us.'

Soon they were sitting down to their meal. Sally complimented Mrs Henshaw on how tasty it was.

'My secret ingredient is bacon rind,' said Mrs Henshaw. 'I fry it until it's crispy, then I use it for seasoning. You have to make the most use of every little thing these days.' Her eyes twinkled. 'Especially now we've got a food rationing expert in the house.'

'I'm not an expert,' said Sally, but she felt pleased all the same. Drinking in the sight of Andrew and wanting to hear his voice, she asked, 'How was your day?'

'Never mind me.' His brown eyes were warm. 'You're the one who's had the first day in a new post. What's your boss like?'

'He's called Mr Overton and he's come out of retirement to do his bit for the war effort. According to the girl I work with, he's distinctly unimpressed with the depot. He sees salvage as women's work. Children's too, now that the Scouts and Guides as well as schools are getting involved in collecting.'

'We all have to do things we'd rather not in wartime,' said Andrew.

'Do you remember when Uncle George and Auntie Sylvia gave your dad a bottle of gin for his birthday?' asked his mother.

Andrew laughed. 'Yes. He was outraged. "Gin is a woman's drink." I remember him carrying on about that. Poor old Dad.'

Mrs Henshaw looked at Sally. 'It sounds like this Mr Overton might be the same. It's the equivalent of expecting a man to do the shopping or the washing. Don't underestimate how hard this must be for him.'

Sally considered that. 'You have a kind heart,' she told her future mother-in-law. 'Anyway, Mr Overton's attitude isn't going to make it easy for Miss Hughes and me. That's another thing. You'll never guess who she is.'

'Judy Garland in disguise,' said Andrew.

Laughing, Sally shook her head at him. 'She's a girl I once tested. You know, when a Food Office person goes into a shop and sees if the person behind the counter will break the rules. Well, I once tested Betty Hughes – and not long ago either.'

Mrs Henshaw's eyes widened. 'Never,' she breathed.

'That's rotten luck for you,' said Andrew.

'It's been a pretty uncomfortable day, actually,' Sally admitted. 'It's not just that I tested her. She lost her job because of me.'

'Not because of you,' Andrew said at once. 'She lost it because she did something wrong and you caught her out.'

'Well, she paid a heavy price,' said Sally, 'and I'm not just talking about the fine.'

'Poor girl,' said Mrs Henshaw. 'She's certainly learned the hard way. She isn't going to make life difficult for you, is she?'

'Well, she was fairly grouchy today,' Sally admitted. Fairness made her add, 'Not all the time, but it felt as if each time she was nice she suddenly remembered she wasn't supposed to like me.'

'Childish,' Andrew remarked, and Sally felt an inner glow at his loyalty.

'Give it time,' Mrs Henshaw advised.

'I'm not sure what difference that will make,' said Sally.

Mrs Henshaw raised her eyebrows in gentle surprise. 'Do you think she won't come to terms with working with the girl who tested her?'

'It's not that,' said Sally. 'It's... well, I worked with my friend Deborah and I loved that because we both knew what we were doing. We were both efficient, but from what I've seen, that word doesn't seem to apply to Miss Hughes.' Sally explained about the women turning up at the depot and then the fiasco of the brooch.

'Mr Overton hauled her over the coals and poor Miss Hughes didn't know where to look.'

'Not very impressive,' said Andrew.

'Exactly,' said Sally.

Truth be told, she wasn't looking forward to having to work with Miss Betty Hughes.

Later in the evening, Andrew disappeared into the front room to get ready to go on duty with his light rescue squad. Sally heard the door click shut behind him. Mrs Henshaw had laid down the law in no uncertain terms when Sally had moved in on Saturday.

'Andrew, your old bedroom now belongs to Sally and you do not set foot in there again. It was generous of Mrs Ibbotson to let us have her spare bed, but it was a squeeze getting it into the front room and you won't be as comfortable in there as you were in your old room, but that's life. Sally, if you and Andrew want some private time together, you may go in the front room, but both of you must sit on the chairs, not on the bed, and you leave the door wide open. I gave your parents assurances that this is a respectable house and I fully intend it's going to remain that way. You're both on your honour not to let down Mr and Mrs White and me.'

Afterwards, Andrew had whispered to Sally, 'Now I know how the boys I teach feel when I haul them over the coals,' and the two of them had giggled like children.

Now, Andrew appeared in the parlour again, dressed in the thick corduroy trousers and old jacket he wore for light rescue.

His mother produced a snap-tin and a Thermos. 'Meat-paste sandwich and a couple of home-made ginger biscuits. That's the last time I'll do this. From now on, this will be your job, Sally.'

Sally smiled happily. She relished any reference to her position as Andrew's intended.

Andrew sat down to put his bicycle clips on, then stood up again.

'Go on, Sally,' said Mrs Henshaw. 'See him off.'

Sally got to her feet. She couldn't wave him off from the step because of the blackout, but she was more than happy to make do with a kiss and a cuddle in the darkened hallway.

After he had gone, Sally and Mrs Henshaw settled down to have a chat while they did some sewing, with the BBC Orchestra playing on the Home Service in the background. As the concert came to a close, the air-raid siren started and they quickly got the house ready before gathering up the air-raid box with its important papers and heading for the Anderson. The raid didn't last long. Half an hour later they were back in the house, switching the gas and water back on.

Mrs Henshaw made Ovaltine and they sat together for a while.

'I must volunteer locally for war work,' said Sally.

'Give yourself a while to settle in,' said Mrs Henshaw. 'You've got a new job and a new home. That's enough change to be going on with. Would you volunteer for mortuary work again?' She gave a little shudder. 'There's a wartime mortuary here in Chorlton on Cavendish Road, up near the station.'

'I imagine they already have as many gas-trained staff as they need.'

'You could come along with me and join the WVS,' Mrs Henshaw said encouragingly. 'You'd be very welcome. The offer's there if you want it.'

As it turned out, Andrew's mother wasn't alone in wanting Sally to join the WVS. The next morning at the depot, when Sally and Miss Hughes were sorting through sacks of mixed salvage, a middle-aged lady kitted out in the full WVS uniform appeared in the big open gateway and stood right in the middle, looking round with a proprietorial air. She held her shoulders back and her chin up. Her gaze swept over Sally and Miss Hughes without stopping. Only when she had apparently surveyed her surroundings to her satisfaction did she look their way and acknowledge them.

She walked over to them, confidence in every line of her appearance, her gas-mask box swinging from one shoulder. She stopped in front of them, planting herself in position, and, even though she wasn't any taller than they were, somehow managed to look down her nose. The sight of the SALVAGE OFFICER band on her arm sent Sally's heart plummeting into her shoes.

The lady looked straight at Sally. 'I take it you're my newest recruit. I am Mrs Lockwood. I trust Miss Hughes is showing you the ropes. It's too bad having two new girls at once, but these things are sent to try us. I'll be keeping a close eye on you, you may be sure.' Her voice, though low-pitched, wasn't soft. Far from it. The politest word for it was 'carrying'. 'I believe you are both new to this area. Therefore I expect you both to join my branch of the WVS.'

'What if we've already signed up for summat else?' Miss Hughes asked.

'Have you?' demanded Mrs Lockwood, pinning down Miss Hughes with her keen gaze.

'Well – no.'

Sally stepped in. 'Neither have I. I used to work in the mortuary where I lived before. I was trained to decontaminate the gas-dead.'

Miss Hughes gave a little gasp. 'How gruesome.'

'Necessary work,' said Mrs Lockwood. 'We've suffered no gas attacks so far, but when it happens... Do I take it you shall be joining the Cavendish Road mortuary?'

'I don't know if they need anyone,' Sally said ambiguously.

'You're not committed, then? Good. I'll expect you both to sign up for the WVS. Go to MacFadyen's Memorial Congregational Church any time, day or night. There is always somebody there. Tell them I sent you. Say you're Mrs Lockwood's salvage girls and that nobody other than myself is to assign any voluntary duties to you. You may leave messages for me there as well.' She gave a crisp nod. 'Carry on,' she ordered as if addressing the troops, then she executed a smart about-turn and left.

Sally stared after her. This must be how the Ancient Greeks had felt when one of the gods descended from Mount Olympus. She turned to Miss Hughes to express her astonishment, but Miss Hughes spoke first.

'Will you go to the mortuary, then?'

'I'd rather not,' said Sally. 'I was never called upon to do anything. Not that I want there to be gas attacks, but waiting for them to happen was a great strain. I dreaded it more with every raid that happened. I hope that doesn't make me sound unpatriotic.'

Miss Hughes tilted her head to one side. 'Says the girl who patriotically tricked shop assistants into breaking the rules.'

'That was patriotic, as a matter of fact,' Sally insisted. 'Rationing means fair shares for all and everyone abiding by the regulations.'

'Of course I can see that,' snapped Miss Hughes, her lovely blue eyes glinting. 'I'm not stupid.'

With a toss of her turbaned head, she left Sally surrounded by salvage sacks and marched across the yard to tidy up a heap of pieces of wood. When the clattering had died down, Sally went over to her.

'I'm confused,' she said. 'I thought Mr Overton was in charge, but that Mrs Lockwood was really throwing her weight around.'

Miss Hughes flicked her a sideways glance. 'And there was me thinking you might be about to apologise.'

'For what?'

'For making a monkey out of me with that food test. I know it was your job, but you don't have to be so self-righteous about it.'

The attack surprised Sally. 'I'm not self-righteous.'

'You are from where I'm standing.'

That hurt. 'If we're saying what we think,' answered Sally,

'then I can't say I'm surprised you failed the test in the shop. You seem pretty easily led to me. First there was Mrs Archer and then there was that girl with the brooch.'

Miss Hughes's creamy complexion was suffused with crimson. 'There's nothing like having your faults pointed out in public, is there? I hope it made you feel good. You might be clever, but at least I'm kind. As for Jenny Baxter – if that was her real name – making a monkey out of me, at least I'm doing something about it.'

'What?' Sally asked, interested in spite of herself.

'I'm planning what we ought to do if someone comes in again asking to have their jewellery back.'

'But the next person might be telling the truth,' Sally pointed out.

'That's why it's taking a lot of thought,' Miss Hughes retorted.

Sally nodded. After the accusation of self-righteousness, she wanted to be gracious. 'Good for you.'

Miss Hughes nodded, a crisp little gesture. 'And just so you know, Mrs Lockwood told me Mr Overton just oversees the depot's day-to-day running.'

Sally didn't fancy in the slightest working for Mrs Lockwood. Talk about overbearing.

At home that evening, Sally talked to Mrs Henshaw about the formidable Mrs Lockwood.

'She behaves like a sergeant major,' said Sally. 'I shan't like working for her at all.'

'I'm not sure you do work for her, as such,' Mrs Henshaw told her. 'Oh, and it seemed like such a clever idea at the time.'

'What did?'

'Fobbing off Mrs Lockwood with salvage.'

'Fobbing her off with it? I don't understand.'

Mrs Henshaw huffed out a breath. 'I'd better explain. Mrs Lockwood was determined to run the local WVS and was furious when Mrs Callaghan was awarded the post instead. Mrs Lock-wood made her life a misery. In the end Mrs Callaghan gave her salvage as a special responsibility as a means of diverting her attention. We all thought it had worked. I'd no idea she was turning up at the depot and laying down the law.'

The next morning, Sally explained the situation to Miss Hughes.

'So Mr Overton is meant to be in charge after all.' Miss Hughes sounded relieved.

'Yes. Unfortunately, "meant to be" are the operative words. If he doesn't put Mrs Lockwood in her place, we'll be stuck with her. I don't like the sound of that.'

'Me neither,' said Miss Hughes, 'but there's nothing we can do about it. We're stuck with her.'

And with one another. The extra words hung unspoken in the air.

CHAPTER TWENTY-THREE

Sitting with the dining chair slightly too far from the table because of having Minnie on her lap, Betty wrote, *So glad you have Saturday off as well, Dad. Looking forward to seeing you* – and then stopped. Dearly as she wanted to put a full stop there, she sighed inwardly and wrote *both*. How she wished it could be just her and Dad on Saturday, but Grace would never allow that. Betty huffed a little sigh, dropping a kiss on Minnie's sleek head. She ended the postcard with *Love, Betty xx* before licking the stamp and attaching it.

She was going to the flicks that evening with the munitions girls and she would pop the postcard into the pillar box on the way. They were going to see *Dark Victory* with Bette Davis, George Brent and Humphrey Bogart. Might there be some good news on the Pathé Newsreel? London was taking a hammering every single night, courtesy of the Luftwaffe, and every single person in the country lived in fear of invasion. Betty thought back to Mr Churchill's stirring speech from last month. 'Never in the field of human conflict was so much owed by so many to so few.' Words had that braced everyone's spirits as they put all their faith and dearest hopes in the brave boys of the RAF.

With what Mr Churchill called the Battle of Britain at an end, Germany's superiority of the air was broken – for now. The threat of imminent invasion had lifted – for now. Even though Jerry was now concentrating on trying to blow London to kingdom come, everyone's spirits were heartened by the sight on the newsreel of Their Majesties the King and Queen visiting areas that were in ruins.

This week was proving to be yet another of air raids and Betty was itching to sign up for voluntary war work. She felt torn about joining the WVS. They had plenty of knowledge and experience of salvage. With Mr Overton not wanting to be involved, it would be good to have that kind of support. On the other hand, it would mean a double helping of Mrs Lockwood, and Betty wasn't keen on that at all. Neither was Miss White. At least that was something the two of them could agree on.

Betty thought again of how she'd been taken for a ride by Miss Butter-Wouldn't-Melt, not to mention Jenny Baxter with the brooch. Something inside Betty curled up whenever she remembered. What a fathead she was. An easy target. She might as well write *Idiot* on her forehead with the laundry-marker pen.

Then to cap it all, her tongue had run away with her and she had claimed to be planning a strategy to prevent the Jenny Baxters of this world from pulling the wool over depot workers' eyes ever again. As if! She hadn't a clue how she could possibly achieve this, but she had to come up with something or Sally White would think her even more of a dolt than she did already.

Betty pictured her darling dad. Might she be able to get him on his own to explain the situation? She would hate having to admit that she had fallen below par – again – but she was sorely in need of his experience. He of all people would surely be able to come up with the sort of idea that Betty needed.

She dreaded Miss White asking if she'd thought of anything yet, but nothing was said on the subject. Miss White had probably given up on her having any useful thoughts.

A lorry drew up on Thursday morning to take away the aluminium collection. It took ages to load it up.

As the lorry pulled away, Miss White was starry-eyed. 'It's wonderful to think of everybody pitching in to help gather metal for the war effort.'

Betty stood tall. 'It never occurred to me before that I might be proud of working in the salvage depot.'

Miss White smiled and Betty was struck by how pretty she was, with her fawny-hazel eyes and the neat features in her heart-shaped face.

'We should all be proud to do war work,' said Miss White, 'no matter what it is.'

'I'm pleased to hear such sentiments,' said Mr Overton, coming across the yard towards them. 'I'm expecting a consign-ment of pig-bins later today. You might want to have a word with the WVS ladies. No doubt they will be happy to deliver them to add to those already on street corners.'

With that, he turned away and headed back into the building.

Betty wrinkled her nose. Nobody liked having the pig-bin outside their house, but it provided an essential and highly effec-tive use for waste food.

'I suppose we should ask Mrs Lockwood,' she said.

'Or,' said Miss White, looking at her, 'we could deliver them ourselves.'

'You what?'

'Why not? We're both new to Chorlton. It'd give us the chance to learn our way around.'

'But folk will see us,' Betty objected.

'Didn't you just say you're proud to do war work?'

She couldn't argue with that. 'How do we get them to the designated places? You're surely not intending us to roll them along the pavement?'

'Sack-trolleys,' Miss White answered at once. 'We've got one here at the depot and I bet we could borrow one from the post office over the road. I can see us now.' Her tawny eyes lit up with delight. 'Marching along, heads held high, pushing our pig-bins. Heigh-ho for the salvage girls!'

Betty couldn't help laughing. Why not? It would get them out and about, doing something different.

Miss White looked thoughtful. 'When each bin is in position, we'll knock on doors and tell people where it is. That would be helpful. Also...'

'Also what?'

'Everyone is used to the WVS running salvage.'

'You mean Mrs Lockwood,' said Betty.

'It wouldn't hurt to let the locals know there's a depot with staff.'

'You've got a real bee in your bonnet about the WVS, haven't you?'

'Not about the WVS, no. I have nothing but respect for them,' said Miss White. 'Just think of everything they do for the community. They look after the elderly and infirm in their own homes. They raise money and run soup-kitchens and knit for the troops. They go out in air raids with urns of hot water so people can have tea. They're marvellous. But we need to get our depot on the map and this is one way of doing it.'

They spent two days delivering pig-bins. If Betty started off feeling embarrassed about pushing the bins around the streets, she soon forgot about it because she was having fun. Yes, fun. After the dullness of long days sorting salvage, this made a welcome change. It was useful too. They found where the local swimming-baths were, as well as the various shops and cinemas and the railway station.

Knocking on doors produced mixed results. Most housewives thanked them. Some were pleased to have a new bin closer to their house, though others were vexed for precisely the same reason. And more than one elderly lady refused to listen to what they had to say because they were too busy berating the girls for wearing *trousers* in *public*. Shameful!

When the last bins were in position, they headed back to the depot for the final time and put the kettle on, Betty smiling to herself.

'Penny for them,' said Miss White.

'I was just thinking. "What did you do in the war, Mummy?" "I doled out pig-bins, darling." Imagine!'

Instead of laughing, Miss White pressed her lips together. 'Someone I used to know at my old job taunted me with being a pig-swill girl.'

Betty kept her tone light, though she chose her words with care. 'It turns out they were right, doesn't it? But there's one thing they were definitely wrong about. If they meant it as a taunt, it shows they had no notion what a lark it was going to turn out to be.'

Miss White brightened. 'Yes, it was a lark, wasn't it? That old lady who waved her broom at you for daring to wear dungarees—'

'And the one who called you a hussy—'

They laughed, enjoying the memory.

'I think we worked well together,' said Miss White.

'Yes, we did,' Betty agreed, realising it was true. A feeling of surprise rippled through her. It was rather a pleasant feeling, actually.

'By the way,' said Miss White, 'I've got something to tell you. It's about ointment tubes. The reason they have to be kept separate from other metal is because they contain tin and lead, which would get lost in the smelting process if they were put in with everything else. I thought you'd like to know.'

Betty was stumped for a reply. She hadn't given the blessed tubes another thought, but it seemed only to be expected that, just when the two of them had worked so well side by side, Miss White should throw something into the conversation that showed her superiority.

Flaming typical.

Mrs Lockwood marched through the gates and positioned herself in the middle of the depot. Lifting her chin, she looked all around, her grey eyes sharply observant, the set of her mouth suggesting a readiness to pounce on any detail that displeased her. Last of all, her gaze settled on Betty and Miss White.

'Good morning, girls.'

Betty braced herself. What did the old bat want this time? But Mrs Lockwood set her sights on the building at the end of the yard and swanned towards the doors. As she vanished inside, Betty and Miss White exchanged shrugs.

A few minutes later, Mrs Lockwood reappeared, followed by Mr Overton, his bushy eyebrows drawn into a deep frown, his deep-set eyes seeming hard and beady. Mrs Lockwood by comparison positively beamed with complacency.

She addressed the girls, her satisfaction dropping in favour of censure.

'It has not escaped my notice that you two girls have not rushed to join the WVS. I do not know if this was defiance or unreliability on your parts, but I warn you I do not care for either. I expect you to look sharp and do as you're told.' Then she drew back her shoulders and puffed out her bosom as complacency was reinstated. 'But it so happens that I don't want you to join the WVS after all. I have found alternative night-duty for you, and I have put all the arrangements in place.'

Beside Betty, Miss White uttered a little gasp of pure outrage but held her tongue.

'You shall become fire-watchers here at the depot,' Mrs Lockwood announced.

'Here?' questioned Betty. 'But I thought—'

Mr Overton said grimly, 'There is a drive on at the moment to recruit a team of fire-watchers for every single street in the country.'

'Precisely.' Mrs Lockwood's voice rang with triumph. 'Mr Overton's current band of men might well wish to do their duty in their own roads, particularly now that we are being bombarded from the skies every night.'

Mr Overton cut across her. 'A new Fire-Watchers Order has been issued. It is the duty of all owners or occupiers of business premises to have designated fire-watchers on duty—'

'—which means that Mr Overton cannot let matters slip,' said Mrs Lockwood.

She might as well have said, 'Mr Overton cannot object to what I have done,' though she didn't need to say it, not really. It was plastered all over her face.

On Saturday morning Betty walked through the familiar, well-loved streets to her home, smiling with pleasure at being back, smiling also because the neighbours who had whispered about her before she left were now stopping her to ask about her new job and her billet.

She had to ring the doorbell when she got home because Grace had taken her key off her before she moved out, laughing as she did so.

'No need for you to take that with you, Betty. It might get lost.'

The door was opened by Dad. Betty felt like crumpling with happiness right there on the doorstep. It was wonderful to see his dear face again. His habitually serious expression crinkled into lines of delight and Betty stepped willingly into his embrace, relishing the feel of his loving arms round her. Oh, how she loved him.

Grace's laughter interrupted the hug. 'Let's at least get the door closed, shall we? Come along in, Betty. Trevor, shut the door.'

Dad gave her a quick kiss before he let go. Betty's cheek tingled beneath the gentle rasp of his moustache.

Grace hung up Betty's things on the hallstand as if she was a guest, then bore her into the parlour, holding her by the arm and depositing her on the sofa. She sat beside her, angled towards her, her face wreathed in smiles. Dad sat in his armchair.

'Tell us everything, love,' said Grace. 'We want to hear all about it, don't we, Trevor? But first I expect you're gasping for a cuppa, aren't you, Betty?' She stood up and went to the door, glancing back to add, 'Don't start without me.'

As soon as Grace disappeared, Betty went to sit on the arm of Dad's chair.

'How are you, Dad?'

'Mustn't grumble.'

'It's lovely to see you.'

'You an' all, love. I've missed you.'

'Have you?' Betty glowed. 'I missed you too.'

'I hope you haven't been homesick.'

'No, I'm all right.' She would have said it anyroad, because she didn't want him to worry, but as she spoke she realised it was true.

When Grace returned carrying a tray, there might have been a look of annoyance on her face, but the smile was back so quickly that it was impossible to say for certain.

'Well, look at the pair of you. But you're a bit old for sitting like that, Betty. You aren't a little girl. Here, take this tray off me.'

When they were settled with tea and home-made rock buns, Betty told them about her digs, and they were pleased she was friendly with the munitions girls.

'That must help you feel settled in,' said Dad.

'You must feel as if you've lived away from home for years,' trilled Grace.

Betty described her work, but not the Mrs Archer fiasco or the brooch incident. She wanted to get Dad on his own to discuss the matter of the brooch and see what ideas he had for ensuring it never happened again. She didn't want to say anything in front of Grace.

Dinner was cutlets with mash and carrots followed by steamed sultana pudding. If Betty had imagined being free to talk to Dad while Grace was busy in the kitchen, she was doomed to disappointment. Grace spirited her away to help, then made a huge fuss of her in front of Dad and called her the cooking pixie.

Dad snoozed while Grace and Betty cleared away. Then Betty suggested going to see Mum. Surely Grace wouldn't accompany her and Dad to the cemetery. But she did, holding on to Dad's arm and patting it comfortingly. Dad covered Grace's hand with his own.

'I'm lucky to have such an understanding woman in my life,' he said, and Betty felt like gnashing her teeth.

Anyroad, that put paid to the brooch matter. There was obviously going to be no chance of getting Dad on his own. Betty was going to have to come up with her own ideas. Crikey.

Then she hated herself for having such thoughts when she should have been concentrating on Mum.

CHAPTER TWENTY-FOUR

Mr Overton wasn't best pleased to have the two girls assigned to the depot as fire-watchers, but there was nothing he could do about it. Betty received her letter instructing her to attend a training session at Darley Court.

'Ooh, lovely. Lucky old you,' said Mrs Beaumont, pausing, toast-rack in hand, when Betty read out the letter at the breakfast table. 'I'd love to go there. It's a proper old manor-house with grounds and everything. The owner offered it as a venue for training and civil defence meetings for the duration. When you go, I want you to take special note of all the furniture and the curtains and what-have-you, so you can tell me all about it when you get back.'

'They're only going to have paintings of crummy old ancestors, Mrs Beaumont,' Stella teased. 'Nobody important like Vesta Tilley or Marie Lloyd.'

Mrs Beaumont stuck her nose in the air. 'Less of your cheek.' But she was only pretending to be offended.

Mrs Beaumont offered Betty the loan of her old boneshaker of a bicycle to get to Darley Court. Miss White's future mother-in-law lent her bike too, so the two girls cycled side by side, carefully following the directions they'd been given. They cycled between two big stone gateposts past the gatekeeper's lodge and up a long drive at the end of which was a handsome house with, protruding at the front, a large porch that you could have driven a motor-car under. The building's many windows were criss-crossed with anti-blast tape, but this evidence of the war was far outweighed by Darley Court's dignity.

Betty braked to a halt and stepped from the saddle, placing one foot on the ground. Beside her, Miss White did likewise.

Some people stood about, smoking and chatting. A man with thin slicked-back hair and half-moon spectacles came towards the two girls as they dismounted. He carried a clipboard and wore an ARP band on the arm of his tweed jacket.

'I know you're here for the fire training, because that's the only course that's running today. I'm Mr Crosby. Your names, please?'

'Betty Hughes and Sally White,' said Miss White.

Betty nodded at Mr Crosby's armband. 'We're being trained by the ARP?'

'Nothing wrong with that,' said Miss White. 'My dad's an ARP warden.'

'I'm not saying there's anything wrong,' said Betty. 'It just seems odd.'

'It's a fair point,' Mr Crosby conceded. 'So far fire-watching has been one of the jobs associated with the ARP, but with the way things are going it won't be long before a separate Fire Guard Unit is established. Well done.' He gave Betty an approving nod. 'Good question. It shows you're thinking things through. Jolly good show.'

Blimey. It had only been a throwaway remark, but she had shot to the top of the class. She hoped Mr Crosby wasn't going to expect her to be today's star pupil.

Mr Crosby indicated a line of bicycle-racks further along the front of the house.

'Leave your bikes there. They'll be fine. We'll go inside in a minute.'

'I can't wait to get inside,' Betty whispered as Mr Crosby moved on. 'My landlady is keen to hear all about it and now that I'm here, I'm keen an' all.'

Presently they went up the shallow stone steps and through a massive door into an impressive hall with a staircase straight ahead. It was like going into a church, Betty thought, with its high vaulted ceiling and sense of grandeur. Mind you, a statue like that one on the half-landing would have no place in a church. Inside an arched alcove, the statue was of a lady in an almost-but-not-quite-revealing robe like the goddesses in a book of Greek myths Betty had once borrowed from the library.

Transferring her gaze to the walls, Betty realised all the paintings had been covered with hardboard. Oh well, it made sense, though Mrs Beaumont might be disappointed.

An elderly lady walked into the hall. She might be advanced in years but she had an air of vigour about her. She must be an old retainer, maybe an old nanny, who had been kept on in comfortable retirement after a lifetime of service to the family.

'Can I help you?' she enquired in an educated voice.

'We're just admiring the place,' said Miss White. 'We haven't been here before.'

The lady nodded. 'Excuse me. I have to place a telephone call.'

Mr Crosby came in, followed by the others as the lady disappeared through a door over to one side.

'I see you've met the owner,' he said.

'That was the owner?' Betty asked in surprise.

'Yes,' said Mr Crosby. 'Miss Brown. She's not as young as she once was, if I may be so indelicate as to refer to a lady's age, but she's as sharp as a tack.'

Betty stared at the door through which Miss Brown had

vanished. She felt she ought to run after her and apologise for
making assumptions.

'Everyone has arrived,' said Mr Crosby, 'so I'll take you
through to the meeting room, where we'll start off by learning
about incendiaries, which is what we'll be training you to deal
with. Later we'll go outside with the equipment and some flash-
bangs.'

In the meeting room – which was furnished with plain tables
and wooden chairs, and not a chintz sofa or a grand piano to be
seen – Mr Crosby and his colleagues sat at the front behind a long
table, looking important. They were all men. They took turns to
speak, standing up and walking over to the end of the table, where
there was a blackboard on an easel. Betty was disappointed to find
that Mr Crosby wasn't a very good speaker, though actually it was
the least talented speaker of all who caused tingles to run up and
down her spine with the information that a Luftwaffe heavy
bomber could potentially start up to one hundred and fifty fires
across a three-mile area.

'And that figure takes into account those incendiaries that
don't detonate or that land on stony ground, where fires can't take
hold.'

It was a harrowing thought, but Betty was heartened to learn
that incendiaries were fairly straightforward to extinguish as long
as they were dealt with promptly. She latched on to that.

But how many could be dealt with when they rained down in
the hundreds – in the thousands?

Sally was deeply impressed as she watched Miss Hughes dart
forward, holding the sandbag in front of her, and then used it to
smother a pretend incendiary before hurrying away in case the
'incendiary' still exploded. She was very good at this. It didn't
matter whether she was called upon to use a sandbag, a shovelful
of earth or a dustbin lid. Her movements were decisive and quick

but not over-hasty. One chap, eager to show off his prowess, had fallen over his own feet. Others were decidedly cack-handed until they got used to what was required, but there was a neatness about Miss Hughes's movements. Sally wasn't just impressed. She felt proud of her colleague.

'You're ever so good at this,' Sally told her warmly when everyone stopped for a cuppa and a potato scone fresh from the Darley Court kitchen.

'Thanks,' said Miss Hughes. 'I want to get it right.'

She accepted Sally's compliment in a completely practical way as if she hadn't realised it was indeed a compliment. It was on the tip of Sally's tongue to be more obvious in her praise, but that might come across as patronising, which was the last thing Sally wanted.

Some time was permitted for general chat during the tea break, then Mr Crosby called for attention.

'Just a few points while we drink our tea, ladies and gents. First off, as I'm sure you know, you'll receive a subsistence allowance for each duty shift. This will be one and sixpence.'

'Coo,' said Miss Hughes, sounding pleased.

Mr Crosby looked at her. 'That's for the men. Ladies get a shilling.'

'We'll all be doing the same duty, though,' said Sally. 'Or...' She faltered. 'Are the men going to be given additional training so they can tackle further dangers?'

'No,' Mr Crosby told her. 'All fire work is the same.'

'But—'

Miss Hughes nudged her, murmuring, 'Hush, can't you? You're making a show of yourself. The men get more because they're men. Simple as that.'

Sally subsided. Miss Hughes was correct. Men always earned more even when they were in exactly the same job, such as teaching or working in a shop. But this was different. This was wartime. They had food rationing to ensure fair shares all round.

Shouldn't there be fair shares of subsistence allowance too? Oh, what was she thinking? Was she being unpatriotic? She shouldn't be grousing about money when there was essential work to be done.

After the tea break, they moved on to training with stirrup-pumps and Redhill scoops. The Redhill scoop was a long-handled shovel, but the 'shovel', instead of being a flat plate like a spade, had a ridge at the sides and at the back.

'You place the scoop in front of the incendiary,' said Mr Crosby. 'With your other hand, use this hoe to draw the incendiary onto the scoop. Then you deposit the incendiary into this contraption here, the Redhill container.' He indicated a sturdy triangular box with an opening at the bottom. 'In goes the incendiary, down comes the door. It is safe to carry the container using the handle on the top. You won't burn your hand.' Straightening up, he looked around the attentive group. 'Half of you will learn to use this and the other half will use the stirrup-pumps, then we'll swap over.'

Sally and Miss Hughes were allocated to the stirrup-pumps first.

'This is a two-man job,' said Mr Crosby, adding with a chuckle, 'or in this case a two-girl job. The pump is placed in a bucket of water. One fellow works the pump up and down while the other aims the hose. I'd like everyone to have a go at both jobs.'

Sally worked hard, determined to show herself ready to do her duty in spite of the difference in the allowances. But honestly, what was wrong with seeing herself and all these others simply as fire-watchers rather than as male and female fire-watchers? But that was the way of the world.

Mr Crosby went from couple to couple, watching and advising. When he came to Sally and Miss Hughes, he observed them for a minute, then said, 'You two work well together. I'm pleased with you.'

'Thank you,' they chorused, then looked at one another. Miss

Hughes's smile and her high chin showed her satisfaction. Sally recognised it because she felt the same.

'First the pig-bins, now the stirrup-pump,' Miss Hughes said in a jokey voice. 'It looks like we're destined to work together.'

'I hope so,' said Sally.

She was starting to realise that there was more to Miss Betty Hughes than she had given her credit for.

CHAPTER TWENTY-FIVE

Betty was pleased when Mr Overton decreed that she and Miss White should do their fire-watching together. It was better than being with a stranger. Besides, they had worked well together. She showed Miss White the way up to the roof. When Miss White exclaimed in delight at the view, Betty felt a twinge of guilt as she recalled being shown up here by Pamela on her first day. She really ought to have brought Miss White up here before now, but she hadn't because... because it would have been a chummy thing to do and she still hadn't wanted to be chummy with Miss Butter-Wouldn't-Melt.

Mr Crosby came to talk them through their duties.

'As well as being responsible for the depot, you've got the part of Beech Road outside it as well. I'll show you exactly which part of the road is yours. The depot fire-watchers haven't had responsibility for part of the road outside before.' The words *so don't make a mess of it* hung unspoken in the air. 'I've looked at the rotas with Mr Overton and your first night will be the last night of September, so you'll go up onto the roof in September and you won't come down again until October,' he said with a chuckle.

'Remember, your duty is to extinguish incendiaries and prevent fires from spreading.'

Later, Mr Overton informed them that the end of September was when the depot's early starts would cease.

'From October, you'll start work at eight, not six thirty.' He gave them a nod and returned to his office.

'Good-o,' said Betty. 'That means we'll have time to go home to have breakfast and get changed after we finish fire-watching at six. That'll make life easier.'

She glanced round. It appeared that Miss White wasn't listening. She was busy eyeing up the heaps of sandbags over in the corner. Oh aye, thought Betty, what's she come up with now?

'If we've got this bit of Beech Road to look after as well,' said Miss White, 'I vote we should start our duty each night by putting some of these sandbags outside the depot along our patch of the road. It'll save time if we have to rush down from the roof. We can lean them against the lamp-posts. What d'you think?'

Tempting as it might be to say, 'Does it really matter what I think?' in a sulky voice, Betty replied, 'That's a good idea.' It was, too. She pictured a mad dash down to the road during an air raid. It was all very well being congratulated for her prowess at extinguishing pretend incendiaries during a training session undertaken in conditions of perfect safety, but she didn't kid herself that the real thing would be as straightforward.

'I'm dying to get to grips with the depot,' said Miss White. 'Mr Overton is the exact opposite of my old boss at the Food Office. He was in charge of every little thing down to the last detail. He never let the clerks give evidence in court even when we were the ones who tested the shopkeepers, and he didn't like me collecting new recipes to give out to housewives. But here, if Mr Overton is going to keep himself to himself, then there's an opportunity for me – for us – to make something of this place. F'rinstance, I think we should make signs to put up to show where all the various different types of salvage need to be put. As well as being useful, it would smarten the place up. What d'you think?'

'I think,' chimed in a new voice – Mrs Lockwood's, 'that you should know your place, Miss White. There's only one person who is going to put their stamp on this depot and that is my good self. You and Miss Hughes are here to do my bidding. You're correct, though, about the place needing to be taken in hand, which is precisely what I intend to do. I approve of your idea about putting up notices and I give you my permission to do so, but in future kindly note that you must make your suggestions directly to me in the first instance and not to the other hired help. Step aside, if you please. I wish to speak to Mr Overton.'

She marched across the yard towards the office, leaving the two girls first staring after her and then staring at one another.

'It isn't Mr Overton you need to worry about,' said Betty. 'It's Mrs Lockwood.'

'But she doesn't actually have any authority here.'

'Try telling her that,' Betty said gloomily.

'It's true,' Miss White said indignantly. 'I know the WVS are heavily involved in salvage – but so are the Girl Guides. That doesn't mean Brown Owl is going to turn up and start laying down the law.'

Betty couldn't help giggling. 'Just imagine if she did.'

'It's no laughing matter.' But Miss White's lips twitched all the same.

'Do you think I ought to inform Mrs Lockwood about my idea to prevent smart alecs from pinching jewellery from us?' joked Betty.

'You've had an idea?' Miss White sounded pleased. 'What is it?'

'I don't know if I should say.' It was all Betty could do to keep a straight face. 'I have to tell the High Priestess of Salvage first, not the hired help.'

'Oh, you!' Miss White chucked a bundle of rags at her and they scattered on the ground.

'I will not tolerate such childish behaviour,' announced Mrs Lockwood, appearing in the yard once more. 'Larking around like guttersnipes – ridiculous! Pull yourselves together. I can see I shall have to pay close attention to this place and its staff in future. I don't expect you to let me down again. Do I make myself clear? Well? Do I?' she demanded, planting herself in front of them, nostrils flaring, clearly with no intention of going on her way until they had been forced to reply, like the children she'd accused them of being.

'Yes, Mrs Lockwood,' said Betty.

Miss White said nothing. Betty gave her a look.

'Yes, Mrs Lockwood,' Miss White muttered.

'Good,' boomed Mrs Lockwood. 'Don't make me have to speak to you in this way again.'

She marched towards the open gates, stopping twice on the way to poke around inside crates of salvage. Just making the point that she was entitled? Witch. When she disappeared through the gates, Betty let out a breath, which made her realise she'd been holding it.

'Well!' said Miss White.

Betty held up a hand to silence her before darting across to the gates and looking outside. Yes, Mrs Lockwood was striding away along Beech Road.

'She's gone,' Betty reported.

'I don't know how you can sound so calm,' said Miss White.

Betty shrugged. 'You meet all sorts when you work in a shop and you always have to be polite, no matter what. It's one of the rules.'

Miss White sighed so deeply that the sound seemed to be dragged all the way up from the soles of her feet. 'I wish Mr Overton would put her in her place. It's very frustrating, the way he lets her ride roughshod over him – and us. I wish he was stronger.'

'Well, he isn't,' said Betty. 'I think he's very unhappy. Remember what I told you about how he feels humiliated by being here?'

'Of course.'

'I'd have thought that you of all people would understand that.'

'How so?' A rosy flush invaded Miss White's cheeks.

'You said that someone at your old place of work called you a pig-swill girl for coming here.'

'She only said it to be unkind.'

'I don't know if folk actually talk about Mr Overton doing a woman's job, but suppose he *thinks* they're all talking about him behind his back?' Betty suggested. 'He used to be a bank manager, you know, one of the important people in the community. Everyone looked up to him. I know we're not supposed to moan and complain about the war work we're given, but it must feel like a real comedown to him.'

'That's more or less what my fiancé's mother said.'

'Did she?'

'And I told her she had a kind heart,' said Miss White, 'so I reckon you must be kind-hearted too.'

'I'm just trying to put myself in his shoes, that's all. That's what my mum would have told me to do. She was a kind person an' all. If you think I'm kind-hearted, that's where I got it from.'

'Your mum sounds like a lovely person.'

'She was. I miss her all the time.' Betty swallowed hard. 'I don't know how we got on to this. We started off talking about Mrs Lockwood.'

'Never mind Mrs Lockwood. I want to hear about your idea for the jewellery,' said Miss White. 'Tell you what. It must be time for our break. Let's bring our tea out here and sit in the sunshine. It won't be long before it's too cold for that.'

Soon they'd made the tea. Mr Overton had his at his desk and the girls carried theirs outside, bringing a saucer to act as an ashtray. Miss White perched on the heap of sandbags and Betty lounged on a pile of empty sacks.

'What would Mrs Lockwood say if she could see us now?' said Betty.

'Please let's forget her for now,' said Miss White. 'I want to hear about your idea.'

'It isn't anything very wonderful,' Betty said, not wanting to get her hopes up. 'If anybody wants to claim something from the jewellery box, they have to describe it in advance without seeing it. There,' she added. 'It's pretty lame, really.'

'It's sensible. It would work.'

'And we can tell anybody who comes to claim something that we're only allowed to hand it back in the presence of a police officer.'

'That would make a fraudster run a mile.' Was that admiration in Miss White's voice?

'And I thought maybe we should ask a jeweller to come every so often to see what we've got. If there's anything of value, we should try to trace the owner in case they want it back.'

'In fact, if anybody brings jewellery in future,' said Miss White, 'perhaps we should keep a note of their address until after we get the valuation.'

'No,' Betty said, surprising herself with how decisive she sounded. 'I've already had my fingers burned that way. I thought I was helping Mrs Archer when she came in wanting to swap her fish-slice, but then she told her neighbours and next news they all wanted to swap things. We can't have word getting round that they can come here for a free valuation.' She took a moment to think about it. 'If it's costume jewellery, we'll accept it. If it's obviously special, we suggest the person has it valued before they make a decision.'

Miss White nodded. 'You're right. But that only applies when someone brings jewellery to the depot. Nearly all of what we receive arrives as a job lot.'

'That's when we ask the jeweller in if something looks expensive or old,' said Betty, 'and we trace the owner if we can. If a lady is happy for us to have her valuable necklace, we arrange for it to be sold and the money goes to the war effort or a charity, like the Red Cross – and we can tell the previous owner how much their necklace raised.'

'I think those are good ideas,' said Miss White, raising her cup of tea as if making a toast. 'Well done, you.'

Betty was pleased. She didn't know where the ideas had come from but, once she'd stopped worrying about it, they had slipped into her mind. 'You see, I'm not so stupid after all.'

'I never called you stupid.'

'You thought it, though.'

'No, I didn't,' said Miss White. 'If you mean because of the butter incident, you're wrong. That showed how trusting you are.'

Trusting? Betty hadn't thought of it that way. It made her feel better about herself.

After a moment in which she looked uncertain, Miss White said, 'D'you think we could be friends? Proper friends, not just colleagues who rub along at work. I haven't lived in Chorlton long and I don't have pals my own age here. I know you've got friends at your billet, but I hope you might have room in your life for someone else.'

Betty warmed to her. 'There's always room for one more. You're all right, you are. I had my doubts about you at first – but my doubts about you were just as much about me being annoyed with myself after the mistakes I made. You're right. We do work well together. On top of that, we'll be spending a lot of time together fire-watching. It would be daft not to be pals, wouldn't it?' She smiled. 'I'm Betty.'

'And I'm Sally.'

CHAPTER TWENTY-SIX

On Sally and Betty's first night up on the depot roof on fire-watching duty, they sat on folding chairs, armed with binoculars and wearing tin hats. They chatted about this and that, enjoying one another's company, though they weren't permitted to smoke up here. Even the tecniest spark of light wasn't permitted in the blackout.

Just after midnight, the wail of the siren lifted into the air, competing with the sound of aeroplane engines. Bright beams of white shone up into the darkness as the searchlights swung this way and that, looking for the planes and then holding them in their sights for the ack-ack guns to take aim.

The girls rose to their feet. Sally watched in horrified fascination as strings of incendiaries streamed down from the skies. That was what they were called: strings. Fortunately these were some distance away, though not, Sally was relieved to see, in the direction of her native Withington.

'The planes are heading this way,' said Betty, an edge to her voice. 'Oh my stars. They're coming straight for us.'

Then came the spine-tingling whistling sound that meant incendiaries were on their way to earth. The whistling turned to a prolonged hiss and there were intense flashes of white light on Beech Road.

'That's our patch!' cried Betty. 'Come on.'

Sally almost lost her footing as she scrambled down the ladder. They clattered down the wooden stairs to the ground floor and spilled outside into the yard. Sally snatched up the stirrup-pump and Betty picked up a bucket of water. Together, they dashed out between the big gates, which stood open – and thank goodness they did. Now wasn't the moment to lose precious time dragging them open.

An incendiary lay outside as if Herr Hitler had sent it specially for them. Sally dumped the bucket of water on the pavement, dunked the pump into it and started pounding the handle up and down while Betty doused the evil contraption, which was roughly the shape and size of a rounders bat. There was no time to feel pleased with themselves. There were other incendiaries to be dealt with.

The bucket soon emptied. Sally ran back into the yard for another full one and returned to see Betty grabbing a sandbag from the base of a lamp-post. She held it in front of her just as they'd been taught, then she stepped forward and thrust it on top of the device, retreating smartly in case the dratted thing went off anyway, but it didn't. Her face was twisted in disgust – well, Sally felt disgusted too. It was appalling to think of ordinary people – women, children, old folk – being targeted in this way. Damn Hitler!

The girls dealt with more incendiaries. Sally was aware of other people up and down the road doing likewise. The raid went on for the best part of an hour all told, the incidents near the depot taking up a frantically busy twenty minutes.

At last the girls returned to the depot roof. Sally felt all fired up and extra-alert lest more incendiaries should come raining down.

'You did well with that sandbag,' she told Betty. 'I saw your face. You looked not best pleased with Jerry.'

To her surprise, Betty laughed.

'I certainly wasn't best pleased about something. Put it this way. What do dogs use lamp-posts for? And if there happened to be a couple of sandbags at the foot of the lamp-post...'

'Oh,' said Sally.

'Oh indeed. I don't think I'll ever feel the same way about these gloves again,' Betty said ruefully, but she laughed as she said it.

That was when the all-clear started to sound. Sally and Betty looked at one another. It was their first air raid on duty as fire-watchers and they had acquitted themselves well.

It was that time of year when, in normal times, people thought of planting bare-root roses and tulip bulbs and starting to gather fallen leaves to tidy up the garden, but this year the lingering scent that hung in the air everywhere wasn't the pungent, ashy smell of gardeners' bonfires but the dull, biting stench of bombed-out houses. Sometimes the atmosphere was fumy and headachy where gas mains had been ruptured and the gas men had raced to heal the damage.

The first time Sally saw a row of houses with one missing, her heart forgot to beat and then took the next dozen beats in a frantic rush. But it was strange what you could get used to. Yes, it was horrible to see a building that had taken a direct hit and was reduced to a mound of rubble, but as the days went by such sights became part of the urban landscape.

At home Sally said, 'It worries me what this must be doing to the children's minds.' She and Andrew were in the front room – with the door open, of course. 'They shouldn't be exposed to sights like this.'

'You're right. They shouldn't.' Andrew held her close, his

arms giving her a sense of shelter and protection as well as love. 'But they seem all right on the whole. Children are more resilient than you think. As for bombed-out houses, they are giant playgrounds. Before the war, cigarette-cards were what every lad collected and swapped, but now bits of shrapnel are far more important.'

Life in the Henshaw household had settled into a steady routine. Something inside Sally wriggled with delight at the thought. The only thing that could improve it would be when she became Mrs Andrew Henshaw.

When she had the chance to introduce Betty to Andrew, she couldn't resist. Andrew did war work after school, effecting small repairs in damaged houses, restoring doors that had been blown off, replacing shelves, mending furniture, replacing floorboards. The other day, he'd told his mother that he was due to do some work in a house on Church Road. That was little more than a stone's throw from the depot. Sally and Betty both had to walk past the end of Church Road on their way home, so Sally invited Betty to come and meet her future husband.

'Just to say how do. It'll only take us five minutes.'

The road was lined on both sides with tall terraced houses with narrow front gardens.

'I'm not sure which house it is,' said Sally, 'but he said it was over the road from the orphanage.'

'That's at the far end,' said Betty.

They hurried down the road, their heels tapping on the pavement. There was nothing in the outward appearance of the houses to suggest that repairs might be in order. Sally felt a bit of a twit. This hadn't been such a good idea after all.

A housewife with a sturdy cloth shopping bag came round the corner and made for one of the houses.

It was worth a try. Sally stepped forward. 'Excuse me. Do you know which of these houses is having repairs done by the Corporation? My fiancé's working in it but I don't know which one.'

'He's in my house, love,' said the woman. 'He's doing a good job an' all. You're lucky to have a chap like that. Shall I send him out to you?'

'Yes, please,' said Sally. 'It'll only take a moment.'

But when the repair man appeared, it was someone else.

'I'm sorry,' said Sally, flustered. 'I thought it was my fiancé working here.' She tried to look over the man's shoulder, thinking that Andrew might appear from the depths of the house. 'Is he in there with you?'

'Working on my own,' said the man, rolling his shoulders to loosen them before taking out a packet of cigarettes and lighting up. He grinned. 'I thought it was odd when the lady said my young lady had turned up. I couldn't imagine why she'd have come all the way from Moss Side.'

'I'm sorry to have bothered you,' said Sally, adding to Betty, 'I'm sorry to have dragged you down here.'

'No harm done,' said good-natured Betty. 'I'll meet him another time.'

Sally went home, where her mother-in-law was preparing toad-in-the-hole with spinach.

'With real sausages,' Mrs Henshaw declared, 'instead of having to make them with oatmeal and herbs.'

'What a treat,' Sally agreed.

When Andrew arrived home, Sally quickly nipped behind the door to the front room just before it opened and Andrew came in. She slipped her arms round his waist from behind and snuggled against him.

'Looking for something?'

He folded his arms over hers. 'I was hoping to find a loving fiancée. Do you know if there's one available?'

Gently unfastening her hold on him, he turned and took her into a warm embrace. Sally angled her face upwards to receive his kiss, her arms snaking up to fasten themselves round his neck, pulling his mouth down to meet hers. He smelled of wood, tobacco and fresh air. When the embrace ended, Sally went into the other room to set the table.

Over their meal, they talked about the day. Sally mentioned taking Betty to the house in Church Road.

'Oh – there,' said Andrew. 'That job got handed to another chap – as you found out.'

'Where are you working now?' asked his mother.

'Here and there. Just small jobs.' Andrew smiled at Sally. 'I'd like to meet your friend Betty at some point.'

'War work permitting,' said Sally.

'October seems to be carrying on where September left off,' said Mrs Henshaw.

Indeed, September nights had brought raid after raid and now October looked like bringing the same. Many bombs and strings of incendiaries fell on places not far from Chorlton – Moss Side, Platt Fields, Fallowfield – and Withington. Sally went cold to the very core of her being when she heard about that, her heart expanding with worry for Mum and Dad, the neighbours, Deborah and her parents, everyone she knew. There were reports of damaged houses, though mercifully the air-raid shelters were mostly doing their job.

'The numbers of casualties could have been far higher,' said Mrs Henshaw when they heard about Withington having had a bad time.

Sally bit her lip. Andrew's mother undoubtedly meant to offer comfort, and what the injury and death tolls would have been without the air raid shelters simply didn't bear thinking about, but that didn't make Sally feel any better about hearing of the deaths in Brown Street and Moorfield Street. Those who died in Moorfield Street, eight of them, had perished when the public air-raid shelter they were in took a direct hit. Public shelters were called surface shelters because they were above ground, unlike the family-sized Anderson shelters that were half-buried in back gardens. Sally might not have known those people personally, but it was all too chilling to imagine their bodies being transported to the mortuary in Embden Street, where she used to work.

As well as the Withington deaths, there were many casualties, who had been transported to Withington Hospital and Christie Hospital. They weren't just from Brown Street and Moorfield Street but also from Allen Road, Davenport Avenue – and Parsonage Road, which was very close to home, so close that a huge tide of longing to see her parents swept over Sally.

'I'm going over to Withington,' she told Mrs Henshaw the moment she walked through the front door that evening.

'If you wait until tomorrow,' said Mrs Henshaw, 'you'll be able to spend longer with them. If you go today, you'll have to hurry back here in time for fire-watching duty.'

But Sally simply couldn't wait. She ate a hurried meal, because Mrs Henshaw refused to let her leave the house without something inside her, then she pulled on the hip-length swing-jacket she'd bought before the war. It had a stand-up collar and cuffed sleeves and she'd loved it on sight. Deborah had called it 'the last word in smartness'. She had bought a new coat as well. Hers was full-length with front panels of leopard-patterned cloth.

'Look at us,' she'd crowed in delight. 'The Swish Sisters. Yours is swish because' – and she laughed – 'it swishes and mine is swish because it's so swanky.'

How proud and delighted they'd been at the time. Their mothers and aunties and all the neighbours had been busy stock-piling tinned goods and toilet rolls while all the men had been occupied digging vast holes in the back gardens to accommodate Anderson shelters – and Sally and Deborah had had one last splurge on good coats. How shallow that seemed now when death was raining down from the skies night after night.

The bus to Withington had to take a detour, which the conductor said was to avoid a 'socking great crater' in the road. By the time she alighted, Sally was clutching her handbag in a tight grip as she battled to keep anxiety from overwhelming her.

To reach her parents' house, she had to pass Deborah's. As keen as she was to see Mum and Dad, Sally went straight to the Grants'. She wanted them to know she cared. She had never stopped caring.

The door was opened by Deborah. Her bright-blue eyes widened in surprise. Then Sally took an unexpected step backward as Deborah launched herself at her. They clung together.

'Are your mum and dad all right?' Sally asked, her words spoken into Deborah's soft hair.

Before Deborah could reply, her mum called, 'Who is it?' and appeared in the doorway.

Sally stared at the woman who had been a second mother to her all her life but who had turned against her for rejecting Rod and then suffered the horrible experience of seeing her beloved son in his true colours. Deborah looked at her mother over her shoulder. There was a moment of charged silence, then Mrs Grant stepped outside and put her arms round both girls.

'You're safe, Sally,' she said. 'Mr Turner from Parsonage Road – he's gone, and so has Olive Busby. The Richardsons from Davenport Avenue.'

The shudder that ran through Mrs Grant vibrated through the two girls as well. Sally's bones seemed to hum with it. Her face wet, she disentangled herself.

'I have to see Mum. Is she – is she all right?'

'As far as I know,' said Mrs Grant, and a sensation of thickness clogged the back of Sally's throat. Times were when Mrs Grant had been in and out of Mum's house like it was an extension of her own.

Sally cleared her throat. 'I'd best cut along. I'm glad to see you.'

Giving Deborah's hand one final squeeze, she ran along the road to Mum and Dad's, throwing herself into Mum's arms when she opened the door.

'Oh my goodness,' said Mum, holding her tight. 'Sally. My girl.'

They sat together on the sofa. Mum would have put the kettle on, but Sally wanted to stay close together, holding hands. She knew that once Mum got over the surprise and emotion of the moment, she would separate herself, not through any lack of love but because that was the way she was. You didn't touch people. You kept your hands to yourself.

It was so very different to the warm hugs she had received from Deborah and her mum that Sally couldn't help saying, 'I saw Deborah and Mrs Grant. I went to their house. I was so relieved to see them, to know they're all right.' She hesitated before adding, 'I asked after you and Mrs Grant said you were all right as far as she knew. Does that mean you're not seeing one another any more?'

Mum sighed, a sad sound. 'The Grants are keeping themselves to themselves at the moment – and can you blame them after what Rod did? It'll take time for them to recover from the shame.'

'You could help by being friends.'

Mum sighed again. This time she sounded vexed. 'What about me? I've got to get over what Rod did as well. He as good as attacked you. I know that's a strong word to use, but he's a strong man and when he made a grab for you...'

'Don't blame his family for what he did,' Sally urged.

'Why not? They're the ones that brought him up.'

'Mum, please,' said Sally. 'That business with Rod was nasty, but the person who was most hurt by it was Mrs Grant. Please don't take it out on her. She doesn't deserve it.'

'Well, I suppose I could give her a knock,' Mum said grudgingly.

Sally left it at that. 'Where's Dad?'

'Civil Defence meeting. He'll be sorry he missed you. We were just saying last night how we haven't seen you.'

Sally immediately felt guilty. 'I'm sorry, but you know what it's like. I've a full-time job and then I've got my fire-watching.'

'And your fiancé. You have to spend time with him. Don't worry. We understand. But you've left a big hole behind. How is Andrew? And his mother?'

'They're both fine,' said Sally. 'I had to come. As soon as I heard about Withington, I needed to see you.'

'And Andrew hasn't come with you?'

Was that criticism? Sally said evenly, 'He's working late. I'll bring him another time.'

'Well, I'm glad you've come. It's good to see you – it's a relief.'

'For me too. I needed to see you and be with you.' Sally pushed down her emotion by asking a practical question. 'Are you keeping busy with the WVS?'

'There's plenty of welfare work to do,' said Mum. 'After every air raid we visit all the damaged houses to make a list of the invalids and the elderly, and we take forwarding addresses if people are going to move in with family. Then there are the folk whose houses are safe, but they need to move out for a day or so because of an unexploded bomb. We have to put them into hostels. One of the gas mains was ruptured the other night, which meant that the next day the local factory workers, nearly two hundred of them, couldn't have hot drinks, so we provided a mobile canteen.'

'It sounds like there's masses to do,' Sally commented.

'A lot of houses take damage just to the upstairs, so we have to provide families with what you might call upstairs necessities. They aren't going to put that in the history books, are they? All those folk needing soap and blankets.'

Sally smiled. 'No, I suppose not.' She waited for Mum to ask the obvious question, but it didn't come. 'Aren't you going to ask me about my work?'

'What is there to ask? You're collecting salvage.'

'It's essential for the war effort.'

'I know it's essential. You don't need to tell me that. It's just that you're capable of so much more.' Mum eased away slightly. Her hazel eyes were questioning as she looked at Sally. 'You loved the Food Office. It was a proper job, something to be proud of. You were a clerk and you dressed smartly. You looked like a proper office girl and I was so proud. Look at you now, working in salvage. Salvage! That's nothing special. What's that compared to being an office girl?'

CHAPTER TWENTY-SEVEN

There were raids that night, though mercifully not over Chorlton or Withington. From the moment the siren commenced its eerie wailing in the small hours until the all-clear finally sounded two heart-pumping hours later, Sally and Betty stood on the depot roof, binoculars glued to their eyes, watching the various lights in the night sky – the powerful beams swinging round, searching for enemy planes to latch onto, the glittering lines of incendiaries falling to earth and, worst of all, the flare and glow of fires that came after the distant *crump* sound that declared a bomb had scored a direct hit.

It was a strange business watching it happen from afar. Adrenaline stormed through Sally's bloodstream, preparing her for the possibility of the attack shifting and coming this way instead. There was pure fear too at the thought of the people on the receiving end. At the same time, there was dry-mouthed, almost giddy relief that Chorlton and Withington were tonight being spared. In a way, that was the hardest part, being grateful to be safe when she knew darned well that her safety and that of her fiancé, his mother and her parents was being paid for by other people being in desperate danger, other people who might lose limbs or loved ones, who might emerge from their Anderson shelters to find a smoking crater where their house used to be.

It wasn't just her own home turf Sally cared about. She cared about Salford too because that was where Betty came from. As far as they could tell, Salford looked safe tonight, but it had suffered badly in recent raids, not least because many of the bombs had contained oil that had caused multiple fires, stretching the fire brigade to the limit. A conflagration had taken hold and rapidly spread after oil bombs had burst through the roof of a huge warehouse containing cotton waste and paper. Another bomb, a high explosive this time, had gone straight through the roof of Salford Town Hall, taking an entire exterior wall with it as well as doing extensive damage inside. Betty knew these details because she had gone to a telephone box yesterday evening and put a call through to the police station where her father worked.

'I've never done it before,' she'd told Sally at the start of their duty shift, 'and he said I mustn't do it again, because it's against all kinds of rules.'

'I bet he was happy to hear your voice, though,' said Sally.

'Oh, he was, and I loved hearing his. I wanted to sob my heart out in pure relief, but that would have been a waste of a telephone call,' Betty added ruefully. 'You're lucky to have your parents fairly nearby. When you said yesterday that you were going over to Withington before you came back here to go on duty, I knew I had to speak to Dad, I just had to.'

Now, at last, six o'clock was approaching and another firewatching shift was coming to an end. A wave of weariness swept over Sally.

'When the war is over,' she said, 'I swear I'm going to sleep for a week.'

'Me an' all.' Betty covered her mouth as she yawned. 'But I'm afraid that's a long way off yet.'

One at a time, they climbed down through the skylight and descended the ladder before locking away the binoculars for safekeeping. Outside, they pulled shut the depot's big double gates and locked them.

'It hardly seems worth it,' said Betty. 'They have to stand open all day when we're here and all the time during night shift. They're only locked when we go home for breakfast.'

'And on Sundays,' Sally said with a smile. 'Don't forget Sundays.'

She walked with Betty to the corner of Wilton Road, then carried on alone along Beech Road, heading for home. Her heart lifted and, in spite of the chilly morning, she felt warmed by the thought of being with her beloved Andrew. He'd been on duty as well last night and, unless he was currently caught up in a complicated rescue, he ought to get home not long after she did.

Mrs Henshaw hadn't been out on WVS duty last night, but she wouldn't be tucked up in bed. She would have set her alarm clock so that Sally and Andrew would arrive home to a hot drink. Sometimes Sally wished – oh, it was horribly ungrateful of her, but sometimes she wished that Mrs Henshaw wouldn't do this. Wouldn't it be wonderful if she and Andrew could creep into the house together and have a bit of time on their own? But she could never say so and she was ashamed for even thinking it. She knew how lucky she was to have such a lovely woman as her future mother-in-law. It was just that there were times when she longed to have her fiancé all to herself.

Soon the Henshaw family was seated together round the table, smoking as they enjoyed mugs of steaming tea. Andrew's face was pale and drawn with tiredness, but as soon as he caught Sally looking at him he brightened, reaching to cover her hand with his own.

'I'm glad you managed to get to Withington last evening,' he told her. 'I know you were worried sick about your parents. I'm sorry you didn't get to see your dad.'

'So am I, but I feel better for seeing Mum.'

'That's not something I ever have to worry about.' Andrew

transferred his smile to Mrs Henshaw. 'It's good that we're together every day, Mum.'

'Keeping an eye on me, are you?' she teased.

'Someone has to.'

'Finished?' Stubbing out her cigarette, Mrs Henshaw leaned forward slightly to glance into their mugs. 'Go and get forty winks if you can. That'll set you up for the day.'

Sally headed upstairs and peeled off her clothes before collapsing into bed. She dozed for a while, but then woke up again, her body seeming to know that it couldn't indulge in a prolonged deep sleep.

Mum's opinion of her war work poured into Sally's mind. It was hurtful to think her own mother didn't respect what she did.

She mentioned it to Andrew over breakfast. 'Everyone knows salvage is important. It's an essential aspect of the war effort, but Mum is more concerned with dressing smartly and sitting behind a desk.'

'Sounds to me as though you like salvage work,' said Andrew. 'Sounds to me as though you're going to be an expert.'

Sally laughed, pretending not to take him seriously, but really she was thrilled to bits.

'Sounds to me...' Andrew began.

'What?' she asked when he paused.

'Sounds to me as though we should celebrate having a future salvage expert in the family,' said Andrew.

Sally was in good spirits as she headed back to the depot. There was still a nip in the air but the October sun was bright, edging the morning with buttercup-yellow light, and the day would no doubt warm up later. Had Andrew been joking when he'd called her a salvage expert? It didn't matter if he had. The thought filled her with pleasure. Could she really find the same sort of satisfaction in salvage work as she had back at the Food Office?

She was sure she could. She'd already made it her business to learn a lot.

She caught up with Betty just as she was about to unlock the door in the fence. Betty smiled at her, which made her sweet little dimple pop into her cheek. She wore that asymmetrical hat she was so fond of and the sunshine caught the rich-blond hair on her shoulders, making it even more golden than usual.

They got changed into their dungarees and came back downstairs to unlock the big gates, each of them then taking one gate and hauling it open. When they did so, there was Mrs Lockwood standing on the pavement, right in the middle, as if they were stagehands who had just swung open the theatre curtains for her to sing an aria that was going to bring an adoring audience to its feet, clamouring for more.

Tossing her head with a sharp jerk that might have sent her felt hat flying if it hadn't been secured by a pearl-topped hatpin, she marched into the yard.

'What sort of timekeeping do you call this?' she demanded. 'Shoddy, is what I call it. I expect this depot to open promptly. Supposing I had brought important visitors with me? What would they have thought? I shall make my views of your lax timekeeping known to Mr Overton forthwith.'

As she stalked across the yard, Betty called, 'He's not here yet. He had to go to a meeting at the Corporation first thing. He'll be in later.'

Mrs Lockwood did a smart about-turn. 'Why was I not informed of this meeting?' She glared accusingly at the girls as if they were responsible. The WVS badge on the front of her hat glinted in the sunshine. 'You should have left a message for me at MacFadyen's. I've told you before how to contact me. What's the matter with you? Standing staring at me. Haven't you got tongues in your heads?' Without waiting for a response, she made a show of looking around at the walls. 'I've come to see the signs that you were supposed to put up, labelling the different areas of the yard, "supposed" being the operative word. Not only are you poor time-keepers, you can't even follow simple instructions. I expect this depot to be properly signed by the time I next visit. Is that understood?'

Mrs Lockwood marched from the premises. Sally and Betty stared at one another, then Betty stuck her head outside to make sure Mrs Lockwood had indeed left.

'Well!' she exclaimed, coming to stand by Sally's side. 'Fancy blaming us for not telling her about the meeting at the Corporation. Flaming cheek! As for those signs, they were your idea, not hers. She just bagged it as hers because it's good.'

Sally's earlier happy spirits had changed to vexation. She could practically feel the steam pouring out of her ears. 'We have to do something to stop that awful woman treating the depot as though it belongs to her.'

'What, though?' asked Betty. 'Believe me, I'm all in favour, but I don't see how we can change her.'

That was when the idea crystallised inside Sally's head. 'It isn't Mrs Lockwood we have to change. It's Mr Overton. We have to do something to give him a boost.'

'A swift kick up the whatsit, more like,' Betty muttered.

'Listen,' said Sally. 'He's unhappy here because he's lost status. We have to give him back some standing in the community. We have to make him see that this isn't such a bad place to be.'

'How?' Betty asked.

'We arrange for him to deliver a talk to the WVS – not our local one, but the one in Withington, so we can be sure Mrs Lockwood won't get wind of it.'

'A talk about salvage?' Betty was doubtful. 'Everyone knows what they need to hang on to.'

'Yes, but not necessarily *why*,' said Sally, warming to her idea. 'Information about what all our salvage gets turned into will be an eye-opener.'

'Everyone knows about saucepans being used for Spitfires,'

said Betty. 'Sorry,' she added. 'I don't mean to pour cold water on your idea, but if we send Mr Overton off to give a talk and it doesn't go well, things could end up worse than they are now.'

'He won't just be telling them what to do. They know that already. In fact, they advise other people,' said Sally. 'I'll find out some salvage information that isn't generally known. The WVS will be impressed at learning something new. It'll be a morale-booster. If Mr Overton praises them for their efforts in the community, they'll feel patriotic too.'

'He's going to praise them, is he?' Now Betty looked amused, her blue eyes twinkling. 'Don't tell me: you're going to write his talk for him.'

'Not exactly, but I'll provide all the notes he needs and, yes, that will include a mention of the WVS's house-to-house collections and so forth. My mum is in the Withington WVS, so I know who their local leader is. I'll suggest the talk to her and then tell Mr Overton that she's invited him. What do you think?'

Betty grinned. 'I think you should work for the Secret Service.'

Sally started work that same day on the content of the talk Mr Overton had no idea he was going to give. She soon found herself absorbed in the information. It reminded her how interested she had always been in the minute details of food rationing and how she had loved gathering knowledge and sharing it with others.

For over a year now, newspapers and magazines had been urging everyone to save food-scraps and bones, paper, rubber and rags, even rabbit fluff. Sally intended to put together all the statistics she could find about what these items were used for, information that would without question increase the WVS's enthusiasm, which in turn would engender increased interest and determination locally.

'It's fascinating,' she told Betty. 'One newspaper, just one single newspaper, can be turned into shell-caps for three twenty-five pounder bombs. Three! Half a dozen books can be made into a carrier for a mortar shell. Every envelope can be turned into a cartridge wad and a dozen letters can make a box to hold rifle cartridges. And it isn't just what goes into the salvage boxes. By using less coal in the home, we can make sure there's more coal for building bomber aircraft. Sorry,' she added, though she was too pleased to feel embarrassed. 'Am I going on a bit?'

'Not at all,' Betty assured her loyally. 'What you've done is impressive. You should be the one delivering the talk, not Mr Overton. You make it sound fascinating, but that's because you're interested in it yourself.'

Now Sally did blush. Yes, she did find it all interesting and it was flattering to know that Betty thought her capable of enthusing others, but putting together all the information was as far as her part in this went. Was it wrong of her – was it big-headed – to wish she could be the one delivering the talk?

CHAPTER TWENTY-EIGHT

Mr Overton wouldn't let Sally and Betty attend his talk to the WVS. He accepted Sally's notes without noticeable enthusiasm. Presumably, as an educated man with a professional past, he added more information of his own, but if he did he didn't say anything to the girls. As he set off, they wished him luck, to which he replied with a polite nod and a word of thanks. Later he returned, every bit as gruff and uncommunicative as usual.

'I'm going to make him a cup of tea,' said Betty, 'and I'll ask him straight out.'

Sally waited eagerly while she did so.

'What did he say?' she asked when Betty came back.

Betty shook her head. 'That it seemed to go well.'

'Is that all he said?'

'What were you hoping for?' Betty asked. 'A blow-by-blow account?'

They looked at one another and laughed.

'Actually, all he wanted to tell me was that the depot is going to house a lorry loaded with paper for the paper mill overnight or maybe for a couple of nights. It's due to arrive on Saturday morning. Apparently, the mill has a backlog because of some problem or other.'

'I'll have to ask my mum about Mr Overton's talk,' said Sally.

She had been due to pop over to Withington in any case that evening. Now she was even more pleased to go, because her mother was a keen WVS member and enjoyed attending talks in the afternoons.

'He was an excellent speaker,' said Mum.

Sally suppressed a feeling of surprise. Why shouldn't Mr Overton be good at public speaking? She hadn't confided her and Betty's plan to either Mum or Mrs Henshaw and now she was even more glad that she hadn't. It meant that Mum's compliment was independent.

She shared it with Betty the next day.

'That's nice to know,' said Betty. 'Getting Mr O to give a talk was a good idea of yours.'

'It's thanks to you, really – well, you and Andrew's mother,' Sally told her. 'The two of you thought kindly of him and that made me want to help him.'

They spent part of the afternoon painting headings on pieces of wood – PAPER, RAGS, METAL, RUBBER and so on. It wasn't easy to get hold of paint these days. It could only be used for work purposes.

'I'm glad Mr Overton was allowed to have this black paint,' said Sally. 'The depot will look better once we put these notices up.'

Betty tilted her head on one side, looking at their artwork. 'Perhaps we should hide the notices and tell Mrs Lockwood we weren't allowed any paint because improving the depot counted as decorating.'

'Don't tempt me,' said Sally.

While the paint was drying, Sally popped down to the dairy to collect the silver-foil bottle-tops that housewives kept and returned to their milkmen – milk-ladies as well these days. This was a little service she had instituted with Mr Overton's permission.

'It would save someone from the dairy having to bring the bottle-tops to us,' she'd said. 'I'm sure they have plenty to do without remembering to do that as well.'

'It's true that they have generally waited until they have a sackful before they bother,' Mr Overton had said thoughtfully. 'Very well, Miss White. Permission granted. But only one of you needs to go, and don't hang about. It isn't a jolly jaunt.'

Now Sally put on her swing-jacket and hat and set off, enjoying the chance to be out and about on such a fine day. It was after four o'clock and some children were playing conkers. One of the conkers was clearly worth a lot of points, because several kids were gathered round, watching intently. Sally crossed Chorlton Green and walked past the Bowling Green pub and down a long road with houses on one side and farmland on the other.

She looked over the garden walls as she went. Next to the vegetables, many householders had hung on to a few favourite flowers, and Sally drank in the sight of the vivid yellow of tall, daisy-like rudbeckia and the feathery yellow of solidago. Other gardens had patches of low-growing asters. There were even some autumn crocuses. Sally turned her face up to feel the sun dancing on her skin.

She hadn't been here before but she recognised the dairy when she saw it, several low buildings set around a long yard on the other side of which were the stables that housed the faithful old horses that pulled the milk-carts. The gates were open and Sally walked inside, her eyes prickling as the scent of straw wafted her way. There was a small building, more of a shed, really, that seemed to be the office. Someone was inside, but with the sun in her eyes she could only make out their height and build, not any details. She waved cheerfully and headed in that direction.

As she did so, a movement caught her eye over at the far end of the sheds and she glanced back to see a familiar figure disappear out of sight round a corner. Andrew! Her impulse was to call to him, even run after him, but the person in the office was waiting for her, so she went to ask for the bottle-tops instead. It took a while for them to be located because one of the milkmen had put them in a safe place without mentioning it to anyone else, but presently Sally had the bag in her possession and was ready to leave.

She stepped out of the little office, looking around eagerly, hoping to see Andrew again, but she was out of luck. For a moment she thought of nipping around the site looking for him, then she thought better of it. If she was away from the depot for too long, Mr Overton wouldn't allow any similar outings again; but she hugged close to her heart the pleasure of having glimpsed Andrew. She might tease him before she let on where she'd caught sight of him.

That evening, Andrew was already there when Sally got in. He and his mother were sitting in the parlour. He got up to kiss her cheek, which made her smile to herself as she thought of the kisses that awaited her when they were on their own.

Andrew returned to his chair and Sally sank onto the arm, wanting to be close to him and delighting in the liberties that a fiancée was free to take but which would be severely frowned upon if a single girl dared behave in such a way.

She saw that she had walked into the middle of a conversation.

Mrs Henshaw said, 'So where was it you were today doing repairs after school?'

It was on the tip of Sally's tongue to join in, but Andrew said, 'West Didsbury,' and the conversation moved along.

'Go and freshen up, Sally,' said Mrs Henshaw, rising to her feet. 'I'll have tea on the table in fifteen minutes.'

Sally quickly did so. Then she ran back downstairs. Andrew

was in the front room, the door standing wide open in invitation. As Sally walked in, her handsome fiancé caught her up in a warm embrace that turned her bones to wax and temporarily banished her question from her mind.

When they broke apart, she said, 'I went to Chorlton Dairy this afternoon and I saw you there. You couldn't have gone to West Didsbury as well. There wouldn't have been time.'

Andrew looked at her for a long moment. 'What took you to the dairy?'

'Collecting the bottle-tops for salvage.'

Andrew nodded, his lips pressed together thoughtfully. 'I love you, Sally White. I never knew I could feel this way about anyone. You've opened up my heart in a way that's never happened before. You mean everything to me and I want to share every single aspect of my life with you – but I can't share this.' Speaking quietly, he asked, 'Do you trust me?'

'Of course.'

'Then please don't ask me again, because I'm not allowed to tell you.'

CHAPTER TWENTY-NINE

Betty checked her wristwatch, trying to do it with the tiniest movement of her arm and the lightest glance downwards so that Sally didn't notice. She didn't want to seem to be a slacker, but she was chilled through and weary to the bone after another night of fire-watching. Half an hour to go, then they could leave the roof – and, oh bliss, it was Saturday and her turn to have the day off.

'Penny for them,' Sally offered.

'I was just daydreaming about going to bed for a lie-in,' said Betty, 'but you know how it is. As much as you long for a proper sleep, it seems like there are better things to do.'

Truth be told, Betty always felt vaguely guilty about having her Saturdays off. It didn't seem fair for her to have the free time when Sally had a fiancé she could be with and Betty was all on her own.

The moment she opened the front door and entered Star House, Betty knew something was wrong. The atmosphere was charged with pain. Betty registered that even before she heard the crying.

Dropping her bag and her gas-mask box, she rushed into the sitting room and stopped in alarm at the sight of four distressed faces and one sombre one. The distressed faces belonged to Mrs Beaumont and the munitions girls. All four of them were weeping. The other person was an older man, stocky and grey-haired, with an air of competence. Was he the doctor? Was someone ill? Aside from being upset, the inhabitants of Star House looked all right.

'What's happened?' Betty asked, scared. 'What's the matter?'

Lottie pushed her fingers through her sandy hair. 'Oh, Betty, you won't believe it.'

Mary's blue eyes were swimming. 'Poor little Minnie. How could anybody be so *vile?*'

Mrs Beaumont seemed about to speak, then she pressed her knuckles to her mouth and shook her head. In her other hand she clutched a silk handkerchief. Heaving a deep breath into her lungs, she managed to say, 'You tell her, Mr Norbreck.'

Betty sank onto a chair.

'I'm the local vet,' Mr Norbreck began gravely.

'Minnie!' Betty exclaimed.

'I'm afraid so.'

'It's worse than that,' Stella blurted out. 'Whatever you're thinking, Betty, it's worse than that.' Fishing out her cigarettes, she struck a match with a hand that shook.

Betty gazed at Mr Norbreck. 'Is – is Minnie...?'

'Dead? I'm afraid so. It was all over before I arrived. At least it was quick. That's the good thing.'

'She was fine yesterday,' said Betty.

'Mr Norbreck says she was poisoned,' said Mary.

'Poisoned?' Betty repeated. 'How could she possibly have got hold of poison?'

'Someone, some swine, did it on purpose,' said Mrs Beaumont. 'Minnie loved snuffling about in the garden. All someone had to do...'

Betty opened her mouth but she was too shocked to speak.

'It isn't the first time I've seen it, I'm afraid,' said Mr Norbreck.

'She was a dachshund, you see. A German breed. People can be cruel.'

'And stupid,' Stella added.

'The real name of the Alsatian breed is the German shepherd,' added Mr Norbreck. 'It had to be changed in the last war for this very reason.'

'But who would...?' Betty asked.

'One of the neighbours, presumably,' said Mr Norbreck. 'You'll never find out unless they tell you and I'm sure they won't do that.'

'Oh, Mrs Beaumont,' said Betty, 'I'm so dreadfully sorry.'

'We all are,' said Lottie. 'We all loved her. She was a proper little character.'

'She's still in the other room, where I examined her,' said Mr Norbreck. 'Would you like me to remove the remains?'

Poor little Minnie. She wasn't a dog any longer. She was just remains. Betty's lungs constricted, making it hard to breathe.

Mrs Beaumont looked as if she might crumple, but then she straightened with dignity. 'No, thank you, Mr Norbreck. We'll bury her in the garden later on.'

'I'll be on my way, then,' said the vet.

Mary saw him out, then came back and sat with the rest of them. They all looked at one another and Betty was sure that the bleakness she saw in the others' eyes must be reflected in her own.

She knew what Mum would have said. She stood up. 'I'll put the kettle on.'

When she returned with the tray, Minnie's little body had been placed in her wicker basket on her red velvet cushion with the gold tassels.

Mrs Beaumont knocked back a cup of tea and polished off a cigarette in record time. She kept rubbing the heel of her hand against her chest.

She stood up. 'This isn't getting the baby bathed. I'll see to the breakfast.'

'We'll do it for you,' Lottie offered immediately.

'I'd rather be up and doing,' said their landlady.

Breakfast was a subdued affair. The girls speculated as to who might have done for Minnie until Mrs Beaumont put a stop to it.

'It's like Mr Norbreck said. We'll never know unless the cowardly brute admits it – and it'll be better for their sake if they never do, because this isn't something I'm going to forget in a hurry.'

After breakfast Mrs Beaumont sent Betty out to the pillar box on Beech Road to catch the eight o'clock collection. As Betty crossed the road to return to Star House, she heard her name being called and there was Sally on her way to the depot in the company of a handsome young man who must be her intended.

As Sally performed the introductions, Betty was struck by what gorgeous brown eyes Andrew had. His build was slim but he looked strong. Well, he worked in light rescue, didn't he, and you had to be strong to do that. Some folk thought that heavy rescue men must be stronger but actually heavy rescue called for men skilled in the use of special equipment. To do light rescue every night, a chap needed the ability to shift rubble and timber by hand for hours on end. That called for stamina as well as muscle.

Betty shook hands with him.

'Pleased to meet you,' he said.

'Charmed, I'm sure,' said Betty.

'Have you been crying?' Sally asked in a voice of concern.

Betty swiped a hand across her face. With a heavy heart, she explained about Minnie.

Sally caught her breath. 'Somebody poisoned her?'

'Looks like it,' said Betty. 'It's too horrid to think about.'

'Your poor landlady,' said Sally. 'She must be dreadfully upset.'

'We all are, but obviously it's much worse for her. Minnie was a sweet little thing and she loved attention. She might have been tiny but those little legs could walk like nobody's business. She loved being taken on the meadows. We're going to bury her in the garden this morning.'

'You'll need to bury her pretty deep,' said Andrew. 'With all the gardens being turned over to vegetable patches, and all eventually being turned back into proper gardens after the war, you wouldn't want to... What I mean is, you wouldn't want to dig her up by mistake.'

'Andrew!' Sally gave Andrew's arm a slap.

'I'm sorry but it's true,' he answered.

'We hadn't thought of that,' said Betty, worried. 'I don't fancy having to tell Mrs Beaumont.'

'I'm sure you'll put it far more tactfully,' said Sally.

'I've got an idea,' said Andrew. 'Let me help you with it. Don't do anything about the garden burial just yet. I'll walk Sally down to the depot and then I need to nip along somewhere else. You'll see why. Then I'll come to your house. Which one is it?' He looked past her.

Betty pointed. 'Star House.'

'I'll be along later,' said Andrew. 'Tell your landlady that Minnie is going to get a good send-off.'

In the sitting room in Star House, Andrew delved inside a large cloth bag and took out a wooden box, showing it to Mrs Beaumont and her billetees. It was larger than a shoebox and was neatly made, with a hinged lid and curvy carvings on the sides.

'Did you make that?' asked Lottie.

Andrew nodded. 'I always have some boxes and what-have-you kicking around. It comes of being a woodwork teacher.'

'It's beautiful,' said Betty. 'It's good to have a skill – but this is more than skill,' she said, looking at the carvings again. 'This shows... creativity and imagination. You're lucky to be so clever.'

'It needs a piece of material to line it,' said Andrew and everyone looked at Mrs Beaumont.

'I think we should use the cover from Minnie's special cushion,' she said.

Stella removed the cushion-pad and Mrs Beaumont fitted the ruby-red cover inside the box, arranging the gold tassels just so. Then she lifted the little body and laid it down tenderly, bending her head to give Minnie a final kiss.

'Fancy Minnie having a proper little coffin,' she murmured. Turning to Andrew she said, 'Thank you.'

'You're welcome,' he replied.

'Are you going to help us bury her in the garden?' Mary asked.

'Actually, I have a different idea – if you like the sound of it,' said Andrew. 'Betty said Minnie loved going for walks on the meadows so I thought we could bury her there.'

After a short silence filled with emotion, Mrs Beaumont said with a catch in her voice, 'That would be perfect,' and the girls chimed in with their agreement.

Betty couldn't help glancing sideways at Andrew. She was fascinated by the idea of Sally's whirlwind romance. Fancy getting engaged to someone you barely knew. It was the ultimate in love affairs. Betty wished a handsome man would sweep her off her feet like that. It wasn't just about romance or Andrew's good looks. For the first time she realised that love was about sharing problems. Imagine having a fella who would say, 'I'll help you deal with that.' Imagine having someone who could be utterly relied on. That would be the icing on the cake.

Putting on coats, hats and gloves, they set off. As they approached the salvage depot, they had to pause for a minute as the truck with the paper reversed into the yard. It was a flatbed lorry, its huge load of paper covered with a tarpaulin held down by ropes.

When the lorry vanished through the gates, the little funeral procession continued on its way to the meadows, Andrew carrying a spade and Stella holding the box reverently in both hands.

They walked for a while. In the October sunshine, the yellow daisy-style blooms of common ragwort gleamed like gold and the tiny white flowers of shepherd's purse looked like a spattering of snowflakes.

Presently Mrs Beaumont chose a place. Andrew dug out a section of bumpy turf, then the girls all took turns helping to dig the hole. Into this Mrs Beaumont placed the box. Andrew covered it first with soil and then with the turf, which he patted into place.

They all gazed at the little grave.

'Ought we to say something?' Lottie asked.

'Yes, please.' Mrs Beaumont wiped her face with her silk hanky, clearly too emotional to do the honours.

Betty drew a breath to steady herself. 'Dear Lord, please take care of the soul of darling Minnie. She was a little dog with a big heart and we all loved her.'

'That was very nice,' Andrew said gently. 'Well done.'

The munitions girls echoed his words.

Mrs Beaumont sighed heavily. 'And now I suppose we'd better go home.'

CHAPTER THIRTY

Dad came over from Withington to see Sally on Saturday evening. When he walked into the Henshaws' parlour, Sally flew into his arms for a hug. As Andrew stood up to shake hands, Sally looked anxiously at her father's beloved face. Although his weary eyes were sunken into caverns of bone, their expression was soft with affection. As always, he brought the familiar aroma of pipe tobacco with him.

'Is everything all right?' Sally asked.

'Of course it is, love. Nothing to worry about. I'm here because I wanted to see you with my own eyes. I just – well, I felt the need, that's all. It's these dratted air raids. They've got everyone on edge with worry about their loved ones.'

'Oh, Dad, it's wonderful to see you,' said Sally, remembering how she had insisted upon going over to Withington on that other occasion even though she'd had to come back to Chorlton in time to go on duty for the night.

'Things have been bad for Manchester recently,' said Dad. 'As ARP wardens, we have to keep a record of every explosive that's dropped, complete with a map. They're called tracings because we trace over a local map, but we only include the relevant information, which makes them easier to read.'

Sally shuddered. 'It can't be easy doing that when you know of the damage that's been done.'

'Not to mention the casualties,' Mrs Henshaw added.

'Exactly,' Dad said in a sober voice. 'Remember when we all had to fill in that census before the war, so the authorities would know exactly who lived where? Well, these tracings will be for the bomb census of Manchester.'

Sally didn't want to hear anything more about that. 'I know it sounds selfish, but the most important thing to me is for the Whites and the Henshaws to come through it safe and well.'

'That's all any family can hope for,' said Andrew.

'Very true,' Dad agreed. 'Long may our luck hold out.'

'If you're not on duty tonight, Mr White,' said Mrs Henshaw, 'you're more than welcome to stop here for the whole evening. I'm going out on WVS duty, but the children will enjoy your company.'

'Honestly, Mum,' Andrew said indignantly but also with affection. 'The children!'

His mother chuckled. 'It doesn't matter how old you get, Andrew. You'll always be my boy. Now I've got Sally too and she'll always be a young lass to me.'

Dad didn't stay. He wanted to get home to Mum. Sally felt a pang as she said goodbye, and found herself having to blink back some unexpected tears. She thought of herself as a sensible person, but right now Withington felt a very long way away and she would have given anything to have her darling mum and dad a lot closer.

Andrew behaved like his normal self as the evening went on, but Sally sensed... something. She decided to have a proper talk with him once his mother had set off for her WVS stint.

As soon as Mrs Henshaw had departed, Andrew caught Sally to him and kissed her, holding her face in his hands. It wasn't what she was expecting but she responded willingly. When the kiss ended, he ran his hands down her arms and back up to her shoulders. Then he leaned his forehead against hers, breathing deeply, his chest rising and falling. When he shut his eyes and left them closed for a long time, Sally became acutely aware once more of whatever it was that she had sensed in him earlier on. Lifting his forehead from hers, he opened his eyes, and a tremor of shock tingled through Sally when she saw the gleam of tears.

'Andrew, what is it?'

He took her hand. 'Come and sit down. I've got something important to tell you.'

They sat on the sofa. Sally moved as close to him as she could get without actually sitting on his knee.

'Darling,' she whispered.

Andrew didn't speak. Had he changed his mind or couldn't he find the words? As much as Sally longed to offer a word of encouragement, some inner wisdom made her hold her tongue and allow him to bring himself to the moment in his own good time.

'That box we put Minnie in,' he started softly. 'I didn't make it at school.' He stopped, then he took a deep breath, and out came what was troubling him so deeply. 'I'm not supposed to talk about this. I'm not supposed to tell you or anyone – ever – and I agreed to the rules, but that was before I met you, before you became the most important person in my life.'

Sally's pulse raced. Her hand lifted of its own accord, but she dropped it back before she could touch his face, stroke his cheek.

'I can't lie to you,' Andrew said earnestly. 'I just can't. I might as well try to lie to myself. When you saw me at the dairy and I said I couldn't tell you what I was doing there... I want to tell you. I need you to know. I need you to understand.'

'What is it?' Sally asked softly.

'It's war work. That's why I was at the dairy. That's where I do it. Not at the dairy itself, but in a building in a little copse behind it. There are two of us, both carpenters. The other chap is an old boy, retired, so he can be there most of the time. But me... I have to have a – a story to hide behind. My story is that I do minor repairs on damaged houses – and I do have to do a bit of that just to keep my story straight. But my main war work, my real war work, is that... that I make coffins.'

Now he moved his head and looked straight at her, deep into her eyes. Sally saw anguish and bleakness in her husband's attractive dark eyes instead of the warmth and kindness she was accustomed to.

'I make coffins,' he said again. 'There are cardboard factories making cardboard coffins for all the unidentified bodies there are certain to be, but wooden boxes will be needed in great quantity as well.' His voice dropped almost to a whisper. 'You have no idea how many people are expected to die – to be killed. It's – it's appalling.'

Sally went hot and cold all over. 'Hundreds and hundreds?'

'It's more than that, my darling. Thousands. Tens of thousands. It isn't just on the battlefields that there will be huge loss of life. It will happen here too. Tens of thousands of civilians. It's bad enough when servicemen are killed – but civilians...'

'It doesn't bear thinking about,' said Sally. Then understanding began to dawn in her. 'But you think about it all the time because of this job you're doing. You're surrounded by the thought of it.'

Andrew nodded slowly. 'I don't just build coffins for adults. I make them for children, for babies.'

Sally uttered a wordless cry. Andrew's fingers tightened round her hand.

He continued, 'And then there are the small boxes for the... well, for what's left when a person or a group of people gets blown to pieces – literally blown to pieces. That's how I was able to produce the box for Minnie when it was needed. I'd already made it. I make so many of these boxes, so many coffins of all sizes. I know it has to be done, but there are times when... when it feels as though I'm inviting death. This isn't like peacetime, when coffins are built to order. These days, we're making them as fast as we can, knowing they're all going to get filled.' After a moment, he added, 'I wasn't supposed to tell you.'

Sally forced aside a sensation of horror. All she wanted was to support her darling fiancé and remove some of the burden from his shoulders. She wanted to show herself to be a worthwhile wife.

'I'm glad you told me,' she said fervently. 'I hate to think of you living with this responsibility and having to keep it to yourself. And all the time you have to present an ordinary face to the world. You must have been under such strain. What can I do to help? I'll do anything.'

'I don't know what you can do. I don't think there's anything.'

Sally's heart swelled. She loved this man so much.

'Listen to me,' she said. 'I know plenty of married couples who share the view that it's the man's job to take care of his wife, to make the decisions, to shelter her from all life's problems, from writing the cheques to driving the motor-car if they're lucky enough to possess one. But that's not what I want for us. That's not the kind of wife I want to be. I will always want you to cherish me and take care of me, but I also want to look after you. I want you to know you can lean on me if you need to. It won't make you any less of a man. It will show that you're a man who trusts and respects his wife and who sees marriage as a partnership. That's the sort of husband I want, a man who has the strength to admit when things are hard, a man who knows the value of sharing life's problems, whatever they may be, a man who knows that I'm strong enough to help carry the burden.'

'It's hard for me to agree to that,' said Andrew, 'because men are meant to be the strong ones, the ones who do all the looking after and shoulder all the responsibilities. I don't want you to think less of me.'

'I would never think less of you for seeing me as an equal partner,' said Sally, looking into his face and searching his eyes. 'I'd love you all the more for it. My mother has never signed a cheque in her life – and that's something she's proud of, because it means she had a responsible father, and now a responsible husband, to do all the men's jobs in the family relationship. But you and I are from a new generation and the war demands that we are capable and independent. It also means we're going to lean on one another all the more for love and support. I'm not just your future wife, Andrew Henshaw, I'm your friend, your best friend. You can talk to me about anything and I'll love you even more deeply because of it, because it will bring us closer. So I'll ask you again. With your dreadful responsibility for making coffins and knowing they're going to be used for the war dead from our local area, possibly even for people you know personally, what can I do to help you carry the burden?'

And at last Andrew smiled, though his warm brown eyes brimmed with sadness.

'You've already done it,' he whispered.

CHAPTER THIRTY-ONE

Betty and Sally were on the depot roof, awaiting the nightly raid. It wasn't a question of *if* a raid would take place. The only question was what time it would kick off. Anxiety sent Betty's insides tightening one moment and quivering the next, but at the same time she set her jaw resolutely.

'I got a postcard from Dad yesterday,' she told Sally. 'He said he'd arrange to be in Etchell's between eight and nine this evening and tomorrow evening too. That's the newsagent he gets his paper from. They have a little booth with a telephone.'

'Were you able to get through?' Sally asked.

Betty nodded. 'I had to queue for ages outside the telephone box, but I got in at ten to nine.'

Sally smiled. 'Just in time.'

'With a bit of luck, we'll have longer tomorrow,' said Betty. She was counting on it.

'It must have been good to hear his voice,' said Sally.

For a moment, Betty couldn't speak. Hearing Dad's beloved voice had warmed her all the way down to her toes. 'Oh, it was. It reminded me how much I love and miss him – which is stupid, because it's not as though I could ever forget those things – but somehow talking to him brought them back in full force. I hate to think of him out on duty in the air raids. Mind you, I'm sure he goes through the same worry on my account.'

'Of course he does. That's why he sent you the postcard. He needed to hear your voice every bit as much as you needed to hear his.'

Betty smiled, glad of Sally's understanding. She didn't ask the question aloud, but she wondered if it was mean of her to relish speaking to Dad on his own, just the two of them. Ever since he had married Grace, Betty seldom got him to herself, or that was how it felt.

Sally changed the subject. 'I heard that Stretford had it bad last night. A long line of incendiaries was dropped all the way across the town from one side to the other. There were lots of serious incidents, apparently. There were casualties in Trafford Park and Urmston too, but there were no gas attacks, fortunately.' She gave a delicate shudder. 'I can't help thinking of my deconta-mination training.'

'It must have been harrowing to do,' said Betty, trying to visu-alise herself in that position. 'Thank goodness no gas-bombs have been dropped – so far. Just the thought of them...'

'We're all scared of gas-bombs,' said Sally. 'People of our age grew up seeing men who were permanent invalids after being gassed last time round.'

'I take it you heard about the bombs that landed on the mead-ows,' said Betty, 'though they were mainly on the Sale side of the Mersey.'

'It's surprising how quickly you get to care about a place,' Sally observed. 'I've lived in Withington all my life, but now I love Chorlton too.'

Betty gave her a nudge. 'And of course it has nothing to do with having a handsome fiancé who's Chorlton born and bred.'

Sally nudged her back, obviously delighted with the tease.

It was then that the siren began its nightly wailing, the eerie tones making the hairs stand up one by one on Betty's arms. Almost at once guns started banging, sounding close by, then more distant, then closer again as the ack-ack guns swung round in different directions in response to the enemy planes droning overhead. Searchlights reached up into the sky, hunting for Jerry.

Instinctively Betty hunched her shoulders as a loud screaming sound told of a whole stick of bombs hurtling to earth. Explosions followed and Chorlton shook, the night lighting up as fires started.

'Incendiaries!' Sally shouted.

Several landed on the depot's roof. Betty froze, then her training took over and she darted towards the pile of sandbags, grabbed one and scurried across the roof to smother an incendiary, Sally doing likewise. They both hurried back to the pile to fetch a second sandbag each to tackle two more. A third dash to the pile saw off the final pair of incendiaries.

The sound of Betty's heart thrashed in her ears. She stared at Sally, knowing all too well that they couldn't use any of the sandbags a second time in case the devices underneath were still active. Now there were just two sandbags left up here on the roof.

'Should we fetch more up?' asked Betty.

'We might need them in the yard,' said Sally. 'And we've got the Redhill up here.'

Betty gazed into the night.

'Here comes another lot,' she said as Jerry dropped incendiaries in a line across their part of Chorlton. Would more land on the depot?

No. Betty's legs went wobbly with relief, not least at the thought of the lorry and its fuel tank in the yard below.

But Sally gave a huge gasp and pointed over Betty's shoulder. Betty spun round, but there was nothing to see.

'It's gone down the chimney,' said Sally. 'Quick! The whole place could go up.'

She grabbed the Redhill container and its hoe. Betty snatched one of the remaining precious sandbags. Opening the skylight, she dropped the sandbag through, then took the hoe from Sally and they both climbed down the ladder, fighting to hang on to the equipment that they couldn't afford to drop for fear of damaging it.

At the foot of the ladder, Betty bent to seize the sandbag and the two girls ran down the narrow staircase to the floor below. All the doors were closed.

Sally pointed. 'That room is above Mr Overton's office, so that's where the chimney is.'

They halted outside. Betty met Sally's determined gaze with a resolute nod, then they both knelt down, one on each side of the door, as they had been trained to do. Betty set down the sandbag within easy reach, holding the hoe's handle in one hand. Then she leaned across to turn the knob and push the door open. That way, any flames or smoke that spurted forth would, God willing, go over their heads.

There was no hot whoosh. There was – nothing. Betty scrabbled in her pocket for her torch and shone it inside. The tissue-dimmed beam picked out the chimney-breast in the far wall, but the fireplace had been boarded up.

There was an audible gasp from Sally. 'If the incendiary has got stuck inside the old grate, we'll have to tear down those boards. We don't have things like crowbars and pickaxes,' she added desperately.

'We ought to check the fireplace in Mr Overton's office before we try anything drastic up here.' Betty reached for the sandbag. 'Come on. If that's where the incendiary has ended up, we need to get down there before it can send the office up in flames.'

They ran downstairs to the ground floor and repeated the procedure of opening the door. Again, no scalding heat emerged. The office itself was not on fire – but the long incendiary could be seen standing inside the fireplace, leaning against the chimney wall. Dear heaven, if it exploded, it would take the entire chimney stack with it and they would lose a whole section of the depot from here all the way up to the roof.

'We need to get it in the Redhill,' said Sally.

There was no time to lose. Instinct might say to edge forward with extreme caution, but the situation necessitated immediate and decisive action. Automatically, the girls split apart, approaching the fireplace from different sides, so that if the worst should happen to one of them the other would still be there to finish the job.

'Shame it didn't bounce out onto the hearth,' said Betty, amazed at how calm she sounded. 'That would have made it a doddle to pick up.'

As it was, the incendiary was propped inside the grate in the ashes from yesterday's fire. Sally positioned the Redhill on the tiled hearth and Betty took a firm grasp on the handle of the hoe.

'Can you lift it out of the fireplace?' Sally asked.

Betty weighed her options. The hoe was supposed to draw the incendiary towards the container, not pick it up. If she picked it up and it rolled off...

She bobbed down, dimly aware of Sally's urgent exclamation of 'No!' behind her. She pulled the metal-barred piece at the front of the grate away from the fireplace, bringing yesterday's ashes spilling out onto the hearth. Then she angled the hoe behind the incendiary and carefully, hardly breathing, brought it forward while Sally pushed the container closer.

The incendiary entered the container and, even as Sally pushed down the protective cover, there was a flash of startling white light. Sally slammed the lid shut, the Redhill shuddering in her hands. There was no time to feel scared or relieved or anything. Betty picked up the sandbag and dumped it into the fireplace just in case. Dust and ashes rose in a cloud and she coughed, but there wasn't even time to catch her breath properly before she found herself doing what the emergency demanded and rushing to the window.

She tried to yell, 'Incendiaries!', but her throat was still filled with dust, so she turned huge eyes towards Sally as she pointed into the yard. They hurtled outside, where several incendiaries lay on the ground, biding their time. Darting across to the pile of sand, Betty snatched one of the spades and thrust it in, balancing it carefully as she hastened across the yard to dump the sand on top of one of the incendiaries. Then she ran back again. Each incendiary would need three or four spadefuls to make sure. She and Sally ran to and fro, working swiftly.

A great hiss and a flash of dazzling light spurted from the top of one of the tarpaulins. Flames immediately began to lick the surface of the sturdy fabric.

'Water!' cried Sally.

Betty grabbed one of the filled buckets and hefted it across the yard. Sally overtook her, carrying the stirrup-pump. Water sloshed as Betty dumped the bucket on the ground. Taking the pump, she plunged it into the water before grasping the handle and thrusting it down and up again, down and up, down and up, while Sally directed the hose. With dust still clogging her throat, Betty fought to breathe through her nose as her shoulder muscles strained to produce the steady flow of water until the bucket was empty. She ran for another bucket, a thrill of alarm passing through her at the sight of another couple of incendiaries lying innocently on the ground, but she and Sally must deal with the fire first and the stirrup-pump was a two-man job.

With the stench of doused fire invading her nostrils, Betty resumed pumping, knowing that they were winning the battle against this particular incendiary. Then her heart leaped as the depot seemed to be suddenly flooded with people bearing sandbags and stirrup-pumps. Reinforcements! Fresh determination coursed through Betty's veins and she felt as if she could fight for ever.

The incendiary on the tarpaulin fizzed into submission, but there was no time for triumph. Helped by two ARP wardens, the girls dragged the tarp to the ground, roughly folding it in on itself.

'Let's drag it out into the middle of the road,' said one of the wardens. 'That way, if it catches fire, it won't do any harm. Leave it to us, ladies,' he added as if Betty and Sally were mere bystanders; but, just as there had been no time for triumph, there wasn't time to feel miffed either.

'Someone ought to drive that lorry to safety,' said Betty.

'What's under the tarpaulin?' asked one of the wardens.

'Paper,' said Betty. 'Can anyone drive?'

'It doesn't matter if they can,' said Sally. 'The delivery man took the key and also a piece from the engine.'

'That'll be the rotor-arm,' said one of the ARP men. 'It's the law. All vehicles have to be disabled when they're parked in case Jerry parachutes in.'

There was nothing to be done about the lorry.

'We ought to check the incendiary in the office,' said Sally.

When they opened the Redhill container and looked at the incendiary, it seemed dead and undoubtedly was dead, but it wasn't worth the risk, not when you'd seen the sort of damage one of these things was capable of.

'Let's get it outdoors,' said Betty.

She carried the Redhill into the yard, Sally holding the doors for her.

Sally gave an exclamation and Betty swiftly followed her gaze in the direction of the lorry. A curling stream of smoke was rising from the tarpaulin that was secured over the paper to the edges of the flatbed. Quickly the girls stowed the Redhill and seized sand-buckets before running to the lorry, yelling for help.

They dumped the buckets on the ground, then Sally helped Betty scramble up before heaving the buckets after her. With a bucket in each hand, Betty tottered across the uneven surface to unload the sand. There was a tear in the sturdy fabric.

Fear poured through her. 'An incendiary has gone straight through,' she called.

'Get down from there,' ordered an ARP man. 'We need to get all the paper off the lorry. There's a chance a fire could have started deep inside. Paper smoulders and then it goes up like a firework.'

Sally assisted Betty to clamber down, then they worked alongside the others to unfasten the rope holding the tarpaulin in position, untying knots and urgently feeding the rope through ringed holes. While the men heaved the tarpaulin out into the road to join the other one, Sally and Betty climbed onto the flatbed and started dragging the bundles of paper to the edge of the lorry and tipping them off. This was easier said than done because the bundles were astonishingly heavy. Betty's arms practically left their shoulder sockets. All the while her eardrums were battered by the roar of explosions and the boom of ack-ack gunfire.

A blast somewhere along the road made the earth shiver. The lorry vibrated and the girls fell over backward, but there was no time to waste feeling winded. They scrambled onto their knees and then their feet and carried on manhandling the bundles, each one seeming heavier and bulkier than the last, and tipping them over onto the ground for the men to drag to safety.

'It's getting hot here in the middle,' Betty shouted.

'Here,' yelled the warden. 'You might need this.'

He threw a dustbin lid onto the back of the lorry. A dustbin lid! They had used these in their training with the flash-bangs. Would a real incendiary prove to be more powerful?

Betty thought of what the ARP warden had said about a smouldering fire, but she mustn't stop. She had a job to do. She was just grateful she'd had the chance to speak to Dad earlier on. If this was the night when she copped it, at least Dad would have the memory of that.

A few minutes later the girls had made their way down to the incendiary – and not a moment too soon. There was a fizz and a dazzle and Betty thrust the dustbin lid on top of it. Sally dragged a bundle on top to hold the lid down.

There was a *whump* from underneath and the girls fell back – literally. The layers of bundles gave a little jump before settling back. The ARP wardens yelled for water and bucket after bucket was handed up to Betty and Sally so they could damp down the paper that was most at risk. Betty was exhausted right down to her bones, but at the same time she felt invigorated and full to the brim with resolution. She would keep at it for as long as she had to.

A couple of men who had until now been tackling incendiaries climbed onto the lorry and started chucking off dry bundles. At long last, only the unsafe bundles, now sopping wet, were left.

'It doesn't matter how wet they are,' said one of the men. 'We can't leave them here, not with fuel in the tank. We can't take the chance.'

So the wet bundles, even heavier than the dry ones, were removed, as was the incendiary, courtesy of the Redhill. The air stank of smoke and dirt.

'Well done, girls,' said an ARP man.

'We'd best get back up to the roof now,' said Sally, 'and check that the incendiaries up there haven't ignited and started smouldering.'

When they emerged from the skylight, it was frankly impossible not to stop for a moment to gaze at the fires in the distance – all the different distances on all sides.

'That must be Didsbury.' Sally stared, her voice hollow. 'My friend's Auntie Winnie and Auntie Maggie live in West Didsbury. And those fires over that way… Hulme. And over there, is that Northenden? Oh my goodness.'

All Betty's attention meanwhile was locked onto where she thought Salford was. Oh please let Dad be safe, and the Tuckers and everyone she knew, Grace included, but most of all Dad, her lovely dad. She couldn't lose him as well as Mum.

In a faraway sort of voice, she said, 'When we were busy rushing around extinguishing the incendiaries, I felt all invigorated and capable of anything, but seeing this now... well, it makes you think. It makes you *feel*.'

How inadequate her words seemed. Sally could probably have expressed it much better, but Betty didn't have the words. All she had was feelings. Their actions tonight had inspired courage and resolution, and now there was the sobering certainty of the damage and the loss of life that had occurred, if not here then elsewhere.

And this was just the beginning of the war. Look how long the previous one had lasted.

CHAPTER THIRTY-TWO

As the time ticked towards six o'clock and the end of their duty, Sally rubbed her gloved hands up and down her arms and lifted the woolly scarf Mum had knitted for her, so that it covered her chin and mouth. Then she had to jerk her chin to free her mouth in order to say, 'We aren't far into October and already the nights are jolly cold. Heaven only knows what it's going to be like up here on the depot roof in the depths of winter.'

Betty smiled wryly. 'Mind you, all that dashing about earlier on kept us warm at the time.'

'Put like that, I'd be happy to freeze,' said Sally. 'I wouldn't wish an air raid on anybody.'

'Hear, hear.'

All the fires were out now, but the smell of smoke lingered in the air. What damage would be seen when daylight emerged? Impulsively Sally turned to Betty and gave her a hug.

'What's that for?' Betty asked in surprise.

'Because we dealt with all those incendiaries and prevented the depot from catching fire. Because we helped with the paper-lorry.'

Betty hugged her back. 'We didn't do badly, did we?' She let go and checked her wristwatch. 'Almost six.'

'Hallelujah,' said Sally.

She wanted nothing more than to race home and see her darling Andrew. He'd been out on duty last night too and she needed to know he was safe. He would certainly have been called out to attend rescues. She wanted to see Andrew's mother as well. Mrs Henshaw had been on duty at the rest centre, looking after people who had lost their homes. There would be plenty more work to do at the rest centre all day and in the days ahead, providing clothing and other necessities for folk who had lost everything, helping them to fill in forms to make their claims, and finding them somewhere to live.

Gathering up their things, the girls climbed through the skylight and down the ladder. They changed their tin helmets for hats and went to the front door. Sally turned back in surprise when Betty didn't follow her outside.

'One of us ought to stay here until a fire officer checks the chimney for us,' said Betty. 'Just in case.'

'I hadn't thought of that.' Sally could have kicked herself.

'You're too busy being keen to get home to your Andrew.'

'Yes, actually. But you're right. Someone ought to stay on the premises for the time being. I'll stay.'

'Why you?' Betty asked in a mild voice. 'You aren't the captain of the ship.'

Yes, why her? Good question. The truth was that, after the interest she had taken in salvage work and the effort she'd invested in this new job, Sally did feel – well, she did feel she took it more seriously than Betty did. Not that Betty wasn't good at it. But Sally had something inside her that revelled in working and made her want to immerse herself in it and be the best at it. Even when she and Deborah had worked in the typing pool, Sally had secretly imagined herself one day becoming the supervisor, allocating the letters and reports to the various girls and checking their work afterwards – though she drew the line at employing her ruler to rap the knuckles of any typist who had made a mistake. As well as being painful, it was humiliating for the girl it happened to, and Sally didn't believe that was the right way to treat people.

So yes, she did feel it was her responsibility to wait for the fire officer. She glanced at Betty, hoping Betty couldn't read her mind. She would hate to give the impression of being a bossy-boots. The last thing she wanted was to put Betty off being chums with her.

She smiled warmly at her colleague. 'Thanks for offering. You're right. I am dying to get home.'

'Take your time,' said Betty. Her peachy complexion was covered in dirt. 'When you come back, I'll dash home.' She smiled and her dimple appeared through the grime. 'Teamwork.'

Sally didn't exactly run home but she certainly walked at top speed. As she approached the house, a van drew up outside, a door was flung open and Andrew jumped down to the pavement, his face smudged with grime beneath his tin helmet. As Sally flew to meet him, he strode forward and clasped her to him. Sally's hat tilted sideways and fell off. After he had kissed her, Andrew bent down to retrieve it.

'That's the best possible welcome home,' he said.

'What, knocking my hat off?'

'Having you racing to meet me.'

Grimy faces grinned at them from the van's bench seat and Sally heard cheering too, but she was too happy and grateful to have Andrew safe and sound to feel embarrassed. She knew what Mum would say. 'Making a holy show of yourself in front of the neighbours.'

'Here comes your mother,' said Sally as Mrs Henshaw, dressed in her green uniform, came along the road. She looked severe but that might have been tiredness. Then she saw them and her smile softened her features.

Sally and Andrew stood with an arm round one other, each of them reaching out their free arm to draw Mrs Henshaw into a family embrace. Warm satisfaction spread through Sally's body and the tiredness she felt at having been up all night changed from exhausting to fulfilling. The Henshaws – she counted herself as a Henshaw – were all together, just the way they ought to be. Sally just needed to know that Mum and Dad were all right and then all would be well with her world.

'We can't stand out here cuddling on the pavement,' said Mrs Henshaw. 'Let's get indoors. I'm dying for a cuppa.'

They went inside. It ought to be the most ordinary thing in the world, stepping over their own threshold. They ought to be able to take it for granted, but you couldn't these days. Everything was different in wartime. Something as basic as opening your front door after an air raid brought gratitude rising to the surface simply because you still had a front door to open. Other folk didn't. Other folk emerged from shelters or returned home after a long night on duty to find a heap of rubble where their beloved home used to be or that the roof was gone or that the whole of the front of the house had been blown off, leaving all the rooms on display, like a giant dolls' house.

'Let's get the kettle on,' said Sally, 'and sort out some breakfast.'

She took a moment to gaze at her handsome, clever, loving fiancé and his kind, sensible mother who had made her so welcome.

The Henshaws. Safe and sound.

'So you've finally decided to turn up for work, have you, Miss Hughes?' Mr Overton said with heavy sarcasm when Betty walked into the depot, having raced home to Star House for a quick wash and brush-up and a bite to eat – well, she'd intended it to be no more than a bite, but Mrs Beaumont took great pride in her breakfasts and Betty had been obliged to sit at the table for porridge and toast.

And now here she was, getting it in the neck from Mr Overton – and after the night she'd had!

Sally was hovering behind their boss. 'Mr Overton, as I've tried to explain—'

Mr Overton made a swatting motion with one hand. 'There's no need for explanations, thank you, Miss White. Clearly you and Miss Hughes believe you can take advantage. The rules are clear. Your fire-watching duty ends at six o'clock and, since you both live close by, that gives you ample time to go home and return here promptly. I personally manage it without any trouble and I live the furthest away, but apparently it's too much to ask the same of you.'

Turning smartly on his heel, Mr Overton marched away, leaving the girls staring after him.

'That's so unfair,' said Betty.

'I did try to tell him why you weren't here on the dot.' Sally's fawny-hazel eyes were filled with concern. 'It's my fault. I should have been quicker at home.'

Betty tried to shrug it off. 'It doesn't matter.'

But it did. By nature she was a follower of rules and it was unsettling to be accused of flouting them. It made her squirm inside, the same way she had when she had fallen out of favour with Mr Tucker.

'Has the fire officer been yet?' she asked.

'Not yet,' Sally confirmed.

They settled down to work. The first job was to refill the fire buckets and sweep the skirts of the sand back into the pile. Then they had to sort through the books that had been donated for paper salvage. Those in the best condition would be sent to public libraries or to the troops abroad.

Sally held out a book for Betty to see. 'Look at this. Leather cover, gilt-tipped pages. It looks old. More to the point, it looks like it might be valuable.'

'How can you tell?'

'Well, I can't, not really,' Sally admitted, 'but maybe we should ask a book expert to take a look. If this is worth something, it would raise money for the war effort.'

'Where are we going to find a book expert?' Betty asked. 'At the library?'

'More likely in a bookshop that specialises in old books, I should think.' Sally gave her head a little shake. 'Anyway, it isn't up to us. I'll show this to Mr Overton.'

She set the book aside and they carried on. They were halfway through when a man walked in. He was tall, with a rangy build and sallow skin.

'Morning, ladies. I'm Mr Garside, the fire officer. I gather there were incendiaries here last night. I'll go and see Mr Overton. His office is this way, isn't it?'

'We were the ones on duty,' said Sally.

'Good-o,' said Mr Garside and headed into the building.

Honestly! As if they couldn't speak for themselves.

They got on with sorting out the books, finding another couple that they set aside. A few minutes later, Mr Overton and Mr Garside emerged from the building.

'I've been up to the roof and that's fine. The yard looks all right as well. Thank you, Mr Overton. I'll add the depot to my report.'

'What about the incendiary that went down the chimney?' asked Sally.

Mr Garside looked startled. 'I knew nothing of that.'

'You didn't ask,' Betty murmured.

Mr Garside took on a completely different attitude. He had seemed rather complacent before. Now he was brisk. 'Show me,' he ordered sharply.

The girls led the way to the office.

'What happened?' asked Mr Garside. 'Tell me exactly.'

'We were on the roof,' said Betty. 'Some incendiaries fell and we smothered them. Then Miss White saw one go down the chimney.'

'We came in here,' Sally continued, 'and scooped it into the Redhill container. We put that sandbag into the grate to be on the safe side.'

Mr Overton's eyebrows climbed up his forehead. 'I hadn't noticed. I don't normally allow myself a fire until the afternoon.'

'Goodness me.' There was a note of alarm in Mr Garside's voice. 'I'll get the whole of the chimney inspected. Well done, ladies,' he added, turning to them with an admiring look on his face. To Mr Overton he said, 'Your two young ladies could well have saved the depot from disaster with their quick thinking and common sense.'

'Thank you, sir,' said Sally.

'You two deserve to get one of these new George Crosses for this,' Mr Garside declared. 'Have you heard of them? They're the highest civilian award for bravery. Named after the King.'

'Crikey,' Betty murmured.

'If I'd been aware that an incendiary had dropped down the chimney, I'd have put you at the top of my list,' said Mr Garside. 'May I use your telephone, Overton? Jolly good show, ladies.'

The girls stared at one another. Betty struggled to take it in. They had saved the depot. They had simply done their duty, done what they'd been trained to do – and, according to the fire officer, they had saved the depot.

CHAPTER THIRTY-THREE

Sally knew she ought to feel proud that she and Betty had saved the depot – and she was proud – but mostly what she felt was... shock. If she hadn't happened to be looking in the direction of the chimney-pots at that precise moment... if the incendiary had had time to ignite...

It was possible to push such thoughts aside to an extent, but her feelings refused to be ignored. At different times throughout that day, she found herself drawing her mouth into a straight line and biting her lip, or squeezing her eyes shut as she touched her throat. Several times her skin went chilly all over.

'It brought home to me how everything could change for ever in a single moment,' she told Andrew and his mother that evening when they were sitting together, smoking and chatting. Sally had been fairly quiet since she got home, but now she wanted to talk.

Mrs Henshaw smiled fondly at her. 'It shows what a good sort you are, love. Plenty would be all puffed up with pride at what they'd done – and I'm not saying you shouldn't feel proud. But you think more deeply than that and I respect you for it. I shall like having a daughter-in-law I can admire.'

'I shall like you having a daughter-in-law you can admire too,' said Andrew.

'Stop it, the pair of you,' said Sally, but it was thrilling to know she was thought well of.

There was a knock at the front door. Sally stood up, blowing out a final stream of tobacco smoke as she ground out the stub in the ashtray. Closing the parlour door to keep the light in, she went along the dark hallway to open the front door.

'Hello, Sally,' said Mum.

Sally drew her into the house, shutting the door before hugging her.

'This is a surprise. Give me your coat.'

When they entered the parlour, Andrew rose politely and greetings were exchanged.

Once everyone was settled, Mrs Henshaw asked, 'What brings you here, Mrs White? Not that we aren't pleased to see you.' She had hardly finished before she added, 'Daft question. You're here to see Sally. You needed to see for yourself that she's all right.'

There was the slightest of hesitations before Mum answered. 'Well, yes – of course.'

Sally could tell that it was something else that had brought Mum here, but all she said was, 'I'm glad to see you too, Mum. Is Dad all right?'

'He's at a meeting.'

'ARP?' Andrew asked.

'Bowls club. They're sorting out the matches for next season.' Mum smiled and her tight expression relaxed. 'I've never before seen the need for ordinary folk such as ourselves to have a domestic telephone, but now I'd give anything to be able to ring Sally after a bad night like last night.'

'I know, Mum,' said Sally. 'I worry about you and Dad too.'

'Your dad says Northenden and East and West Didsbury copped it last night,' said Mum.

Sally remembered seeing the fires from the depot roof. It gave her no pleasure to have been correct in her guesses. 'I'm glad Withington was spared.'

'I'd rather the bombs dropped on me than on you,' said Mum.

'Many a mother feels that way,' said Mrs Henshaw. 'Your lovely daughter was a heroine last night.'

And out came the tale of the incendiaries that had fallen on the depot. Mum pressed splayed fingers to her bosom when she heard about the one that had dropped down the chimney and how Sally and Betty had raced downstairs to tackle it.

'There's no doubt the girls saved the depot from going up in smoke,' said Andrew, pride shining in his brown eyes. 'The fire officer said so when he went to do his inspection this morning.'

'Well, I don't know what to think. I'm proud of you, Sally, obviously, but it sends shivers down my spine to picture you in danger.' Mum shook her head, huffing out a breath. 'I must say that wasn't what I expected to be talking about when I came round.'

'What did you expect?' Sally asked. She knew there was something.

'If it's private, Sally,' said Mrs Henshaw, 'you can take your mother into the front room.'

'No,' said Sally even as her mother started to get to her feet, causing Mum to freeze halfway. Sally looked squarely at her. 'There's nothing that can't be said in front of Andrew and his mother,' she said firmly.

Mum sank down again. 'Oh. Well.' Then she pushed back her shoulders and gave Sally a straight look. 'Your father didn't want me to say. He said there was no need to tell you.'

'Tell me what?'

'It's Rod,' said Mum.

'Rod?' Sally exclaimed, fire springing into her cheeks. '*Mum!*'

'You're the one who wanted me to say,' Mum retorted.

'What about him?' Andrew asked in a calm voice.

'He's got married,' said Mum.

'*What?*' said Sally.

'You heard. On a special licence. It came as a bolt out of the blue to his parents. Rod sent them a letter from up in Barrow. They haven't even met this girl. It's the talk of the street.'

'Is this the fellow Sally left Andrew for?' asked Mrs Henshaw in a mild voice that didn't quite conceal her avid interest.

'Yes,' said Mum.

'He didn't waste any time,' commented Mrs Henshaw.

Sally spoke from her heart. 'I just hope he treats his wife better than he treated me.'

'We all hope that.' Mum twitched her shoulders in a theatrical shudder.

Andrew cleared his throat. 'I think that's enough on this particular subject.'

'I agree,' said Sally. 'Thank you for telling me, Mum. I wish Rod well and I'm glad he's found happiness elsewhere.'

'Well, I hope he has, for his sake,' said Mum, adding darkly, 'or is he on the rebound?'

'It's really none of our business,' Sally said, but she was thinking about the new Mrs Rod Grant and praying the girl never had reason to rue the day.

When the time came for Mum to leave, Sally helped her on with her coat and opened the front door.

'Step outside a minute and pull the door to,' said Mum. 'I need to ask you something.'

Sally stifled a groan. 'Oh, Mum, this isn't about Rod, is it?'

'No, it isn't. Pop your coat on. It's cold out.'

Sally did as she was bade and the two of them stood outside.

'What's this about?' asked Sally.

'You and Andrew,' said Mum. 'Andrew's a teacher. He ought

to ask for a post in an evacuated school in the countryside and he could take you with him.'

This was so unexpected that it took a second to sink in.

'I don't know whether he'd be allowed to ask for another post,' said Sally.

'I don't see why not,' Mum said in what Dad called her stubborn voice. 'They need teachers all over the place. In some of these evacuated schools, the children have to be crammed into the local schools, and there are so many children that they have to split the teaching and the children can only have lessons half the time because there are too many of them to sit in the classroom all at once.'

'Andrew moving to the country wouldn't miraculously make the village school able to accommodate more pupils at the same time.'

'Don't answer back.' Mum made Sally sound like a ten-year-old giving cheek. 'What I'm saying is, they need more teachers. Your Andrew could take a class in a village hall or a church hall.'

'You're grasping at straws, Mum,' said Sally. 'I know you're doing it out of love and concern for me.'

'Can you blame me?' Mum demanded. 'I'd do anything to make sure my daughter, my one and only child, is safe. Andrew is in a reserved occupation and I bet he could go and work somewhere else if he really wanted. Then you could be safe too. Don't you want him to be safe?'

'That's not fair,' Sally protested. 'Of course I do, with all my heart. Everybody wants their loved ones to be safe, but we can't all move into the country.'

'How do you know if you haven't asked?' Mum challenged her. 'I'm serious, Sally. You're brand new in that job. They'd soon find someone else. Anyone can sort through a bit of salvage. And Andrew can teach anywhere. They'd probably be glad to have a man teacher. Good for discipline.'

'I don't know, Mum. We'd rather be here. It's where we live. It's where we belong.'

'Here, with all the bombs? You know how bad it's been.'

'Oh, Mum,' said Sally.

'You think about it, Sally. Me and your dad can't bear to think of our precious only child in danger and you should feel the same way about Andrew.'

'Of course I don't want him to be in danger.'

'What about all those teachers who weren't given a choice about being evacuated?' said Mum. 'There must be some who want to come home. I bet Andrew could swap with one of them.'

'I don't know if he'd be allowed. In any case, I'm his fiancée, not his wife. I wouldn't be permitted to go with him.'

'Find out,' Mum urged. 'That's my advice.' She grasped Sally's hands and looked deep into her eyes. 'We waited such a long time before you came along. How would we ever live without you now? I know you, Sally. I know you've spent all day today thinking *what if?* What if you hadn't happened to be looking at that chimney at the right moment? I'll tell you what went through my head when you told me. What if the incendiary had exploded and the chimney had gone up in flames? You and that other girl – you might have escaped – but what if you'd been trapped on the roof. What if...?'

'Don't think that way,' breathed Sally.

'How can I *not* think that way? Every mother thinks that way. I don't want you to have to face something like that ever again – and you shouldn't want Andrew to have to face it every time he enters a damaged house to rescue someone. It's in your power to do something about it, Sally.' Mum looked straight at her. 'If you arrange to be evacuated – I'll give you permission to get married.'

* * *

Sally didn't know what to think. She felt stunned. Mum had finally given the permission Sally and Andrew longed for – but at what price?

'You look thoughtful,' Mrs Henshaw observed when Sally went back indoors. 'Are you dwelling on what happened last night?'

'No,' Sally told her. 'It was something Mum said.'

'You mean that Rod Grant fellow?'

Sally's skin tingled unpleasantly. 'No,' she said at once. She couldn't have Andrew and his mother thinking that.

'I'm about to start listening to a comedy play on the wireless,' said Mrs Henshaw. 'Shoo, you two. I'm sure you've got plenty to talk about.'

Sally and Andrew went into the front room. It was cold in here but they couldn't have a fire because of saving coal.

'It's a good excuse to snuggle close,' said Andrew. 'Not that I need an excuse, what with you being as gorgeous as you are.'

'I'm sorry Mum announced Rod's business like that.'

'No harm done. Is there?' Andrew asked casually.

'What?' Sally exclaimed. 'No! Of course not. If you're asking if it made me question if I did the right thing in getting engaged to you, then no, absolutely not.'

Andrew smiled. 'I didn't really think so, but it's good to hear you say it. Can we have that snuggle now?'

She cuddled into him. 'There is something else we ought to discuss.' Sally explained Mum's idea, then waited anxiously for his response.

'Your mother will let us get married if we promise to move away.' Andrew spoke wonderingly.

'All I've wanted ever since we got engaged is to be your wife,' said Sally. 'I hate having to wait.'

'So do I,' Andrew agreed. 'I've seen so many injuries and deaths in my rescue work. Every single time, my thoughts leap towards you, as if thinking about you can keep you safe. You're my world. I can face whatever I have to as long as I have you. I want more than anything for you to be my wife. I've never forgotten racing round the hospitals that time, knowing if I tracked you down, all I would get was confirmation of your presence but no details as to your condition.'

He brought Sally's palm to his lips.

'I feel exactly the same,' she said softly. 'We're meant to be together. In times like these, it's wrong to wait to get married. No one knows how much or how little time they'll have together. Every moment is precious.'

Andrew laid his forehead against hers. 'And every moment should be spent together. Or if not side by side, then together in the sense of being married, being officially a couple.'

'Mrs and Mrs Andrew Henshaw,' Sally whispered.

It was what she longed for. It was what would make her life complete.

Andrew lifted his forehead from hers and they looked deep into each other's eyes.

'But there's a price to pay,' said Andrew.

'I know,' said Sally. 'I wish Mum hadn't asked it of us. I wish she had just accepted that marriage is right for us.'

'So do I.'

'Would we be able to move, do you think?' Sally asked. 'I'm not saying we should, but would the opportunity be available?'

Andrew's mouth formed a sort of upside-down smile as he considered. 'I honestly don't know, but if there is a teacher out in the sticks who wanted to come back here...'

'What about your... other war work?'

'Presumably there are carpenters all over the country constructing coffins in secret. Put it this way. If we were to pursue this idea, it wouldn't just be the Board of Education I'd need permission from.'

In the ensuing silence, Sally pictured the countryside. Trees, meadows, a pretty stream sparkling in the sunshine as it gurgled along. A village, cottages, thatched roofs, a Norman church. And herself with a gold band beside her engagement ring. It ought to feel perfect... but it didn't.

'Some people are sitting out the war in the West Country,' she said. 'People with money, who can afford to live in a hotel for however long. Everyone really rather despises them, don't they?'

'Yes, but we wouldn't be like that,' Andrew pointed out. 'We'd be working. I'd be teaching and doing my secret work and you'd find something.' He brushed his hand against her hair. 'If there's one thing I know about you, it's that you love working and you take your responsibilities seriously.' His brown eyes filled with tenderness. 'That's what it all comes down to, isn't it? Responsibility. Duty. Doing what's right. It doesn't matter how right it is for us to get married. There is a much bigger rightness than that.'

Sally nodded. It was a serious moment, a moment of duty, reflection and acceptance.

'Our place is here,' she said. 'I know Mum wants to keep me safe, but I'm not a child to be evacuated. I'm an adult and I have my duty. Everyone does. Yours is to teach the lads who have been left here or who were sent home, and build coffins, and rescue people from the rubble.'

'And yours,' Andrew said quietly, almost like a prayer, 'is to keep the salvage depot running and to watch for fires and deal with incendiaries on your patch.'

'I want with all my heart to be your wife,' Sally told him, 'but not if we have to run away and shirk our duty.'

'Manchester is our home,' said Andrew, 'and we must fight for it. Whatever happens, like everyone else, we must see it through to the end.'

CHAPTER THIRTY-FOUR

'Have you heard about the nurses' home belonging to Manchester Royal Infirmary?' Mrs Beaumont asked, placing a plate of mince-and-onion tart, boiled carrots and a jacket potato in front of Betty. She and the munitions girls were, for once, all eating at the same time, but Stella, Lottie and Mary had all eaten their main meal at dinnertime in the munitions canteen, so now they were having parsnip soup and meat-paste sandwiches.

'Take a direct hit, did it?' asked Mary, looking concerned.

'A bomb went straight through the top two floors,' said Mrs Beaumont. Having served all the food, she sat down, crossed one knee over the other and took out her cigarettes, slotting one into her holder. 'It caused ever such a lot of damage when it went off.'

'Any casualties?' Stella asked.

'No, thank God. The nurses were all elsewhere, either working or in the shelters.' Mrs Beaumont tilted back her head and her throat moved slightly as she blew a perfect smoke ring.

Lottie waved her soup spoon in Betty's direction as she remarked, 'Sounds a bit like you and that incendiary that went down the chimney.'

'Except that you prevented your incendiary from going off,' said Mary.

'I'm glad the nurses are all safe,' said Stella.

'And so say all of us,' Lottie added.

'Are you on duty tonight?' Stella asked Betty.

'No,' said Betty. 'I'm looking forward to some sleep – in so far as anyone gets any shut-eye during air raids,' she added wryly.

There was bound to be another raid tonight – if not more than one. As arranged, Betty was due to speak to Dad again this evening. This time, she set off in loads of time, hoping to reach the front of the telephone queue somewhat earlier than she had yesterday. She imagined Dad sitting in the newsagent's booth, anxiously awaiting her call.

When she got through, he asked her how Chorlton had fared last night. Betty was tempted to make light of it so as not to worry him, but what if he heard through other channels? He was a police officer and was very likely to hear all the news about local raids. Better not to try to keep it from him. Besides, she would hate it if he kept information from her. So she described what had happened.

'And you dealt with all that yourself?' There was pride in Dad's voice.

'Not on my own.'

'You're a good girl, Betty. I always knew you had it in you.'

'Really?' she asked in surprise.

'Oh aye, you're a capable lass, and never let anyone tell you otherwise.'

Betty would dearly have loved to ask him exactly what he meant by that, but Mum had always said that only selfish folk fished for compliments, so instead she asked if Salford had been targeted last night, shuddering as Dad told her about the deadly oil bomb that had hit a public air-raid shelter, though by some miracle only two people had been injured, and also about the considerable damage to Albert Park Library. Betty's heart swelled with love and concern both for her darling dad and for her home town.

'Is that a little crack I can hear in your voice?' Dad asked. 'No tears, love. This is how it is. Air raids every night. We have to be strong. We have to show Hitler what's what.'

'I feel guilty for being over here when the place I grew up in is having a bad time. I feel as if I should be there with all of you.'

'Now then, our Betty,' Dad gently chided her. His voice was kind but it carried a firmness that made Betty stand up straight inside the telephone box. 'You work hard in that salvage yard and you're doing your best for your country. That's the most any of us can do and it doesn't matter where you are when you do it. Don't feel guilty about being away from home. It's just as dangerous where you are. I'm proud of you, Betty.' And then he added the words that brought tears to Betty's eyes. 'Your mum would have been proud an' all.'

He couldn't have uttered any words that would have meant more to her and she placed a hand over her heart.

It also made her realise that, as deep as her affection was for her Salford roots, she had settled into her new life. She enjoyed living at Star House with Mrs Beaumont and the munitions girls; and, after their bumpy start, she'd found a good friend in Sally. She hadn't much liked the salvage depot to start with, but that was before Sally arrived and started making the most of it. That business with the incendiary had made a difference too. Being praised for saving the depot had made Betty feel the place belonged to her. Was that barmy? Even if it was, it didn't alter the way she felt.

Fancy that. She actually cared about the salvage depot.

Betty and Sally had constructed a staff room of sorts in the room above Mr Overton's office. When he had his little fire burning, the heat went up the chimney and warmed the chimney-breast in the room above. The girls had furnished the room with a couple of chairs and a table they'd found dotted about in the building's various rooms. Sally had brought in an ashtray she had found on the market.

By pulling the chairs close to the boarded-up fireplace, they could feel the warmth behind it.

'Do you think Mr Overton would reinstate the fireplace for us?' Betty asked. 'It wouldn't be a big job.'

Sally shrugged, then smiled mischievously, and her tawny-hazel eyes sparkled. 'With winter on its way, he might face a straight choice between giving us a fireplace of our own or sharing his own fire with us.'

They both laughed at the very idea. It was a cosy moment in spite of being not quite warm enough. Mugs of tea stood on the table in front of them and their tobacco smoke curled in the air above them.

'Do you miss all the customers from your days at the shop?' Sally asked.

'Sometimes,' Betty admitted, 'but I'm used to this now and I like it.'

Sally nodded. 'I know what you mean. I'm the same. I used to love the contact I had with the general public at the Food Office.' Seeing Betty's face, she quickly added, 'I don't mean doing tests on shopkeepers. I mean the advice sessions I used to run.'

Betty laughed, relieved. 'I thought you meant—'

'I know what you thought. Just so you know: I hated every moment of those tests.'

Betty kept it to herself, but she was putting aside a bit of her wages every week to save up and – eventually – pay Dad back for the money he'd been obliged to stump up to reimburse Mr Tucker for his own hefty fine and Betty's fine. It wouldn't be kind to say that to Sally, though – and that in itself showed that they were true friends. Not so long ago, Betty would have made a point of rubbing Sally's nose in every last detail of that incident and its painful aftermath. She smiled to herself. It was good to have a friend.

Sally leaned forward and knocked the ash from her half-smoked cigarette into the ashtray before stubbing it out, firmly enough to extinguish the ciggie but carefully enough that it would be possible to light it up and finish it later.

Betty supped the last of her tea. 'Back to the grindstone.'

They returned to the yard.

'Just in time,' Sally murmured, nodding at the open entrance where a van had just pulled up and Mrs Lockwood was climbing out. 'Imagine if she'd caught us having a tea break.'

'Slacking, more like,' Betty whispered back with a wink.

The shared moment of levity vanished as Mrs Lockwood came marching into the yard, looking around, patrician nose in the air as if she owned the place.

'Good morning, Mrs Lockwood,' said Sally. 'Can I help you?'

Mrs Lockwood regarded her with disdain. 'No, thank you. I am here to speak to Mr Overton about handing over the reins to me.'

Betty's jaw dropped. 'Come again.'

'Handing over the reins,' Mrs Lockwood repeated a fraction more slowly, as if Betty was the dunce of the class. 'He has been given a new post in the Town Hall. Apparently, he gave a talk to the ladies of the Withington branch of the WVS and he was pleased with how it went. I took the opportunity to suggest that he might wish to apply for a vacant post in the accounts department, where his banking knowledge would be of value.'

Sally looked stunned. 'He hasn't said a word.'

'And why should he?' Mrs Lockwood enquired loftily. 'He isn't obliged to confide his private business to the likes of you.'

'But we work for him,' said Betty.

'Precisely. You're the workers. That means you do what's required of you, which does not include poking your noses into the business of those of us who make the important decisions. I shall expect a better attitude from the pair of you when I officially assume responsibility here.'

Sally's head jerked back. 'D'you mean you're taking over the depot?'

'Of course I am. I'm surprised you even need to ask.' Mrs Lockwood twisted her arm slightly to display the SALVAGE OFFICER band she wore on the jacket sleeve of her smart green uniform. 'I am the obvious person to run the depot efficiently. I possess all the necessary knowledge and I will expect you two to knuckle down and work your hardest.'

'We already do,' said Sally.

Mrs Lockwood's grey eyes turned to flint. 'I shall also expect a higher standard of respect and good manners from both of you. It did not escape my notice that one or both of you arranged for Mr Overton to deliver his talk to the Withington WVS. A friend of mine is in that group and she asked why I was not the one to give the talk, since I am in charge of the Chorlton Salvage Depot. That was the first I'd heard of the talk taking place and I was not amused. A few discreet enquiries soon furnished me with the information that it was one of the salvage girls who approached the Withington branch with the suggestion. Disgraceful! Any talks should be delivered by me. In future, they will be. Do I make myself clear?' She stopped talking to give them the full benefit of a wrathful glare. 'Continue with your work.'

She walked across the yard. Standing side by side, the girls stared after her until she disappeared indoors. Finding her mouth open, Betty shut it with a snap.

'Well!' she exclaimed. 'I can't believe it.'

'You'd better start believing it toot sweet,' Sally said in a tight voice, 'because it looks like she's our new boss. When I had the idea of arranging for Mr Overton to give a talk, I hoped it would make him see the depot in a new light. I didn't want to buck him up to the point where he would leave.'

'We have Mrs Lockwood to thank for that,' said Betty. 'She brought the new job to his attention.'

Sally groaned. 'So much for my big idea. Without that, Mr Overton would have stayed on here and Mrs Lockwood wouldn't have thought of prising him out of the depot. Now she's going to take over and it's all my fault.'

'Look,' said Betty. 'We've got more company arriving.'

Into the yard walked two gentlemen in pinstripes and bowlers. One had a large paunch, puffy cheeks and a trim moustache. The other, broad-shouldered and straight-backed, used his rolled-up umbrella as if it was a walking-cane, tapping the metal ferrule smartly on the ground with each step he took.

Seeing Betty and Sally, the men halted and politely raised their bowlers.

'Good morning, ladies,' said the portly gentleman. 'I am Mr Pratt and this is Mr Merivale. We are from the Corporation and we are here to see Mr Overton regarding the future of this depot.'

Betty's eyes widened. This really was happening.

Beside her, Sally said, 'Mr Overton is in his office. I'll show you the way.'

'There's no need, young lady,' said Mr Merivale. 'We've been here before. You just carry on doing what you're doing. Jolly good show.'

Mr Pratt smiled at them and his eyes crinkled above his chubby cheeks. 'If one of you good fairies would kindly pop the kettle on presently, I'm sure we'd be very grateful.'

So saying, the two men from the Corporation headed for the office.

'They must be here to rubber-stamp handing over the depot to Mrs Lockwood,' Sally observed in a flat voice.

Betty looked at her friend, trying to read her facial expression. 'This must be extra-hard for you. You've made a difference here.'

'Not really.'

'You've made a difference to *me*,' Betty said. 'It was just a job when I first came here, and a jolly dull one at that, but you've taken a real interest in salvage and that's ended up making it interesting for me. If anybody should be given the job of running this depot, it's you. You deserve it, Sally White, and what's more, I'm going to tell them so.'

'You can't—'

But Betty was already on her way. She felt all fired up and that wasn't like her. She marched to Mr Overton's office, knocked and walked straight in without waiting to be invited.

'Here's the good fairy with the tea,' said Mr Pratt.

'No, it isn't,' said Betty, remembering to add 'sir' at the last moment.

Mr Overton sat behind his desk. His three visitors were crammed into the rest of the space. They all looked smart and official and Betty suddenly felt clumsy and lower-class in her dungarees and turban. Cripes. What on earth did she think she was doing?

She almost backed down. She almost apologised and took a big step backward out of the room; but then she thought of Sally, who had done her best for the depot. That was all Betty needed to spur her on.

'I'm here to speak up for Miss White,' Betty announced. 'If you're looking for someone new to run this depot, she's the one you should choose. She knows all about salvage, not just what to collect but what happens to it, what it gets made into. She knocked on umpteen doors to tell housewives the locations of their new pig-bins. It was her idea to paint the new signs showing where to put things; and she wants to bring in a book expert to identify valuable books. She even found out why ointment tubes have to be kept separate from other metal things.'

'Ointment tubes?' Mr Merivale repeated, looking bemused.

'Aye – ointment tubes,' said Betty. 'And don't forget how brave she was the night when the paper-mill lorry was here and the fire started. That was the night when the incendiary went down the

chimney an' all. Miss White showed true courage and determination.'

'So do other people all the time these days,' Mr Merivale
pointed out, 'and thank heaven for it. It's what Britain needs just
now.'

'That's true,' Betty agreed, 'and Miss White is as good as
anyone. Mr Garside, the fire officer, said she deserved the George
Cross for what she did. On top of that, she finds salvage interesting – not just a duty or a necessity, but interesting in its own
right, which has made me find it interesting too.' She addressed
Mr Overton. 'Just think of all the facts and figures she dug up for
you when you gave your talk to the WVS.'

'That's true,' Mr Overton conceded.

'She has a way with the public an' all,' Betty went on. 'When
she worked at the Food Office, she had to deal with all sorts – a
wedding one minute, a funeral the next – and she understands the
best way to talk to people. They like her. They respect her.
They—'

'If you have quite finished blowing off steam, Miss Hughes,'
Mrs Lockwood interposed grandly, 'please return to your duties.'
She cast a sideways glance at the men and made a show of rolling
her eyes heavenwards.

Betty felt startled and a little breathless at being cut off in full
flow. She looked at the gentlemen, but she couldn't tell what they
were thinking. None of them invited her to continue making her
point. Silence sat heavily in the room and she felt awkward. She'd
barged in so confidently and now it seemed she would have to
skulk out with her tail between her legs.

Tilting her chin in the way that always made Grace utter a
tinkling laugh and call her obstinate, Betty withdrew. She shut the
door softly and leaned against it. She had acted for the best, but
had she scuppered Sally's chances with her outburst? That was
the very opposite of what she had hoped to achieve.

She returned to the yard. Sally looked at her. To Betty's

surprise, she said, 'Thank you for standing up for me and for thinking well of me. It means a lot.'

'To be honest, I might have done more harm than good,' Betty admitted. 'But you and me are friends and I know how hard you've worked. I know what you have to offer an' all. You could really make something of this place. You could make the locals see it differently, not just as somewhere to dump their salvage, but as a place to get information and – and inspiration.'

'Inspiration?' Sally repeated. 'You're joking.'

'No, I'm not. If anyone could get folk really interested in salvage, it's you. That's what I think, anyroad.'

'Here they come,' Sally said quietly.

With Mr Merivale once more tapping his umbrella on the ground with each step, the four important people emerged into the yard. They approached the girls.

'Miss White,' said Mr Pratt, 'after some discussion, we have decided to offer you the post of manager of the Chorlton Salvage Depot.'

Sally didn't utter a sound, but Betty drew in a gasp of delight and beamed at her friend.

Sally looked stunned. 'You want me to run the depot?' she asked. 'Me?'

'This is very much against my better judgement, Miss White,' declared Mrs Lockwood. 'Make no mistake about that, but it seems I have been outvoted.' She took a step closer to Sally. 'I shall be watching you very closely, you may be sure, and,' she added in a voice that dared the men to disagree, 'I shall be ready to step in at any moment. I have no doubt my expertise will be called upon once the mistake of appointing you is seen for what it is.'

Mr Merivale cleared his throat loudly. 'Um, yes, well, Mrs Lockwood.'

The three gentlemen looked expectantly at Sally.

'What d'you say, Miss White?' asked Mr Pratt. 'Are you up to the job?'

'Look at her,' Mrs Lockwood said scornfully. 'Too over-whelmed to make a simple decision. I told you this was a mistake. You should withdraw the offer immediately if you know what's good for the depot. We can't have a chit like this blundering along, making mistakes left, right and centre, which is what will undoubtedly happen.'

That seemed to bring Sally to life. She straightened her slender shoulders and her tawny eyes became bright and alert. A pretty smile played across her lips as she addressed the three gentlemen.

'Thank you for your faith in me. I promise I won't let you down.'

CHAPTER THIRTY-FIVE

Sally could barely believe what had happened. Instead of the salvage depot being handed over to the haughty and disagreeable Mrs Lockwood, it had been offered to her. Her! When she had come to work this morning, she hadn't even known a new manager was required – and now she was going to take over when Mr Overton left.

Betty was singing 'Deep Purple' under her breath as she worked.

'You don't mind the position being offered to me, do you?' Sally asked.

Betty stopped singing and looked at her. 'Mind that they want you instead of the Duchess of Lockwood? Give me one good reason why I should mind that.'

'That's not what I meant,' said Sally. 'I mean – well, that they chose me over you.'

Betty laughed and her blue eyes shone. 'Of course I don't mind, you daft ha'porth. I'm perfectly happy being a foot-soldier and always have been.' Her cheery manner melted away and she added in a serious tone, 'Congratulations, Sally. You deserve it. I'm nothing but pleased for you, honest injun. I'd better go and have a word with Mr Overton and say sorry for butting in on his meeting. Not that I'm sorry really,' she added with a cheeky grin.

Sally watched her disappear inside. What a good friend she was. Fancy pushing her way into the meeting like that.

After a minute or two, Betty returned.

'You'll never guess what,' she said. 'Mr Overton has just put me in my place good and proper.'

'I'm sorry to hear it,' said Sally, 'but it's not exactly unexpected, is it, after what you did?'

Betty laughed. 'Wrong!' she sang. 'There was me, apologising for barging in and sticking up for you, and Mr Overton was at pains to point out that he spoke up for you an' all.'

'He didn't,' Sally said in disbelief.

'He jolly well did,' said Betty, 'and he made it clear to me that I had no business taking the credit because you'd not have been offered the job if it hadn't been for him.'

Well! That was the last thing Sally had expected.

'I suppose I ought to thank him,' she said.

'Be my guest.' Betty smiled and her dimple popped into place. 'You'll find him in his office.' Her eyes twinkled. 'In *your* office, I should say.'

Sally went to the office and knocked.

'Enter,' came Mr Overton's voice.

She went inside. Mr Overton was seated behind his desk, filling in paperwork.

'What is it, Miss White?'

'I came to thank you for speaking up for me in the meeting. I appreciate it very much.'

'Do you indeed?' Mr Overton asked drily. 'It might interest you to know, Miss White, that I didn't do it for your benefit. I did it for mine. Should Mrs Lockwood take over here, it would set the seal upon the notion of my having been obliged to do women's work. I would be a laughing-stock in my new post in the Town Hall. Before you say anything, yes, I know you're also a woman.

But you're young and capable, not middle-aged and bossy. If you take over on my recommendation, it shows me in a good light. It tells everyone that I have trained you up to do the job and follow in my footsteps. I find that acceptable.'

'Oh.' What else could she say? Sally returned to Betty and relayed the information. 'It's a bit of a kick in the teeth.'

'No, it isn't,' Betty said at once. 'Do the whys and wherefores of how you came by the post really matter? This is wartime and we've all got to do our bit. This way, Mr Overton saves face and you get the job you were born to do. Congratulations, Miss Depot Manager.'

Sally couldn't wait to get home and tell Andrew her wonderful news. The thought of running the depot, of actually being its manager, sent little sparks of excitement chasing through her. What a marvellous opportunity. And fancy Betty speaking up for her like that. She owed her friend a great deal.

It was one of those days when Andrew was home before her, so Sally could share her news immediately. As she drank in the sight of the smile that Andrew couldn't have contained if he'd tried, she felt like running a victory lap round the block. He pulled her into his arms, lifting her off her feet and swinging her in a circle, while his mother laughed at the pair of them.

When Andrew put her down, Mrs Henshaw gave Sally a warm hug. 'Well done, Sally. I'm proud of you.'

Sally drew in a deep breath. The pride shining in Andrew's brown eyes filled her with joy and satisfaction.

'When I'm in the queue outside the butcher's tomorrow,' said Mrs Henshaw, 'I'll tell everyone I see that my future daughter-in-law is all set to be the new boss at the salvage depot.'

Sally and Andrew exchanged glances. They hadn't uttered a word to Mrs Henshaw about Sally's mother's attempt to bribe them into an immediate marriage. They had agreed last night that Sally would go and tell Mum this evening what they had decided.

When Sally was ready to set off, Andrew asked, 'Are you sure you don't want me to come too?'

'I'd much prefer us to do it together,' said Sally, 'but Mum will probably find it easier to hear it from me on my own. I'll tell her about my new job as well.'

Andrew walked her to the bus stop and waited with her for the bus. It was small attentions like this that made Sally feel special. She knew Andrew would always make her feel cared for and looked after.

When she arrived at her parents' house, Mum opened the door, looking over Sally's shoulder into the darkness.

'On your own?'

'Yes.' Sally stepped inside. 'I hoped we could have a good natter about things. I've got something special to tell you.'

Mum looked pleased. 'Dad is round at Mr Ridgeway's comparing ideas for their allotments, so it's just us.'

They entered the parlour. Instead of offering to put the kettle on, Mum sat down and got straight to the point.

'Have you discussed my idea with Andrew?'

'Yes. We had a long talk.'

'Good.' Mum smiled. 'And I can tell from your glad expression what your answer is – and I'm more than happy to give my consent.'

Sally hurried to correct her. 'No, Mum, it's not that. We decided that, as much as we want to get married, we want to stay here.'

The smile dropped off Mum's face. 'Well! I never thought you'd say that.'

'We want to do our bit for the war.'

'Well, you can't want to get married all that much, that's all I can say.'

'Mum! What a thing to say. Of course we want to get married.

But we aren't prepared to run away from our wartime duty in order to do it. Please try to understand. I know how much you want me to be safe, but duty is important too.'

Mum's lips tightened into a thin line. She stood up. 'I'll put the kettle on.' Her voice was tight too.

She left the room and Sally didn't follow. It seemed best to give her a few minutes on her own to let off steam in private. Sally knew how Mum hated to be thwarted when she'd set her heart on something. After all, Sally reminded herself, she had been driven by an entirely understandable desire to see her only child at a safe distance.

When Mum returned with the tea-tray, she nudged the door to with her hip. Sally waited for her to sit down.

'Anyway,' Sally said, 'I do have some good news for you. I've been promoted. I've been given the post of manager at the salvage depot. Isn't that exciting?'

'I'd rather you'd been made the manager of the local Food Office.'

'Mum, please don't spoil it,' Sally begged.

'I'm not going to lie to you, Sally. You know how I feel about you working at that salvage place. It's a comedown for a girl like you.'

'I'm sorry you feel that way.' Sally spoke in a formal voice, determined not to show that Mum had riled her. 'Personally, I'm proud of what I do.'

Mum huffed an exaggerated sigh. 'Oh well, there's nothing I can do about it if your job means more to you than Andrew's safety.'

'That's not fair,' exclaimed Sally. 'I've already explained why we decided not to take you up on your offer.'

'I hope you're completely sure,' said Mum, 'because I shan't make the offer again. I thought you'd jump at the chance to get married, I really did.'

The door, which hadn't closed properly when Mum nudged

it, now swung open and Dad stood there, the vertical lines between his bushy eyebrows deeper than usual.

'Eric!' Mum looked startled. 'I didn't hear you come in.'

'That's because I came in the back way. What's this about Sally jumping at the chance to get married – or not jumping at it?'

'It's nothing.' Mum made it sound as if it had been a joke.

'It sounds very much like something to me,' said Dad.

Mum answered in an airy voice that didn't fool Sally for one moment. Mum was flustered. 'I said I'd give Sally permission to marry if she and Andrew would move to the countryside. I'm sure Andrew could wangle it if he tried. I just wanted Sally to be safe,' she added in an anguished voice.

'But that's...' Dad shook his head. 'I hesitate to use the word "blackmail" when I'm talking about my own wife. I want you to know, Sally, this is the first I've heard of it. All I want is for you to be happy. From the moment I first saw you when you were half an hour old, that's what I've wanted. The day you got engaged, you went round to the Henshaws' and ended up in their air-raid shelter. I wasn't on ARP duty that night and I sat in our shelter with Mum, wishing you were with us. I comforted Mum by telling her you must be in the Henshaws' Anderson shelter and that you'd be safe. That was when it struck me.'

'What did?' Sally asked softly.

'It was where you most wanted to be. You wanted to be in the Henshaws' Anderson – with Andrew. He's a good man and I've seen with my own eyes how much he loves you. I respect the pair of you for putting duty before marriage. It shows what you're made of.' Dad addressed Mum. 'It shows they've put patriotism and maturity before their whirlwind romance. It also shows them treating their relationship as long-term. They haven't been swept away on the tide of emotion and daydreams.'

Tears welled up in Sally's eyes as she absorbed Dad's words of praise. She wanted to say, 'Thank you' but all she could do was mouth the words.

'I know you want Sally to be safe,' Dad said to Mum. 'So do I – but this isn't the way to do it. This is about the importance of being able to hold your head up. It's about being able to say with pride, "This is what I did and why I did it." You and Andrew have just done that, Sally. Believe me, in years to come, you'd have hung your heads in shame if you'd had to tell your children, "We ran off to the country to get married and live safely while everyone we knew was in deadly danger." Now you'll be able to tell them, "All we wanted was to get married, but we put our duty to our country first." Your children will respect you all the more for it and so will everyone who knows your story. I certainly will.'

'Oh, Dad...' Sally whispered.

'Eric—' Mum started to say.

'The only reason I didn't give you permission to marry before, Sally, was out of respect for Mum. Now she's said that you can marry if you move to safety. Well, what I say is that you can get married if you stop here.' Dad jutted out his chin as he nodded. 'Have we got any of that good writing paper left? I'll write my permission here and now and be proud to do it.'

CHAPTER THIRTY-SIX

To Sally's great relief and gratitude, although her plan to send her daughter to safety hadn't worked, Mum threw herself into her role as mother of the bride. Dad was happy for Sally and Andrew to marry as soon as possible, even on a special licence if that was what they wanted, but Mum was keen to have time to organise what she called a proper wedding, by which she meant a full white wedding.

'They've gone out of fashion,' Sally explained, 'especially now we're having air raids all the time. The feeling now is that brides should aim for simplicity. Lots of girls are getting married in smart costumes and pretty hats. It's much more sensible than a long white dress you'll never wear again.'

Mum sighed, but she went along with it. Sally was able to get an afternoon off work and they went into the middle of Manchester and spent the afternoon going round the shops. Sally tried on a few costumes but without falling in love with any of them.

'I said you should have worn white,' Mum murmured.

Then they went into Ingleby's on Market Street, where they

found a lovely forget-me-not-blue suit. The jacket had padded shoulders and a buckled belt that would show off Sally's trim waist. The skirt was knee-length with a panel of pleats down the front.

'I don't need a new hat,' said Sally. 'I'll wear my straw hat with a scarf round the crown.'

The shop assistant found a floaty scarf in a mixture of hazy blues that complemented the forget-me-not perfectly. Sally couldn't stop gazing at herself in the long mirror in the changing room. Her wedding outfit! She loved it.

The sound of the air-raid siren jostled her thoughts aside. The shop assistants ushered their customers downstairs to wait out the raid. Sally, still in her wedding costume, filed along with everyone else into the basement, which was kitted out with chairs and benches. A notice on the wall said LADIES, PLEASE KNIT FOR THE FORCES AT INGLEBY'S EXPENSE above a table with needles and balls of wool. Several women immediately chose wool and started to cast on.

'It'll be a fine story to tell your children one day,' said Mum, 'how you were trying on your wedding clothes and you had to shelter from an air raid.'

'Ooh,' said a lady close by, 'is that your wedding rig-out, love?'

'Stand up and let's have a look,' another customer said encouragingly.

Sally laughed, thinking she was joking, but other voices joined in.

'Yes, do.'

'It'll give us summat nice to think about instead of Hitler's bombs.'

Sally did as she was asked and received admiration from all sides. The atmosphere was light-hearted and hopeful as everyone swapped wedding anecdotes. When it was time to leave the basement, Sally's ears were ringing with good wishes for her wedding.

'Well, wasn't that jolly?' said Mum. After a moment, she added, 'It made me feel quite weddingy.'

'Didn't you feel weddingy before?' asked Sally.

'Yes and no. I always imagined a white wedding and months of planning. But this afternoon in the basement has quite perked me up. It was very special to see my beautiful daughter being admired in her finery.'

Something inside Sally melted. 'Thanks, Mum.'

'I never got the wedding I wanted. Satin and lace at the age of eighteen was what I grew up hoping for, and of course that never happened. I was thirty-seven when I got married. No one said, "Congratulations" – or if they did, I don't remember it. What I do remember is folk saying how lucky I was to find a husband at my age – aye, and the surprise in their voices when they said it.' She turned to look at Sally as she said earnestly, 'That's why I want it to be perfect for you.'

'But it is perfect,' Sally said gently. 'It's perfect because it's Andrew and me. That's all I need – well, no, not all I need. I need my mum to be happy for me. Every daughter needs that.'

'Oh, love.' Mum went misty-eyed. 'Let's make this the best wedding we can.'

'Even if it's taking place quickly on a special licence?' Sally asked with a tease in her voice.

'As I said, it's not what I wanted for you, but I can see that it's what you want for yourself – and that's good enough for me.'

Sally hugged her, right there in the middle of Ingleby's.

'You're the best mum ever.'

Sally spent the night before her wedding back at home in Mum and Dad's house. Betty had slept here too. She was going to be one of the bridesmaids.

'But you've only known her for such a short time,' Mum had started to object when Sally told her, but Sally had laughed.

'Then she'll fit in perfectly, because I've only known the groom since the beginning of August. In fact,' she added mischievously, 'I met Betty before I met Andrew, so I count her as a very old friend.'

The girls were both able to have Saturday off, because Betty had prevailed upon Mr Overton to open the depot.

'It's good of him,' Sally had said gratefully to Betty.

'I told him it would be his wedding present to you,' Betty told her before adding with a twinkle, 'And I might just have mentioned that, if he didn't do it, I might have to approach Mrs Lockwood.'

'Heaven forbid,' Sally had exclaimed.

'That's a coincidence,' Betty answered. 'That's exactly what Mr Overton said.'

Sally was delighted to have her new friend as one of her bridesmaids – and also her very oldest friend as her other one. After the horrible falling-out she'd gone through with Deborah, they were friends again now, and Deborah was going to fulfil her childhood promise of being an attendant at Sally's wedding.

Betty and Deborah were to wear their best dresses in their role as bridesmaids, something that had drawn forth a little sigh of regret from Mum, who was no doubt imagining the matching satin floor-length dresses and headdresses of dainty flowers she had dreamed of for years.

Betty was going to wear a pretty lilac dress. Deborah was originally going to wear blue until Sally bought her own forget-me-not blue suit, whereupon Deborah switched to a dress with stripes of cream and apple green. Deborah was going to wear a dainty pillbox hat and Betty had brought her stylish asymmetrical hat with her.

After breakfast Deborah came round to the Whites' and the three girls helped Mum make meat-paste sandwiches and vegetable rissoles.

'It'll be a decent spread with what others are providing,' said Mum. 'It's a shame we can't have an iced cake, though.'

'Never mind,' said Sally. 'Your trench cake is always delicious and it keeps so well.'

As well as being given a slice to eat that afternoon, each guest would be offered a slice wrapped in greaseproof paper to post to a loved one fighting overseas. Trench cake was so-called because it was perfect for sending abroad to the troops, as it contained no eggs, which meant it was certain to last well.

Dad stumped up for a taxi to take Sally and Mum across to the Henshaws' house with the food. That was where they were going to hold the reception. Nobody had wanted to hold it in the local hall where Rod had proposed to Sally.

'It should be Betty or me taking the food with your mum,' said Deborah, 'not you, Sally.'

'I don't want to miss out on a single thing today,' said Sally. She laughed happily. 'Including delivering the food.'

When they arrived in Chorlton, Mum made Sally wait in the motor while she ensured that Andrew wasn't in the house, so there would be no danger of his seeing the bride.

'Isn't it me in the dress he's not supposed to see?' asked Sally.

'I don't know about that,' said Mum, 'but you in your turban with your rollers poking out at the front might scare him off.'

Sally beamed. It was good to hear Mum making a joke.

'Apparently, he's round at the neighbours' that lent their spare bed,' said Mum.

Sally nodded. She knew that the Ibbotsons' spare bed, which had been lent for Andrew to sleep in, had been dismantled this morning and returned to its owners. Andrew's other job for the morning was to move his own and Sally's things into the double bedroom that so far had been his mother's room. Mrs Henshaw was moving into the smaller bedroom, which originally Andrew's before Sally came into their lives. Sally had felt awkward about her and Andrew having the big bedroom, but Mrs Henshaw had insisted, and it did make sense. That was where the newly-weds were going to sleep tonight, while Mrs Henshaw stayed with one of the neighbours so they could have their privacy.

Mum and Sally carried the food into the kitchen, where the rissoles were placed beneath a fly-net while the plate with the sandwiches had a damp tea-towel laid over the top to stop the bread drying out.

Mrs Henshaw wiped her hands on her apron. 'The next time you come through that front door, Sally, you'll be carried over the threshold by your new husband. You'll be Mrs Andrew Henshaw. I want you to know, Mrs White, how very happy I am that your daughter is marrying my son. I couldn't ask for a better wife for him.'

'I'm sure Andrew will make her a good husband,' said Mum. 'He's a decent man – honest, reliable. I know me and Sally's dad can trust him to take care of her.'

Sally and her mother-in-law-to-be shared a warm look. They had got along well right from the start and the relationship had strengthened since Sally had moved in. It felt right to hold the wedding reception here. It was where Mrs Henshaw had thrown the impromptu engagement party, which made today's reception feel like coming full circle.

Sally and Mum went home again. Neighbours popped in, offering good wishes and small presents, a pair of pillowcases, a honey-spoon, cotton reels with useful colours, the sheet music for two popular songs, a darning mushroom.

'Practical things,' Sally said, pleased. 'I'm not one for fripperies.'

'You wait,' said Mum. 'If this war goes on as long as the last one, that honey-spoon will be a frippery and young couples will be grateful for a tin of tuna or a flour-sieve.'

It was already difficult, if not downright impossible, to get hold of all sorts of ordinary, everyday items, such as needles and pencils. Although Sally knew in her head that things were going to get worse, because everyone kept saying so, somehow her heart found it harder to accept.

When it was time to get ready, she gave herself a strip-wash and got dressed, helped by Betty and Deborah. Emotion swelled inside Sally at having these two friends here sharing these special moments. Mum fussed over her too.

Sally had just a small mirror on top of her chest of drawers. The big mirror was on Mum's dressing-table. Warmth spread all through Sally as she gazed at herself in her forget-me-not-blue wedding suit.

'Put the hat on,' Mum urged her.

The scarf with its mixture of hazy blues looked pretty and summery wound round the crown of Sally's straw hat.

Sally couldn't tear her gaze away. She might not be the satin-and-lace bride Mum had always dreamed of and she herself had always imagined, but she was a blissfully happy and excited bride all the same.

Mrs Andrew Henshaw.

'Come and stand with me,' she said to the other girls.

The three of them crowded in front of the mirror, Sally in the centre. Sally looked at Deborah in her striped dress, her bright-blue eyes sparkling and her smile filled with joy. Did part of that joy stem from being reunited with her childhood friend? Then Sally looked at Betty dressed in lilac, her complexion smooth and creamy, her dimple popping for all it was worth as her smile widened.

'Come on, Mum,' said Sally. 'There's space for one more if we all breathe in.'

Laughing, Mum joined the smiling group.

'This is what everyone will see when they look at us this afternoon,' said Sally. 'Happy people.'

.   .   .

When the taxi pulled up outside the registry office, Andrew was waiting on the pavement. He looked handsome in a two-piece suit, its double-breasted jacket showing it to be pre-war. He opened the door and helped Sally out.

'You look beautiful,' he told her, his brown eyes drinking in her appearance.

Mum, Deborah and Betty clustered around her, sorting out the flowers. Sally's bouquet was of mauve and lilac asters with trailing greenery, provided by the neighbours. Having a bouquet to which her lifelong neighbours had contributed made it all the more meaningful. Deborah and Betty carried posies. Dad already wore his buttonhole and there was another buttonhole for Andrew, which Sally pinned into place.

Even though her eyes were on the flower, she could feel Andrew's gaze on her face. Sally smiled but felt unaccountably shy all of a sudden and she stepped away, taking her bouquet from Deborah and fussing over it.

'Are you all right?' Mum asked quietly.

'Andrew and I have lived under the same roof for some time and we know one another all the more closely because of it, yet here am I feeling all shy.' Sally looked at her mother. 'Am I being silly?'

Mum smiled kindly. 'I think,' she said, 'that you're feeling like a bride.'

They all went inside and were directed to the place to wait.

'Looks like a busy day for weddings,' Dad remarked, taking his pipe from his pocket to while away the wait. 'Either that or you've invited lots of extra folk without telling me.'

There were two other groups in separate clusters in the gloomy foyer between the registry office and the staircases leading to other parts of the building. Everyone was smartly dressed and Sally smiled to see a pair of excited little girls in pink satin. The other two grooms, smoking nervously, were both in uniform.

'Are we behind all these people?' asked Mum.

'Not necessarily,' said a lady from one of the other parties. 'We're very early.'

The door on the far side opened and a wedding group spilled out, led by the bride and groom. When they had gone, a gentleman appeared in the doorway.

'Private Sullivan and Miss Bridge, please.'

The party with the pink-clad children followed him inside and the door closed. A clerk appeared beside Sally and Andrew.

'Mr Henshaw and Miss White? Come with me, please. We need to do the paperwork.'

In a small office, Sally and Andrew answered the necessary questions so that their marriage certificate could be filled in correctly. The clerk already had Dad's letter of consent, which Sally had had to hand over a few days ago when the wedding was booked. The clerk wrote down their full names and addresses. When he realised they already lived at the same address, he gave them a sharp glance before quickly lowering his head.

Then he asked them to confirm their status as bachelor and spinster.

'And your profession, please, Mr Henshaw?'

'Woodwork teacher.'

'Thank you.' The clerk wrote *Schoolmaster*. 'And your job, Miss White?'

Sally lifted her chin. 'Salvage worker.'

They were then asked for their fathers' names and professions. The clerk wrote *Retired* under Dad's details and *Deceased* in brackets beneath Andrew's father's.

'And the two mothers are going to be your witnesses, I believe. Good. I need to come and have a word with them to check how they sign their names. That's everything. I will have your certificate ready for you after your wedding.'

Sally and Andrew returned to their guests. A few relatives had arrived while they were in with the clerk and there were greetings and introductions. Mrs Henshaw introduced her sister and brother-in-law to Sally and her parents, and Dad introduced his sister Rose to the Henshaws. Sally hovered close to her husband-to-be. Her shy feeling had vanished now. What she felt was pride in Andrew. He was a talented carpenter and joiner who had followed his vocation to teach. He was a brave man who took part in dangerous rescues, and – just as bravely – he coped with having to build endless rows of coffins in secret. It took real strength of character to do that.

Another group entered the waiting area. This bride wore white.

'At least you can tell who their bride is,' Auntie Rose commented in Sally's hearing.

'Anyone can see who our bride is too,' said Dad, 'because she looks radiant.'

The far door opened once more and the wedding party emerged, followed by the registrar.

'Mr Henshaw and Miss White, please.'

Andrew led their group into the room. Dad knocked out his pipe into a full ashtray on a small side-table, putting it in his pocket as he and Sally, Deborah and Betty hung back. Dad was going to give Sally away.

The door shut behind the guests and a shiver of excitement passed through Sally. How long would it take for everyone to sit down? She slipped her arm through Dad's and they smiled warmly at one another, then they turned and looked behind them at Betty and Deborah holding their posies. Sally couldn't think of anyone she wanted more to walk with her as she approached her husband-to-be. Deborah, her lifelong friend, and Betty, whom the war had brought into her life.

Andrew's uncle opened the door with a broad grin on his face. Dad gave Sally's hand a little squeeze and Sally drew in a deep breath, then they walked into the long room. Sally was aware of smiling faces all turned their way. She had planned to smile around at all her guests as she made her way to the front, but instead her gaze locked on Andrew as he stood watching her and she thought she might cry with pure happiness.

This was what she wanted with all her heart.

A LETTER FROM SUSANNA

Dear Reader,

A warm welcome to my new Second World War book, *The Home Front Girls.* I am so proud and excited to be able to write those words! I loved creating Sally, Betty and all the other characters and I hope you loved meeting them and getting to know them too.

If you did enjoy my book, and want to keep up to date with all my latest releases, just sign up at the following link. Your email address will never be shared and you can unsubscribe at any time.

www.bookouture.com/susanna-bavin

It was my history teacher Miss Smith who gave me my love of history and it is because of her that I now write novels set in the past. In particular, I am fascinated by social and domestic history and the ordinary everyday lives that people led, often in very difficult circumstances. The way people lived on the home front is a strong example of this. Every single aspect of ordinary life changed. The blackout was enforced. Rationing was introduced for food, clothing, furniture – even soap. Small items that everybody took for granted vanished from the shops. And of course nightly air raids brought the war to the civilian population.

Everyone did war work of one sort or another. In *The Home Front Girls,* Sally and Betty both get jobs working in a salvage depot. Salvage (what we today call recycling) was a massive part of the war effort. With everything in increasingly short supply, reusing was essential. Many items were redirected into another purpose. 'Saucepans into Spitfires' was the popular and inspirational slogan for a drive to collect aluminium in the summer of 1940. The housewives of Britain proudly gave up their pots and pans, vacuum-cleaner tubes, coat hangers etc. Throughout the war, everything was salvaged – paper, string, metal, glass, rubber, rags. Food-waste went into the pig-bin, except for the bones, which went in the bone-basket (to make glue, explosives, soap, fertiliser and animal-feed). Silver-foil milk-bottle-tops were kept and given back to the milkman. In the spring of 1943, it became an offence to throw away waste paper.

Thank you for choosing to read *The Home Front Girls*. I would love to hear your thoughts on it in a review. These are so important not only for letting authors receive your personal feedback but also for helping new readers to choose their next book and discover new authors.

I love hearing from my readers – you can get in touch with me on social media. I hope you'll follow me on Facebook. My author page is a warm and friendly community where you'll find all the latest news about my writing and forthcoming books (no spoilers, I promise!) as well as photos of my beautiful home town by the sea and my favourite garden plants, and the regular 'What are you reading this weekend?' feature.

Much love

Susanna xx

www.susannabavin.co.uk

facebook.com/MaisieThomasAuthor

x.com/SusannaBavin

ACKNOWLEDGMENTS

Many thanks to my agent, Camilla Shestopal, and my editor, Susannah Hamilton, for their support while I wrote this book. Susannah, it is a delight to be working with you again. Thank you for giving the first draft a jolly good shake and turning it into a much better story.

Thanks also to everyone at Bookouture for welcoming me so warmly, especially Kim Nash and Emma Davies. Jen Gilroy, Annette Yates, Beverley Ann Hopper and Jane Cable for all they do to support my writing. And the staff at Llyfrgell Llandudno Library.

Milton Keynes UK
Ingram Content Group UK Ltd.
UKHW010910080424
440801UK00004B/305

9 781837 907861